The Truths Our Secrets Tell

A.T. Rhode

VAILED PEN
PUBLICATIONS

A.T. Rhode

The Truths Our Secrets Tell
Copyright © 2025 by A. T. Rhode

Published by
Vailed Pen Publications

For permission requests, write to the publisher at:
anu@vailedpenpublications.com

This is a work of fiction. Names, characters, places, and incidents are either
products of the author's imagination or used fictitiously. Any resemblance
to actual persons, living or dead, or actual events is purely coincidental.

ISBN: 979-8-9933493-4-3 *eBook*
ISBN: 979-8-9933493-5-0 *Paperback*
ISBN: 979-8-9933493-6-7 *Hardcover*

First Edition

For those who forgave, even when it hurt.
Letting go is how we move forward.

Table of Contents

The Truth Beneath 1

Where It Begins 17

Breaking Lines..45

The Edge of Everything..80

The Unmaking of Self..112

Tracking the Invisible 145

The Turning Point..176

Becoming Whole 201

Connection Points..230

What Binds Us Together...267

A House Made New..307

The Heart of the Mansion..332

Full Circle of Love's Foundation 339

Thank You for Choosing Change..348

About the Author..349

More Titles from Vailed Pen Publications 350

Chapter 1

The Truth Beneath

DUST MOTES DANCED in the soft afternoon light filtering through the attic's grimy round window. They settled on Abbeline's updo, unwelcome stars on her meticulously pinned hair. She sneezed, the sound echoing through the cramped space.

She patted near the crown of her head, where a pin jabbed her scalp. The humid air had begun to loosen her sleek bun, and rebellious strands now slipped free around her temples. After five weeks without a visit, tomorrow's hair appointment couldn't come soon enough—she was losing the battle with her natural curls.

After thirty minutes of searching, Abbeline surrendered to the inevitable defeat. Her feet throbbed in her Louboutins. She wiped a patch of dusty floor with an old rag, then sank down cross-legged beside a worn leather trunk. Her fingers traced its faded monogram: B.H. Beatrice Hartwell. History lingered even in Beatrice's smallest corners.

"Under all that dust, there's another layer," Beatrice called from below, her voice warm with teasing.

"You're right!" Abbeline called back with mock exasperation. "I found one of your law school papers!"

"So I *did* pass contracts," Beatrice laughed.

The lid creaked as Abbeline opened it, unleashing a cloud that smelled of cedar and old paper. Inside lay stacks of letters tied with ribbon, yellowed newspapers, and black-and-white photos.

She picked up the photo on top and blew off a gentle puff of dust. Two children smiled at her. A girl of about seven or eight held a baby wrapped in blankets, blonde-haired with wide, surprised eyes.

"Just like me and your Grandma, Elisabeth." Beatrice appeared at the top of the stairs with a dust rag and a grin. She settled beside Abbeline, peering at the photograph. Her hands dusted off her slacks absently, but one thumb kept circling the edge of a worn silver ring. "That's me holding your mom, Abbie. Not exactly Dad's idea of a perfect holiday card."

Abbeline handed her the picture. "Was he always so... controlling?"

"He had his moments." Beatrice smiled at the photo. "But some things I couldn't let him win."

The memory of her grandfather's voice lingered in the attic like a ghost of conversation. *Family history matters,* he'd insisted when she protested about visiting Beatrice. His sternness had surprised her. For years, even her smallest wish had been met with kindness.

So why had this particular "wish" felt non-negotiable? What exactly was he afraid she'd find up here?

"We did have a dramatic flair for scandal," Beatrice continued, tying the photo bundle with care. Her eyes brightened with mischief. "Speaking of which—"

"Scandal or drama?" Abbeline interrupted playfully.

"Both." Beatrice nudged her shoulder. "I'm getting your favorite for dinner tonight."

"I have that dinner thing with Madison and Chance's family," Abbeline said, hesitating.

"Priorities," Beatrice teased, rising and brushing off her knees.

Abbeline sighed, laughing despite herself, as she stood to follow. The dim attic played tricks on her imagination, making her almost believe Randolph watched from the shadows.

"So what's for dinner?" she asked.

Beatrice paused at the door, smirking. "Crème brûlée cheesecake."

Abbeline shook her head in mock dismay. A thrill ran through her as she imagined the buttery crust, silky filling, and crackling burnt sugar lingering on her tongue.

"You play dirty," she groaned. Beatrice just chuckled.

As they descended the attic stairs, the wood creaked beneath their feet. Abbeline brushed her fingers along the banister in passing, her mind drifting—

—to an hour ago, in the study, when everything still felt composed.

Randolph's study smelled of old books, leather, and wood polish. A faint, sweet scent lingered in the air; she couldn't place where it was coming from.

She watched Randolph sign another check with his usual flourish. The pen scratched against the paper.

"You spoil me, Grandpa," Abbeline said.

Sunlight streamed through the window, lighting the elegant study. Golden rays fell across the mahogany desk and Randolph's stoic figure, catching on his neatly combed gray hair and the signet ring on his finger.

That ring had once felt cool against her cheek during those moments of childhood praise. Each compliment about her "manageable" hair or "refined" look had pulled her further from who she might have been.

"Nothing's too good for my best girl." His smile—the one that always made her feel like the most precious thing in his world—held something unfamiliar.

Something that looked almost like guilt. But that was ridiculous. Randolph Hartwell didn't do guilt.

"Just promise you'll stop by Beatrice's first. That school project won't complete itself."

"Do I have to?" She pouted, already plotting to reschedule. "The attic is filled with spiders. I'm having dinner with Madison's family tonight. They're considering me for junior league committee chair."

"Abbeline." His tone carried that rare note of steel she knew better than to challenge. "Family history matters. You'll understand that someday."

She had nodded then, but something in his tone lingered. Not warning—more like caution. Like he feared she might actually uncover something.

As she descended from the attic, a sheet-draped easel caught her eye. Her fingers twitched, remembering how they once held paintbrushes. A skill she'd learned to hide, just like her curls and her laugh. The faint scent of old art supplies hung in the air: linseed oil and warm paper.

A memory surfaced. At thirteen, her grandfather had picked her up from Beatrice's for a surprise weekend visit. Her hands were covered in paint. His quiet disappointment on the drive home cut deeper than anger. *Hartwells present themselves in a dignified manner, Abbeline.* She'd abandoned finger painting, and every other art form, that day. Her grandfather hadn't brought it up again, but the memory stayed.

Now she only painted when certain no one would see.

Mixing colors, losing herself in the brush's rhythm, had once meant freedom. But after that car ride, covered in green and ochre, she'd scrubbed her hands raw, as if shame could be rinsed away.

Since then, art had become a private indulgence, a secret habit. The canvas still called to her sometimes, though its voice had grown quieter.

Now, an hour after arriving at Beatrice's house, Abbeline descended the final stairs from the attic.

In Beatrice's kitchen, sunlight poured through the windows, painting warm patterns on the floor where leaf shadows danced. The smell of smoked meats and sweet barbecue sauce wrapped around them.

"I can stay a little while," Abbeline relented, kicking off her heels by the door.

Beatrice laughed softly, pulling plates from a cupboard. "That's my girl." She set the table with mismatched dishes, each one telling a piece of family history—delicate florals and vintage flourishes.

The table filled with pulled pork sandwiches, coleslaw, and dishes of pickles. Abbeline leaned back as they ate, savoring both the meal and the rare feeling of ease.

"So what's their angle?" Beatrice asked, one brow arched.

"Who?"

"This family you're having dinner with tonight."

Abbeline rolled her eyes with a sigh. "They're looking to make me junior league committee chair."

"And what do you think?"

She hesitated, picking at a crumb on her plate. The sauce's sweetness lingered on her lips like a secret she wasn't ready to share. "I'm still figuring that out."

Beatrice squeezed her hand. The warmth calmed her in ways words couldn't.

"What about you?" Abbeline deflected. "Ready to face the judge and jury tomorrow?"

"Oh, I'll survive." Beatrice smirked. "I've been dealing with your grandfather longer than you've been alive."

They talked until the food disappeared. Time slipped away. Abbeline glanced at the antique grandfather clock and gasped.

"I'm going to be late!" She grabbed her bag for her phone, but it wasn't there. She patted her pockets, then moved plates around. "My phone—I thought I had it…"

Realization dawned. She bolted from the table and ran back up the attic stairs.

In the attic, she retraced her steps.

"If I find it now, I can still make it on time."

"This is the worst timing ever," she muttered.

She didn't want to be late. Beyond poor etiquette, she wanted to avoid Randolph's lecture on responsibilities.

In her haste, she knocked over a box. Glancing at the spilled contents, she froze.

Beneath the toppled container was another trunk, similar to the first.

She continued searching, but something tugged at her attention. "A.H.," she whispered, the letters reverent.

She returned to the trunk and brushed it off. The initials were clear: A.H. for Abigail Hartwell.

"Mom's trunk," she breathed, fingers tracing the letters.

There was no dust where the initials were carved. The fallen box had shielded that spot.

She possessed so little from her mother. Her only inheritance was the silver chain around her neck, a gift from Beatrice on her eighteenth birthday—the necklace that once belonged to Abbie.

She had never seen anything else marked with her mother's initials.

Kneeling before the trunk, she opened it gently. The hinges creaked with a sound like thunder.

Three hours earlier, Abbeline stepped through Beatrice's front door. The familiar scent of smoked spices and worn wood washed over her.

She knew every corner of the charming two-story house—except the attic, a dark, dusty space she always avoided.

Dressed in Chanel, she carried herself with deliberate elegance. The antique mirror in the foyer reflected a woman polished to perfection—not a strand out of place, not a hint of uncertainty. Just the way her grandfather liked it.

Even now, her heels clicked with precision, a cadence drilled into her over years of "proper" entrances.

"Auntie Bea?" she called, her voice carrying the practiced lilt she'd honed at cotillion.

No response came—only the distant ticking of the grandfather clock filled the room, the same one her aunt refused to replace despite her grandfather's offers to "modernize" her home.

He'd called it outdated more than once. Abbeline had never said so aloud, but she liked that it kept ticking anyway.

A family photograph on the wall caught her eye, one of the few that included her mother. Abigail's wild blonde curls and bright, dimpled smile seemed to mock Abbeline's careful poise. Their arms were around each other, grinning in worn denim and windblown curls—so unguarded, so real. She couldn't remember the last time she laughed like that, without checking a mirror first. A tightness gathered in her chest, an ache without a name.

Something inside her itched—guilt, maybe. Or grief she'd never learned to name.

She turned away quickly, trying to shake the feeling.

"Aunt Bea?" she called again.

"I'm in here," came Beatrice's voice, slightly muffled.

Abbeline followed the sound around the corner, smiling as the sweet smell of barbecue pulled her into the kitchen. Beatrice laughed at Abbeline's carefully curated appearance.

She wiped her hands on a floral apron, then gave a slow, affectionate once-over like she was checking for armor.

"Sugar, you're not exactly dressed for digging through old junk."

"You mean family history," Abbeline teased back. "I hope you made enough for two," she added, popping a piece of cornbread into her mouth before hugging her aunt.

"Try enough for ten. I always cook for a platoon," Beatrice said, kissing her cheek.

"How much longer until the food's ready?" Abbeline asked, hanging her purse on the chair. She took out her phone and slipped it into her blazer pocket.

"About thirty more minutes," Beatrice said, tasting her special barbecue sauce on the stove.

"Perfect. That gives me just enough time to find what I'm looking for," she said, turning toward the attic.

She turned on the light and climbed the stairs, pausing at the top—this was her least favorite room in the house. The air grew cooler as she ascended. She stepped inside carefully, avoiding dusty boxes.

At the top, she hesitated. Silence pressed down like the dust on every surface. The attic had always unsettled her—too many shadows, too many secrets tucked into forgotten corners.

She'd always blamed the dust. But maybe it was something else. Maybe some part of her knew this place held things not meant to be found.

***

Now at her mother's open trunk, a scent wafted out—not just mothballs and age, but something that yanked her fully into the present. It was eerily familiar.

"Mom's perfume," she whispered. Jasmine and vanilla. The same fragrance that clung to the few possessions of her mother that remained.

The scent curled around her like memory, warm and aching.

At first glance, the trunk held only yellowed linens, moth-eaten clothes, and fine-bound books. But as she dug deeper, her fingers brushed something flat and rectangular beneath a cashmere shawl—an envelope, age-worn with softened edges.

Inside, she found photographs.

In the first, Beatrice and her mother stood side by side in front of a wooden cottage, arms linked. Beatrice looked to be in her twenties; her mother, barely out of her teens. Their faces glowed with youth, laughter frozen in silver tones.

The second photo took her breath away. Her mother perched alone on a cottage railing, surrounded by wildflowers. Blonde hair caught the sunlight. A dreamy, secretive smile played on her lips. A book lay forgotten in her lap. She looked like someone on the brink of something extraordinary.

But the third photograph stopped her heart.

Her mother again—this time locked in an embrace with a strikingly handsome Black man. His hazel eyes were fixed on her with unmistakable tenderness. They seemed lost in their own world, she gazing up at him with a love that defied the stillness of the frame.

A folded page fluttered from the envelope. She smoothed its brittle creases with shaking fingers and held it to the light.

The handwriting was bold and masculine:

My darling Abbie,

I see you in every sunrise, in every wildflower that dares to bloom between city sidewalks. When you smile with real joy—not just a polite grin—the world seems to pause in wonder. I want to spend my life collecting those real smiles, protecting them from anyone who would dim their light.

Forever yours,

Edward

Her fingers rose to her neck, touching the delicate silver chain she always wore.

In the grimy attic window, her reflection stared back. Stubborn curls had escaped their pins. She glanced from her reflection to the photo and back again. Her mother's eyes. His warm skin tone. The curve of his smile. Her mom's dimples.

A trembling truth began to form.

A truth her reflection had hinted at for years—but one she'd been trained to silence.

Her heart pounded, each beat echoing with possibility and dread. Secrets like this had no place in her grandfather's world. His plans were blueprints: precise, unyielding. She'd followed them for so long; she could no longer tell where his expectations ended and she began.

And if this changed who she was, what would he do to keep it buried?

She placed everything back in the trunk with care. But the photographs and letter—those, she tucked gently into her jacket pocket.

As if on cue, her phone buzzed with a notification. Her earlier search forgotten.

Grabbing it, she hurried down the stairs.

"Sugar, did you find it? You're really running late now," Beatrice called from the kitchen, her voice tinged with concern.

Abbeline paused, the words stuck in her throat. She took a deep breath before meeting her aunt's eyes.

"You'll never believe what I found," she said, trying to keep her voice steady—but the tremor was impossible to hide.

Beatrice's expression shifted, sensing the change in her niece.

The way her brow lifted, ever so slightly, told Abbeline this moment mattered.

"Honey," she said softly, "what did you find?"

Beatrice paused before answering. Her eyes moved between Abbeline's shaking hands and her bulging pocket. Abbeline watched recognition—and fear—wash over her aunt's usually composed face.

"You found your father," Beatrice said softly. Her voice was calm, but her eyes betrayed a storm. It wasn't a question; it was an admission.

"My father." The words felt foreign on Abbeline's tongue, a name she'd never dared whisper. A man her grandfather had declared dead rather than acknowledge. She said it again, more certain this time: "My father."

Saying the words aloud felt like snapping a thread no one wanted her to tug.

"Oh, Sugar." Beatrice reached for her hand.

Abbeline's phone buzzed—likely Madison, wondering about her absence. She ignored it.

The raw truth made her dizzy. Years of half-answers and shadowed doubts evaporated in an instant. She emptied her pocket onto the kitchen table and sank into a chair. Beatrice joined her. The photos and letter lay between them like evidence at a crime scene. Only the steady ticking of the grandfather clock broke the silence.

Abbeline's hands trembled slightly on the wood, but she didn't pull them away. *Let her see,* she thought. *Let her know I'm not okay.*

"Why didn't you ever tell me?" Her voice sounded small.

"I was going to, when the time was right." Beatrice's eyes clouded with memory. "But your grandfather thought he knew best, like always."

She clasped her hands tightly in her lap now, knuckles pale from pressure.

Abbeline heard the pain in her voice—regret woven through years of careful omissions.

"Well, here's your 'right time.' Tell me about them." Her voice cracked despite her best effort to control it. "The real story. Not Grandfather's version."

Beatrice picked up the photo showing only Abbie and studied it, as if buying time. When she looked up, her eyes held pain and resolve that made Abbeline's heart stutter.

"Your mother," she began, "was extraordinary. Not because she was a Hartwell, but because she dared to be herself in a world that demanded conformity." She paused, studying her niece's face—features echoing Abbie's, the coloring hinting at a different heritage. "They both fought for that right. Every day."

Her voice softened at the end, as if still unsure whether to speak hope or warning.

Abbeline held the photo with reverence, tracing her parents' faces. Her mother's wild blonde curls against his darker skin. Both radiated joy she'd never seen in any of her grandfather's family albums.

"What was his name?" she asked, even though she already knew. She needed to hear it out loud.

"Edward," Beatrice said. The name hung in the air, heavy with decades. "Edward Stuart. He worked security at your mother's eighteenth birthday gala. Former military, highly trained. He served with Claremont Securities—an elite firm that hired veterans for high-profile clients." A faint smile crossed her face. "And he loved your mother desperately."

"And she loved him?" Abbeline asked, her voice catching.

"More than anything. Enough to walk away from everything your grandfather offered. Enough to choose love and freedom over wealth and its baggage."

Abbeline's phone rang again—probably Madison, angry about the missed dinner. She silenced it with a tap.

It was remarkable how small that life felt now—committee chairs, table settings, even the perfect updo.

"Grandfather told me he caused Mom's death," she said, the words tasting like ash. "That he used her, preyed on a naive rich girl, then left when there was nothing more to take."

Beatrice's face hardened. "Another carefully crafted lie. Your mother died from complications during childbirth. Your father..." She paused, the pain showing. "Your father loved you both more than his own life."

"Then where is he?" The question burst out. "If he loved me so much, where has he been for twenty years?"

The words came sharper than she intended. Part accusation. Part plea.

"That," Beatrice said quietly, "is a much longer story."

She stood and walked to the antique secretary desk in the corner. Her fingers trembled as she withdrew a worn leather journal.

"Before I continue, you need to understand something. What I'm about to share won't be easy. Are you sure you're ready?"

She held the journal to her chest for a beat, as if bracing for ghosts.

Abbeline looked again at the photograph. Her mother's dimpled smile. Her father's protective embrace. Everything she thought she knew had been a carefully built cage of half-truths and omissions. The party, the nomination, the straightened hair—none of it mattered now. This changed everything.

Her scalp throbbed from the pins securing her updo. Without thinking, she reached up and pulled free the one that had been digging into her skin. The relief was immediate, like a full breath after being underwater. One pin came out, then another, and another. Each made her feel lighter. She had worn the pressure so long, she no longer noticed it. A curl popped free by her cheek, then another by her temple. Her hair finally rebelled after years of taming.

"I'm ready," she said. Her voice was stronger than she felt.

Whatever came next, she would face it without the mask.

Beatrice opened the journal, releasing the scent of old paper.

"It began," she said softly, "with a birthday party. Your mother's eighteenth..."

Afternoon light faded into evening shadows as Beatrice spoke. Abbeline listened in silence as the story unfolded—the unlikely meeting, the secret courtship, the defiance of expectations, and her grandfather's rage. Each word stripped away another layer of her crafted identity, exposing something raw and painful beneath.

When Beatrice finished, Abbeline felt hollow—stripped bare of everything she believed about herself.

But in its place, something new began to form: anger, grief, wonder... and deep down, an unfamiliar sense of freedom.

"All this time," she whispered, "he knew. He watched me straighten my hair, cover my skin, become the perfect Hartwell heiress. And all along, he was erasing half of who I am."

She clenched the journal tightly now, as if trying to hold the truth together with her own hands.

Beatrice didn't speak right away. She just nodded, her eyes full of sorrow.

"Yes," she said simply.

Abbeline turned to the window, searching for something—maybe air, maybe clarity. Twilight had fallen. Long shadows stretched across Beatrice's garden. The old oak tree reached toward the sky, its leaves catching the last light of day.

Her reflection in the dark glass startled her. Loose curls framed her face. Her makeup had smudged from tears she hadn't noticed.

Her phone buzzed again from her purse. Without looking, she knew Madison was wondering where she was. Yesterday, that dinner had felt so important.

For the first time, she powered her phone off without reading the message.

She turned back to Beatrice. Her eyes, though rimmed with tears, were clear.

"Tell me more," she said, her voice steady despite the ache. "Tell me everything."

Because now, she needed the truth more than the comfort of pretending.

Chapter 2

Where It Begins

EDWARD STUART ADJUSTED his tie in the bathroom mirror of his East Atlanta apartment. His fingers moved with military precision on the Windsor knot. The fluorescent light flickered, casting sharp shadows over the thin scar on his jaw—a souvenir from his second tour in Afghanistan.

He picked up the Security Advance memo from the sink.

"Abigail Hartwell," he muttered, studying the photo clipped to the file. Gray eyes stared back at him, defiant even in the formal pose.

"Just graduated from Point of Grace. Starts UAG in the fall."

He set the memo down.

Looks like money tried to iron out the fire, he thought. The girl in the photo wasn't soft—those eyes were alert, unyielding. Not your average trust-fund brat.

The mirror reflected his dark hair, cropped in a military style. His shoulders remained squared, posture straight even in civilian clothes. He adjusted his earpiece, the weight familiar against his skin.

His phone rang: Jax, former commanding officer, now his boss at Claremont Securities.

"Stuart here."

"Ed, just checking you're good for tonight." Jax's voice carried a hint of tension. "Randolph Hartwell's a big client. We can't afford any hiccups."

"It's babysitting duty, Jax. I can handle one spoiled princess."

"Just remember who signs your checks. These society types—they're different."

"Different how? More dangerous than Taliban snipers?"

"Pay your dues, kid. Everyone starts somewhere." A pause. "And Ed? Leave the body cam at home. These people value discretion."

The line went dead. Edward stared at the phone, then at the small camera clipped to his lapel. Jax had told him to leave it. "These people value discretion." But discretion didn't save Sanchez or Kaplowitz. Orders didn't catch the red flags in Kandahar. *His gut had.*

He left it on.

He switched off the bathroom light. The floorboards creaked under his polished shoes as he moved through the apartment. Through the window, the Bank of America Tower caught the sunset, its glass reflecting gold. Forty-five stories of wealth and power that felt a world away.

In the kitchenette, last night's coffee mug sat in the sink. The living room held a secondhand couch and a TV he rarely used. His bedroom showed military-tight sheets and not much else. The apartment was functional—just a place to sleep between jobs.

His watch read 6:15. With good traffic, Buckhead was thirty minutes away. He grabbed his keys from the counter.

At the door, his fingers brushed the lone framed photo on the side table. Five men in desert camo, arms slung over shoulders, grinning through the dust. Sanchez. Miller. Washington. Kaplowitz. All gone. He tapped the frame twice— left, then right. His ritual before each assignment. Then he locked the door, *leaving his real life behind.*

Beatrice Hartwell watched her sister twirl before the mirror in their downtown condo. The custom gown caught the light in every crystal bead. At twenty-seven, Beatrice was already a top mergers and acquisitions lawyer at Hartwell Industries, and part-time emotional anchor to her eighteen-year-old sister.

"You look beautiful, Abs," she said, reaching to tame a stray blonde curl. "Mom would be so proud."

Abbie's fingers touched the silver chain at her neck—a gift from Beatrice.

"I wish she was here, Bea."

Beatrice swallowed. Their mother's death when Abbie was sixteen had thrown her into a maternal role while still launching her own career. She moved behind her sister, meeting her eyes in the mirror.

"She is here. In your smile. In how you see the world through your art."

The mirror reflected their contrasts. Beatrice, in a tailored navy dress, her chestnut hair swept into a sleek chignon, the pearls at her neck. Abbie, radiant with honey-blonde curls and eyes full of excitement—and something else. Something that looked like rebellion.

"Dad wants me to network tonight," Abbie said. "Make connections for business school."

"And what do you want?" Beatrice asked, already knowing. She'd found the hidden sketchpads beneath sweaters in Abbie's dresser. Beatrice had followed the expected path—Harvard, Stanford Law, Hartwell Industries—and thrived. But Abbie was different. More like their mother, Elisabeth.

"I want to paint," Abbie whispered. "I want to tell stories with colors."

Beatrice turned her to face her. Steel-blue eyes met gray.

"Then that's what you'll do. I'll handle Dad." She smoothed Abbie's dress. "But tonight, dance, laugh, eat too much cake. Deal?"

Abbie's dimpled smile surfaced. "Deal. But rescue me if Caroline starts talking about Yale boys again."

"Scout's honor," Beatrice laughed, checking her watch—the Rolex their mother gave her when she passed the bar. "Car's waiting. Ready for your grand entrance?"

In the private elevator, Beatrice touched her mother's pearls. *I'm trying, Mom. Trying to give her both wings and roots.*

Some days, the weight of being the responsible one pressed so hard she could barely breathe. She smiled, straightened her shoulders, and prayed Abbie would never have to carry this kind of balance—between love and duty, between truth and silence.

Outside, humidity pressed against their skin. The scent of magnolias clung to the air, mingling with car exhaust and a trace of distant rain. Their driver waited by the open door with a gentle smile.

Abbie paused, one hand at her necklace, the other smoothing her gown.

"Last chance to back out," Beatrice teased.

Abbie slid into the car. "No backing out now. Besides, Chef Maurice is making chocolate soufflé."

As the car pulled away, the streetlights flicked on above them, one by one—like stars being born.

At the gala, the ballroom blazed with crystal light. Edward stood by the grand staircase, tracking every entrance and exit. The weight of his concealed holster pressed against his ribs. Chandeliers scattered fractured light across marble floors. Champagne flowed on silver trays borne by white-gloved servers. Perfume marked women who never looked his way.

He divided the room into quadrants. North corner: three security personnel, easy to spot by earpieces and posture. East wall: wait staff moving in practiced rhythm. Central floor: Atlanta's elite circling like sharks in designer water.

He spotted Abigail Hartwell among a pack of giggling debutantes. But tension pulled at her shoulders. Her fingers kept drifting to the silver chain at her neck.

A server brushed past too close. Edward's hand twitched toward his side, then stilled.

Two young men burst in, flushed and laughing, tuxes rumpled, bow ties loose. Drunk. Edward tracked them to the bar, noting how they sliced through personal space.

To his left, a voice said, "Stuart."

He turned to face Randolph Hartwell. The man's Boston-cut features projected control. The resemblance to Abigail was clear—they shared the same gray eyes, though hers held warmth where his were cold.

"Watch Abigail tonight," Randolph said. "It's her eighteenth birthday. I won't have unsavory types sniffing around." His gaze flicked to the newcomers.

"Yes, sir." Edward straightened instinctively.

Beatrice Hartwell approached, cutting in.

"Daddy, the Whitmore acquisition team wants to speak with you. Something about those terms we discussed?"

Edward watched Randolph shift—stern father one second, business titan the next.

"Ah, yes. Excuse me, Stuart." He patted Beatrice's shoulder. "Always on top of things, aren't you, dear?"

As Randolph walked off, Beatrice turned to Edward. Her eyes dropped to the bulge beneath his lapel—the body cam.

"Mr. Stuart," she said quietly, "my sister isn't just another trust-fund princess to be managed. She's special."

Their eyes met. He saw the warning in hers, and something more—an assessment.

"I understand, Ms. Hartwell," he said. Though he wasn't sure he did.

Laughter buzzed around Abbie like static, all champagne sparkle and designer gossip. She nodded along, fingers absently tracing her necklace, but her thoughts were miles from the ballroom.

"Abbie, are you even listening?" Caroline pouted, her gaze drifting. "Oh my God, who is that? The new security guy? He's gorgeous!"

"Speaking of gorgeous," another girl chimed in, "Bea looks amazing tonight. Is it true she's dating that attorney? Roderick something?"

Abbie suppressed a smile, picturing how her sister would roll her eyes at the gossip.

"Bea and Roderick are just colleagues. They're working on that children's advocacy initiative together."

"Don't even think about it, Care," another girl giggled, eyeing Edward. "Daddy would have a coronary if you dated the help."

The casual cruelty landed like a cold hand on Abbie's chest.

These were her friends—girls she'd grown up with, vacationed with, posed beside in countless debutante photos. But lately, every conversation felt like play-acting a life she no longer believed in.

She let her fingers drift from her necklace, remembering her mother's voice.

"True worth isn't in what you own, darling, but in how you treat others."

"I need some air," she murmured, already slipping away.

Edward remained at his post, watching Abigail move to the edge of the crowd.

When she thought no one was looking, she pulled a small sketchbook from her evening purse. Her fingers moved quickly, confidently, sketching the angle of a chandelier, the slope of a shoulder. This wasn't distraction—it was survival.

Then, just as swiftly, she tucked it away.

You could learn a lot about a person by what they did when they thought no one was watching. Edward had seen the sketchbook, saw how her expression changed—focused, alive.

Abigail Hartwell's hidden sketches made him wonder what else she kept behind that polished smile.

The gala spun around Abbie in a blur of crystal and practiced smiles. Her father introduced her to several business school representatives, each conversation more strained than the last. His questions about her "five-year plan" tightened the knot in her stomach.

"I'm thinking about finance," she said for the third time that evening, her words hollow even to her own ears.

Across the room, Beatrice navigated business discussions with the Whitmores effortlessly. Her sister wielded warmth and professional polish in perfect balance. Abbie touched her silver necklace, wishing for even a fraction of that grace.

The weight of expectations pressed heavier on her shoulders than the gown she wore. She needed to escape, if only for a moment.

"Would you excuse me?" she said to the Princeton representative, offering a polite smile. "I should greet our other guests."

She moved through the crowd, nodding at familiar faces without stopping. Every superficial interaction chipped away at her patience. Her fingers ached for her sketchbook. The Whitmore twins slouched by the dessert table, boredom etched in their posture. Mrs. Caldwell squinted into her champagne like it had wronged her. The room brimmed with unguarded moments begging to be captured.

She found a quiet alcove near the French doors. After making sure no one was watching, she slipped her sketchbook from her evening purse. Her pencil moved quickly, confidently, capturing the orchestra. Each musician revealed something in posture—some rigid with focus, others swaying with the melody.

"Miss Hartwell."

The voice startled her. Abbie snapped the sketchbook shut, heart jumping as she turned to face the security guard—Stuart. His expression gave nothing away, but his eyes missed little.

"I'm not doing anything wrong," she said, more defensive than she'd intended.

"I didn't say you were." His tone was neutral, which somehow made her feel more exposed.

Up close, she noticed what she hadn't before—the faint scar along his jaw, his precise stance, his eyes scanning the room even as he spoke. Military background, she guessed. There was a coiled energy about him, power held carefully in check.

"Your father asked me to check on you," he said. "You've been absent from the main floor for fifteen minutes."

"He's keeping tabs now?" she muttered, surprised by the sharpness in her own voice.

The corner of Stuart's mouth twitched—not quite a smile, but close.

"Security protocols. Periodic check-ins for the guest of honor."

She doubted that was standard, but appreciated the discretion. Her sketchbook was still clutched to her chest.

"Are you an artist?" he asked, nodding toward the book.

The question caught her off guard. No one at these events ever asked about her art.

"Just a hobby," she said automatically—the dismissal her father had trained into her. But something in Stuart's direct gaze invited honesty.

"I like to observe people when they don't know they're being watched. That's when you see who they really are."

Stuart noted how her posture changed. Her spine straightened, her voice steadied, her eyes lit with something real.

"May I?" he asked, gesturing to the sketchbook.

Abbie hesitated. These drawings were private, her unfiltered view of the world. But his stillness didn't feel judgmental—it felt curious. She opened the book and handed it to him.

Edward turned the pages slowly. His expression stayed unreadable, but his focus was total. Abbie studied his face, bracing for the usual dismissive politeness—like her father's friends offered when they entertained her "hobby."

"You have a gift for capturing what people try to hide," he said, stopping on a sketch of an elderly couple. The woman's hand just barely reached toward her husband, whose arms remained stiff behind his back.

"This tension: it tells an entire story."

Something uncoiled in her chest. He saw it—really saw it. Not the technique or linework, but the meaning. The woman's quiet yearning, the man's restraint.

"Most people just say they're pretty pictures."

"I'm not most people," he said, flipping to the next page. He paused over the orchestra sketch, his finger hovering just above the paper.

"You notice things others miss."

He spotted the two young men from earlier approaching the alcove. One nudged the other, grinning as he pointed toward Abbie.

"Your admirers approach," he said, closing the sketchbook and handing it back.

"Unwanted ones, I'm guessing."

Abbie followed his gaze and stifled a groan.

"Bradley Thompson and Marcus Reed. They've been circling me all night."

Edward shifted subtly, positioning himself between her and the newcomers without drawing attention.

"Would you prefer to avoid them?"

"God, yes," she said, forgetting to filter her tone. "But that would be rude, and Hartwells aren't rude in public."

"Perhaps a security matter requires your attention elsewhere," he offered, tone cool, though a faint glint in his eye gave him away.

Slipping the sketchbook into her purse, she nodded, grateful for the out.

"Lead the way, Mr. Stuart."

He guided her through a service corridor. The muffled thrum of the party faded behind them, replaced by quiet and the crisp air near the garden entrance.

"Thank you," Abbie said, drawing a deep breath. "For the rescue—and for what you said about my sketches."

"I only told the truth." His hands remained behind his back, his posture watchful as he scanned the garden.

"That's refreshing," she said with a faint laugh. "Truth is in short supply at these events."

Before he could respond, a server approached with a message from Randolph: Abbie was needed for the cake presentation. The moment dissolved.

"Back to the performance," she murmured, lifting her chin and summoning her Hartwell smile.

Edward watched the transformation—the artist vanishing beneath the polished mask. She turned to go but glanced back. In that single look, gratitude flickered before she disappeared into the corridor.

He'd expected petulance, vanity, maybe boredom. Not precision. Not insight. She watched the room as closely as he did—only through a different lens.

After the party, Edward returned to the alcove where they'd spoken. On the chair, her sketchbook lay open.

He reached for it, intending to return it, then paused.

A sketch of himself stared back: captured in profile, alert, eyes sweeping the room. Unlike her other subjects, he wasn't caught off guard. She'd drawn him with awareness.

Beneath the image, in delicate script:

"The only one who sees rather than looks."

Edward closed the book carefully and tucked it into his jacket. Technically, he should leave it with lost and found.

But he'd return it personally—just to see what else she might be hiding.

***

The stillness of Edward's apartment struck him again as he returned from the gala. He tossed his keys onto the counter, the metallic clatter echoing through the bare space. He loosened his tie and rolled his shoulders, releasing the tension from hours of vigilance. The microwave clock glowed 2:17 a.m., its digits sharp against the dim kitchen light.

He removed his holster, secured it in the lockbox beside his bed, then detached the body cam from his lapel. Protocol required reviewing the footage before his next shift, but he'd already broken orders by wearing it, so he set the device aside. His thoughts lingered instead on the evening's unexpected turn.

From his jacket, he withdrew Abigail Hartwell's sketchbook. The leather cover showed wear at the corners, evidence of frequent use. He held it a moment, aware he'd already crossed an invisible line by bringing it home.

Security protocol said all lost items went to the Claremont office. But he'd already broken one rule tonight.

Edward settled onto his secondhand couch and opened the book. Under the harsh apartment lighting, he noticed things he'd missed earlier. An elderly woman watched young dancers, her eyes filled with echoes of her own youth. Waitstaff exchanged knowing glances behind champagne trays. Randolph Hartwell appeared exhausted, his shoulders low and mouth drawn tight, caught in a rare unguarded moment.

These weren't just illustrations—they were windows. Abigail Hartwell had the rare ability to see people in the spaces between performances.

He turned to the final page. His own likeness stared back, drawn with intent rather than accident. She'd caught the tension in his shoulders, the vigilance in his eyes. But more than that— she'd seen something he believed he kept buried. And that, more than anything, unsettled him.

His phone rang. Jax's name glowed on the screen.

"It's after two, Jax," Edward said, setting the sketchbook aside.

"Got a call from Beatrice Hartwell. Something about a missing sketchbook."

Edward glanced at the book on his coffee table. "Found it after they left. I'll drop it at the office tomorrow."

"Good. Return it first thing."

"Understood."

Jax paused. "And Ed? Hartwell's daughter needs transporttation to Athens tomorrow. Her sister's tied up with a board meeting."

"Let me check my schedule—"

"It wasn't a request. Be at the Hartwell mansion at nine sharp. You've been specifically requested."

The line went dead.

Edward stared at the phone. Beatrice Hartwell had requested him? After the body cam, after keeping the sketchbook off record? Something didn't fit.

He stood, stretching the stiffness from his spine, and moved toward the shower. Hot water pounded his shoulders, but his thoughts wouldn't settle. Abigail's sketches, her guarded honesty, the way her posture shifted when she spoke about art—all of it clung to him more than sweat or steam.

"Just a hobby," she'd said. But her eyes had told a different story.

Later, in his bedroom, he dressed in worn sweatpants and set his alarm for 7:00 a.m. As he lay in the dark, the sketchbook still on the table outside, he acknowledged what he hadn't said aloud: Abigail Hartwell was no longer just another client. She wasn't what he expected. *She wasn't even who she pretended to be.*

Morning arrived with the harsh buzz of his alarm. Edward moved through his routine with practiced discipline—push-ups, stretching, a cold shower, protein shake. He suited up in his Claremont uniform, polished shoes, earpiece aligned, everything in place.

He picked up the sketchbook. Something had shifted—he couldn't deny that anymore. The book wasn't just filled with drawings. It was a ledger of what mattered to her. And now, part of that ledger included him.

At the door, he tapped the photo of his fallen comrades—left side, then right. The ritual felt heavier. They'd known him beneath the mission-ready exterior. Now, someone else had seen past the uniform, too.

Edward stepped into the bright Atlanta morning. His drive to Buckhead awaited. The sketchbook rested on the passenger seat beside him, its presence quiet but undeniable. In war, seeing beneath the surface had saved his life more than once.

What it meant in civilian life—especially in the world of the Hartwells—remained to be seen.

Edward arrived an hour early at the Hartwell mansion and waited in the company car. The sketchbook tucked securely inside his jacket. Through the windshield, he watched Abigail embrace her father on the front steps.

Her transformation from the night before startled him. The polished debutante had vanished. In her place stood a young woman in a simple cornflower sundress that stirred in the morning breeze. Her honey-blonde hair fell loose, catching the light in ways her formal updo hadn't allowed.

Randolph Hartwell stood beside her, his tailored suit projecting authority. Edward observed their interaction with professional detachment. Randolph's hand rested on his daughter's shoulder. She shifted slightly under the contact but maintained her smile. Her posture told a truth her words didn't touch.

Edward exited the car as they approached.

"Good morning, Mr. Hartwell."

"Ah, Stuart. Prompt as expected." Randolph's gaze swept over the vehicle with the scrutiny of a man accustomed to evaluating assets. "Jax speaks highly of your professionalism."

"Thank you, sir."

"I expect my daughter in Athens by one. She has an appointment with her academic advisor." His tone allowed no room for negotiation.

"Yes, sir. I've mapped the route."

Abbie glanced at the car while her father continued issuing instructions, as if she were cargo to be logged and transported. When Randolph finally addressed her, his expression softened marginally.

"Now, Abigail, remember what we discussed about Professor Thompson's business ethics seminar. It's essential for establishing the right connections."

"Yes, Daddy," she replied, her voice polished and bright. "I've prepared all my questions."

Beatrice appeared in the doorway, brow slightly furrowed. Unlike her sister, she wore a crisp navy suit, already immersed in the day's business. She approached with a small envelope.

"Abbie's apartment keys," she said. "And the building manager's contact information."

"I have all that, Bea," Abbie said, the edge in her voice faint but unmistakable.

"I know." Beatrice gave her sister's hand a brief squeeze, then turned to Edward. "Mr. Stuart, a word?"

They stepped a few paces aside.

"The route I suggested avoids construction on I-85," Beatrice said, all efficiency. Then, more quietly, "My sister values her independence, even within careful boundaries. Please respect that."

Edward met her gaze. "I understand, Ms. Hartwell."

Something in his tone satisfied her. She nodded and rejoined the others while Edward loaded Abbie's bags into the trunk.

From a distance, they looked like a close family, but up close, the seams showed—in posture, in pauses, in what wasn't said.

As Randolph and Beatrice departed—he to Hartwell Industries, she to her board meeting—Edward opened the car door for Abbie.

"Wait," she said, hesitating. "Shouldn't I sit in the back? Isn't that protocol?"

"Your choice, Ms. Hartwell," he said evenly. "Front or back."

She studied him for a moment, then, with quiet decisiveness, slid into the front passenger seat. "Front. And please, call me Abbie. 'Ms. Hartwell' makes me sound like my sister."

Edward closed her door and circled to the driver's side. As he started the engine, he noticed her watching him.

"Your sister seems protective," he said, steering them out of the circular driveway.

"Bea stepped in after Mom died," she said softly. "She was barely out of law school, but she put everything on hold for me."

Edward nodded, guiding them through Buckhead's exclusive streets. Mansions gave way to upscale boutiques, then to more modest storefronts. Atlanta's social hierarchy shifted with each mile.

They drove in silence for several minutes. Abbie gazed out the window, lost in thought.

"I believe this belongs to you," Edward said, retrieving the sketchbook from his jacket once they reached a straight stretch of highway.

Her eyes widened. "Where did you find it?"

"Found it under a chair at the gala," he said, passing it to her. "I should've turned it in immediately."

"But you didn't." Her voice was even, unreadable. She traced the worn leather cover, relief and apprehension flickering across her face. "Did you look inside?"

"Yes," he answered, without hesitation.

She held the book close. Silence stretched between them.

"You're angry," he said.

"I'm... I'm not sure what I am. Those sketches aren't for others. They help me understand what I see."

"They're good," Edward said simply. "Honest."

She studied him, searching for condescension. Finding none, she relaxed slightly.

"You didn't tell my father?"

"That's not part of my job. I don't betray confidences."

Abbie tilted her head, reevaluating him. "You're not what I expected, Mr. Stuart."

"Edward," he said. "And what did you expect?"

"The usual. Someone who sees the Hartwell name first and the person second." She opened to the last page—her sketch of him. "But you notice things. At the party, you shook your head when Caroline snuck champagne. Your mouth twitched when Mrs. Whittington counted her steps."

He tightened his grip on the wheel, eyes narrowing slightly. "Noticing details is part of security work."

"Is that why you kept my sketchbook? Professional curiosity?"

"At first. Then I saw what you captured. Not just appearances—truth, emotion, humanity."

"Like how I drew you?"

"Yes." He met her eyes, then looked back to the road. "Few people look past the uniform."

"Few people look past the Hartwell name either."

They shared a glance. Something passed between them—quiet and electric.

"So," he said, shifting the mood, "you're studying business at UGA?"

"That's the plan," she said carefully.

"But not your plan?"

She turned to the window. "It's complicated."

"Most worthwhile things are," he said, thinking of his own transition from soldier to civilian.

She turned back, curiosity blooming. "Is that why you left the military? Complications?"

He tightened his grip on the wheel. "What makes you think I served?"

"Your posture. Your haircut. How you track exits without looking like you're tracking exits. Plus, you have that look."

"What look?"

"Like you've seen things most people haven't. My sketch captured it."

He nodded. "Army Rangers. Two tours in Afghanistan."

"And now you're driving debutantes to college," she said, not unkindly.

"It's quieter," he replied. "Safer. Most days."

She nodded, accepting his answer. "Sometimes, the path laid out for you doesn't match who you are."

The comment lingered longer than he expected. "Is that why you chose an apartment twenty minutes from campus?"

She looked at him, surprised. "Yes."

He smiled faintly. "Creating distance from expectations."

Their silence after that was different—not empty, but understood.

The road stretched ahead, sunlight bouncing off the windshield. Beside him, Abbie sketched—quiet, observant, unguarded. Edward kept his eyes on the road, but for the first time, not just out of habit.

"Turn here," Abbie said suddenly, pointing to a weathered sign reading Big Joe's BBQ.

Edward glanced at the roadside establishment. Its faded wooden exterior and gravel parking lot stood in stark contrast to Buckhead's polished venues. A few pickup trucks dotted the lot.

"Best pulled pork in Georgia," she added, answering his unspoken question. "Trust me." She smiled.

Edward eased the car off the road and into the lot, parking beside a rusted Chevy.

"This isn't on the way to Athens."

"Consider it cultural education." Her smile revealed those dimples again.

"Security professionals should know local landmarks."

Inside, the scent of hickory smoke and sweet sauce wrapped around them. Checkered tablecloths covered scarred wooden tables. Faded photographs of local sports teams lined the wood-paneled walls. A waitress with "Darlene" on her name tag lit up when she saw Abbie.

"Sugar! Been too long." She enveloped Abbie in a warm hug.

"Your usual spot's open," Darlene said.

Abbie led Edward to a corner booth with a clear view of both the entrance and the kitchen. He noted the tactical advantage, wondering whether the seat was chosen by instinct or design.

"My mom used to bring us here," Abbie explained, sliding into the booth.

"Said it was the one place in Georgia where people didn't care about your last name."

Edward's instincts had him scanning exits and logging faces, but the restaurant's relaxed atmosphere gradually eased his guard. Darlene returned with glasses of sweet tea before they'd even ordered.

"Get the pulled pork platter," Abbie advised.

"And save room for peach cobbler."

"Yes, ma'am," he said, the Southern drawl slipping into his voice, surprising them both.

When the platters arrived—heaped with pulled pork, coleslaw, and cornbread—Edward watched Abbie dive in without hesitation. Her usual polish gave way to genuine appetite.

"So," she said between bites, "what did your file say about me?"

Edward considered his response.

"Standard background. Family, school records, usual movement patterns. Nothing about your art, or that you can quote Whitman from memory."

Her eyebrows lifted.

"How did you know that?"

"You murmured 'I contain multitudes' when that Princeton guy brought up conformity guidelines."

"I didn't think anyone heard that." She studied him.

"What else did you notice?"

"That you scan for exits like I do. That you note security camera blind spots. That your grip in that photo on your father's desk suggests formal shooting training."

She smirked, not denying it.

"Bea insisted after Mom died. Said Atlanta wasn't always kind to young women alone. I have a standing appointment at Peachtree Range every Thursday." She took another sip of tea.

"Your turn—what's not in your file?"

"That's not how this works."

"No? I thought we were trading truths."

Edward hesitated.

"My father was military. Third generation. Never forgave me for leaving the Rangers before making colonel."

"Why did you leave?" Her voice held no judgment, only curiosity.

He stared at the scratched tabletop.

"Lost four men under my command. Bad intel. Command cleared me, but…"

"But you couldn't clear yourself," she finished.

Their eyes met across the table. No explanations needed.

"Peach cobbler," Darlene announced, placing two steaming bowls before them.

"On the house for Abbie and her friend."

The conversation lightened as they savored the dessert. Edward shared stories about his grandfather's fishing boat. Abbie described her first failed oil painting, how the canvas tipped and ruined her mother's favorite rug. Laughter came easily, filling the space where tension had lived.

An hour later, they stepped into the heat, both slowed by full stomachs. The lot had filled while they ate. Their car was now one of the last from the earlier crowd.

"Well?" Abbie asked as they reached the car.

"Was I right about the BBQ?"

"Best in Georgia," Edward admitted, opening her door.

"Though I notice you still haven't told me that shooting range score."

She paused, grinning.

"Maybe next time, Stuart. Can't reveal all my secrets at once."

Back on the road—the air between them had changed. The driver-passenger boundary had quietly dissolved somewhere between cornbread and shared memories. Edward switched off his body cam. He no longer felt like a guard performing a role. *For once, he didn't need the distance.*

When they pulled up to Abbie's off-campus apartment, Edward was surprised by a feeling he hadn't anticipated: he didn't want the drive to end.

"I can carry my own bags," Abbie said, watching him retrieve her suitcase.

"Humor me," he replied.

Her dimples flashed.

"If you insist."

At her door, she turned to him.

"This is me. Number 309."

"You're all set then?"

Abbie paused before answering, fingers brushing the strap of her bag. Then, with a breath:

"Can I give you my number? I'd like to continue our conversation sometime."

Her directness surprised them both.

Edward blinked, then nodded and handed her his phone.

"I'd like that."

She entered her number, typed quickly, then hit send. When he looked at his screen, it read: Your unexpected surprise here, call me.

"There," she said, her voice lighter.

"Now it's official."

"That was one of the best conversations I've ever had," she said.

"Thanks for the drive, and for listening."

"Same here," Edward said.

"It was my pleasure."

He watched her go, then slid into the driver's seat. The unexpected nature of the day settled around him like calm after a storm. Abigail Hartwell had become something more than a client.

That evening, Beatrice's phone rang as she reviewed merger documents.

"Everything okay, Sugar?"

"We stopped at Mom's place," Abbie said softly.

Beatrice's hand stilled on her pen. Big Joe's. Their mother's retreat from expectations. After her death, it had become Abbie's.

"You took him there?" Beatrice asked gently.

"He felt different, Bea. Real." She paused.

"Is that crazy?"

Beatrice thought of the careful steps she'd taken to keep her heart locked and her path safe.

"No, Sugar. Sometimes the crazy choices are the most honest ones." She hesitated.

"Just... be careful with your heart, okay?"

"You sound like Mom," Abbie laughed.

"Well, someone has to," Beatrice said, her throat tightening.

"Did you get the pulled pork?"

"And peach cobbler. I saved you some."

"My hero," Beatrice smiled, remembering summer afternoons in that weathered booth—their mother whispering truths that had nothing to do with society. Truths about kindness, worth, and the quiet power of seeing people as they really are.

✳✳✳

Beatrice placed orange slices in her mother's chipped glass bowl and wiped her hands on a linen towel. Edward stood nearby, flipping cornbread in a cast iron skillet. Abbie, barefoot, leaned against the counter, sketchbook open as she softly hummed a tune by Joni Mitchell.

"You're early," Beatrice said.

"She insisted," Edward replied, nodding at Abbie. "Said today was a special one."

Abbie looked up. "I've decided to turn down the Caldwell internship," she said quietly.

The room felt suspended.

Beatrice set the bowl on the table with a soft clink. "You're sure?"

"I want to paint," Abbie replied. "The Atlanta Collective offered me a fall exhibit."

The coffee pot hissed. Edward didn't speak—not because nothing needed saying, but because his silence said enough.

Beatrice smiled gently. "What do you want?"

"To paint."

"Then that's what you'll do. I'll handle Dad."

Beatrice thought of all the Sundays before this—the first brunch with Edward, where he'd sat rigid, to this one, where he now moved easily through her kitchen.

Over time, Sundays had become a ritual—debates over art, laughter over fresh bread from Edward's favorite bakery, quiet acceptance of each other's rhythms. Edward's response to Abbie's choice came without a word—he squeezed her hand beneath the table.

She remembered one late-night conversation over wine—Abbie's fork poised, the air loose with candor.

"He's not what I expected."

"Rigid?" Abbie teased.

"Both—and he quotes Frost and actually makes soufflés."

Abbie laughed. "Once you pass the perimeter, he barely looked away from protocol."

At another brunch, Abbie twirled her mother's silver necklace and asked, "What would Mom think of him?"

Beatrice answered softly, "She'd be proud you chose someone who sees your heart," then added, "That's worth everything."

One Sunday, Edward came early. Beatrice found him adjusting a shelf, then pausing before their mother's framed photo.

"She had Abbie's smile," he said quietly.

"Other way around," Beatrice replied, handing him coffee. "Abbie has her smile, and her fire."

Edward paused, mug in hand.

"Thank you... for trusting me with her. I know that costs you."

"You mean with Dad?"

"With everything. You've protected her a long time. That kind of trust doesn't change easily."

Beatrice met his gaze.

"Just... don't ask her to shrink."

"I wouldn't," he said firmly. "Not ever."

———

Summer came again. Abbie called late to say, "We watched the meteor shower. He held my hand."

Minutes later, Edward's text to Beatrice read: "She's special. I don't deserve her."

She typed back: "That's exactly why you might."

Spring followed. Mimosas and sun lit the next brunch.

As the third anniversary approached, simple moments marked its passage—Abbie referring to our apartment, Edward's toothbrush a quiet fixture in her bathroom. Their lives were no longer separate paths.

That evening, Beatrice found Edward waiting in her dim office lobby. His posture was stillness, but his eyes carried gravity.

"Something on your mind, Stuart?" she asked.

He inhaled. "I'd like to talk with you. About Abbie."

Beatrice felt that familiar weight—but this time, it felt like hope.

"Let's get coffee," she said.

Chapter 3

Breaking Lines

BEATRICE STEPPED OUT of her downtown condo just as
Abbie shut the truck bed, her hiking gear already loaded.
Morning traffic hummed, commuters flowing along the
sidewalks. Abbie moved with a new sharpness, so unlike the
quiet girl who'd barely touched her toast that morning.

"You've got the trail map?" Beatrice asked, handing her a
thermos of coffee.

"Yes, and the emergency contacts." Abbie accepted it with
a smile that didn't quite reach her eyes. "And yes, I'll be careful."

"You'll call from the summit?" The question carried more
than surface meaning, a tradition born after their mother's
death, when Beatrice had tracked Abbie's first solo hike through
nervous hourly check-ins.

"Always, Bea."

Abbie climbed into the passenger seat, laughing at
something Edward said. The truck eased into traffic and

vanished around the corner. Beatrice lingered a moment longer, arms folded against the chill, before heading inside. She had a nine o'clock deposition to prepare for, but her mind stayed with the truck long after it disappeared.

—

Edward's fingers tapped the steering wheel as they climbed into Georgia's northern hills. Pine trees pressed close to the winding road, their piney scent drifting in through a cracked window. The trailhead lot was nearly empty—just a red Jeep and a mud-splattered pickup.

Perfect.

"Ready?" he asked, cutting the engine.

"Race you to the top?" Abbie's fingers curled around the door handle, eyes lit with challenge.

He grinned. "No head start this time."

"Don't need one."

The trail climbed, steep and steady. Pine needles cushioned their steps, releasing a sharp, familiar pine scent. Sunlight dappled the forest floor, shifting across Abbie's honey-blonde curls as she led the way. They didn't talk much, saving their breath for the climb, but the silence felt easy, almost sacred.

At the summit, Abbie dropped her pack onto a sun-warmed boulder, her cheeks flushed with triumph.

"Told you." She wiped her brow with her sleeve, barely winded.

"I let you win." The lie slipped out easily, his grin giving him away.

"Sure you did." Her smile widened.

Edward's chest tightened. *These hikes, these hours off-grid—they were theirs.* And they'd built something real in the quiet. Today, the air between them felt charged, like they were teetering on the edge of something more.

Abbie stepped to the overlook. Atlanta shimmered in the distance, a glittering mirage. Wind lifted her hair, and for a moment, she seemed carved from the sky—luminous and unreachable.

"Come here often?" The old joke slipped out, his voice low, trying to mask the ache in his chest.

"Only with handsome tour guides." She didn't turn, but her voice warmed.

He moved beside her, close enough to catch the familiar blend of jasmine and vanilla. A hawk circled below, silent and graceful. On impulse, he snapped a photo—her figure framed against the sky, a stolen moment he never wanted to lose.

"You're staring again." Her lips curved, still facing the valley. "What is it? Trail mix in my hair?"

"No, I..." He stepped closer, voice quieter now. "I was thinking about the first time I saw you."

She turned, catching his gaze. "At the gala? When you thought I was just another spoiled princess?"

"When I thought I knew exactly who you were." His eyes flicked to her lips, then back. "I've never been so glad to be wrong."

Color rose in her cheeks, but her gaze didn't waver. "And who am I, Edward Stuart?"

The question lingered. He could list the details—the way she scanned exits, her uncanny aim, the truth she captured in sketches—but none of that encompassed what she truly was to him.

"You're my best friend, Abs." The words came out rough, scraped and raw. "And I'm scared to ruin that."

Her breath caught. "Why would you ruin it?"

He looked out at the horizon, the endless stretch of possibility and consequence. His instincts screamed at him to retreat, to hold the line.

But silence, suddenly, felt like the bigger danger.

"Because I'm in love with you." The words left him like an exhale. "Have been for too damn long. And I know there are a thousand reasons this is a bad idea—your father, my job, our friendship."

"Edward?" She stepped in, closing the space between them.

"Yeah?"

"Shut up and kiss me."

For a heartbeat, he searched her face—for doubt, for hesitation—but saw only certainty. He cupped her cheek, brushing his thumb across a freckle, and kissed her.

It was both a beginning and a homecoming. She fisted his shirt, anchoring him. The world shrank to the warmth of her lips, the press of her hand against his chest, the steady drumbeat of something long denied.

When they finally parted, her smile was radiant.

"Took you long enough," she whispered.

A laugh rumbled in his chest. "I was trying to be professional."

"You wore a body cam to drive me to college."

"And you called me out immediately." He tucked a strand of hair behind her ear. "I think I started falling for you right then."

"Really? Not when I outshot you at the range last month?"

"You know I let you win that too." His tone was pure surrender.

She kissed him again—soft, sure.

When she pulled back, her expression turned quietly serious.

"I love you too, you know. Have for years." Her fingers traced his jaw. "Every visit. Every phone call. Every dumb grilled cheese text. I just... kept falling."

He rested his forehead against hers. "Your father's going to hate this."

"Probably." Her fingers tensed slightly against his chest. "But I learned something from you."

"What's that?"

"Sometimes the best things in life happen when you break protocol."

He held her tighter, breathing her in. Below them, Atlanta sprawled like an afterthought. But up here, with her heart pressed to his, nothing else mattered.

"I love you," he said again, just because he could.

Her smile rivaled the sunset. "I know. I've got sketches to prove it."

———

Beatrice's phone rang just as darkness settled outside her office window. Legal briefs lay forgotten, the Burton case half-drafted.

"You reached the summit?" she asked, their hiking-code now shorthand for everything important.

"Bea." Abbie's voice brimmed with joy. "He loves me. He actually loves me."

Beatrice sank into her chair, eyes stinging with tears. She thought of their mother's words—*love is always worth the risk.*

"Oh, sugar. He'd be a fool not to."

"I'm scared," Abbie admitted softly. "What do we do now?"

"Now?" Beatrice glanced at a photo on her desk—their mother, laughing in her wedding dress. "Now you love him back. With everything you've got. And let me worry about Daddy."

"You're the best sister-mom ever, you know that?"

Beatrice's laugh cracked through the tears. "Don't you forget it. Now spill it. Every single detail."

And as Abbie's story tumbled out, Beatrice leaned back and listened, her whole heart in it.

***

The Midnight Owl Coffee Shop bustled with Tuesday afternoon crowds. Edward claimed their usual corner table, positioned with clear sightlines to both exits. Three days had passed since the summit confession, and still, his lips remembered the shape of hers. Focus came harder now.

"Two lattes," the barista called over the espresso machine's hiss.

He nodded his thanks and retrieved their drinks. Another hidden meeting, another calculated risk. The pattern repeated weekly—sometimes even daily: a diner on Auburn Avenue with faded booths, the sculpture garden behind the High, hidden from cameras, a remote trail along the Chattahoochee. Every location was chosen with the precision he'd once used in Kandahar.

Abbie slipped through the door, scanning the room until she spotted him. That smile of hers—unguarded, radiant—sparked heat in his chest. She wore paint-splattered jeans and an oversized sweater: her real self, not the version curated for her father's public image. Edward watched her weave through the tables, counting the seconds.

"Sorry I'm late," she said, sliding into the seat across from him, her knee brushing his under the table. "Professor Davis wanted to go over my portfolio submission."

"Good news?" He nudged her latte toward her, noting a smudge of blue paint along her jawline.

Her dimples appeared. "He's recommending me for the summer showcase."

"That's amazing, Abs." He resisted the urge to wipe away the paint. Public displays of affection were a luxury they couldn't afford. "I'm proud of you."

She blushed, fingers curling around the mug. "It's just a university thing."

"It's a beginning." Their eyes held, and something unspoken passed between them—a beginning of her own path, not the one her father had charted.

Their conversation flowed easily, voices low amid the café's noise. Edward committed every detail to memory: the way her curls caught the afternoon light, how her hands moved with her stories, the particular glint of her gray eyes when she laughed. Small things. Precious things. Stored for the nights he couldn't see her.

But the quiet evenings at Beatrice's condo were his favorite. There, he could finally exhale.

Later that evening, butter sizzled in the pan as Edward flipped a grilled cheese. Abbie sat cross-legged on the worn couch, sketchbook balanced on one knee. The scratch of her pencil met the low hum of kitchen sounds—domestic, easy, theirs.

"You're humming that march again," she said without looking up.

"Am I?" He lifted the edge of the sandwich, checking for that perfect crust.

"Mmhmm. You always do when you're happy." Her pencil paused, a smile in her voice.

He slid the sandwich onto a plate. "Something about seeing our debutante princess in paint-stained sweatpants just does it for me."

"Careful, soldier." She glanced up, eyes gleaming. "These are designer paint stains."

The front door clicked open.

Beatrice swept in, sleek in a black dress that could command both courtrooms and cocktail hours. She kicked off her heels before reaching the living room, gym bag slung over one shoulder.

"Sorry I'm late," she called. "Roderick needed backup at the Children's Legal Defense Fund event. Not my scene, but he had donor sharks to navigate." She rolled her shoulders. "Had to skip jiu-jitsu too. My instructor's going to kill me—demo next week."

She sniffed. "Something smells amazing. Tell me there's enough for three? Those fundraiser canapés were basically edible air."

"Always," Edward said, already reaching for more bread. He'd come to admire Beatrice—not just for backing their relationship, but for the tactical sharpness she brought to everything, from boardrooms to triangle chokes.

"Did you have to save Roderick from talking juvenile recidivism over champagne again?" Abbie asked, shifting to make room.

"Worse. He tried explaining guardian ad litem appointments to the mayor's wife." Beatrice dropped onto the couch, posture straight despite exhaustion. "What that man needs is an M&A lawyer's instinct for when to shut up and close."

She accepted a glass of wine from Edward with a grateful nod. "Speaking of closing... I tied up loose ends on your 'independent study' today." Her gaze turned sly. "Though I doubt it included the picnic basket I saw you packing this morning."

Abbie blushed. "You're getting too good at this, Bea."

"Five years of jiu-jitsu teaches you to anticipate your opponent's next move," she quipped, sipping her wine. "And you two aren't exactly subtle."

Edward smiled at Beatrice's remark, then turned to Abbie and gestured to her sketchbook. "What's the masterpiece today?"

Abbie turned it toward them. A scene from Big Joe's BBQ—Edward laughing, Abbie stealing fries. In the corner, Beatrice at her booth, phone to her ear.

"This is how we look to other people," Abbie said quietly. "When we don't have to hide."

Edward placed the plates on the table and sat beside her, his thigh brushing hers as he kissed her temple. "We won't have to hide forever."

"I know." She leaned into him. "But sometimes I wonder... am I being selfish? Asking you both to sneak around? Your job at Claremont—"

"Hey." He gently tilted her chin. "You're not asking me to do anything. I'm exactly where I want to be."

"But Daddy's company is Claremont's biggest account. If he finds out—"

"And you're the most important person in my life." His thumb brushed her cheek. *He'd trained to assess risk. But this wasn't a mission. This was the reason.* "I've got savings. Old contacts. I'll figure it out."

"And I've got a spare room," Beatrice added, stretching. "Though full disclosure—I've converted the den into a gym. Jiu-jitsu doesn't mix with furniture."

Her voice was light, but her gaze held steel. Beatrice had her own arsenal when it came to dealing with Randolph Hartwell.

"How's the Stevenson merger going?" Edward asked. He genuinely liked talking shop with her over Sunday brunch. "Still wrangling those international subsidiaries?"

"Closed it yesterday. The fundraiser was our victory lap disguised as charity." Her smile thinned. "One of those wins that reminds the male partners I still exist."

"Their mistake for ever forgetting," Abbie said loyally.

Beatrice's phone buzzed. Her smile turned impish. "Martinez sisters are at Phantom tonight. They've got a spot for me at their table."

She stood, draining her wine. "Shower, wardrobe change, then downtown before the good DJ starts."

Abbie looked between them. Her sister in motion. Her boyfriend smiling like he had a secret. "Look at us. Three exciting Friday night plans."

Edward pulled two tickets from his pocket. "Speaking of plans... how do you feel about a weekend in Savannah? Art festival, decent cover story. Far enough from Atlanta."

Abbie kissed him before he could finish. Almost knocked over their dinner.

"You planned a whole weekend?"

"Strictly professional research for your art elective," he said solemnly. "Very important gallery reconnaissance."

"And the romantic bed and breakfast?"

"Best sightlines in the historic district."

"Perfect timing," Beatrice called, reappearing as her nightlife self—statement jewelry, hair down, ready for anything. "I'll be buried in depositions all weekend. Text me when you get there?"

"Oh—Edward. Roderick mentioned needing your help with that new children's center. Surveillance system design. He liked your insights at the fundraiser."

"Tell him I'm in," Edward said. "Just let me know when."

"I'll connect you two tomorrow." Beatrice checked her phone. "Car's here." She grabbed her clutch, then paused. "Don't wait up. Devon's DJ-ing tonight." Her gaze lingered. "And Edward—thank you."

The door clicked shut behind her, leaving the apartment quiet.

Edward looked at Abbie, warmth blooming in his chest. "Dance with me?"

"There's no music," she said, already moving into his arms.

He hummed that same quiet march, guiding her in a slow turn around Beatrice's living room. City lights shimmered beyond the windows like a constellation of their own.

Abbie's head rested on his chest. "She started jiu-jitsu after Mom died," she said quietly. "Dad wanted her to see a therapist, but Bea said she needed to physically work through things. Five years later, she terrifies junior associates."

"It suits her," Edward said. "That focus. That fight."

"It's armor," Abbie murmured. "The mergers, the clubs, the martial arts—it's all armor."

They swayed in silence. The city glittered around them.

"What about you?" he asked. "What's your armor?"

Abbie looked up, eyes luminous in the dim light. "I don't need armor when I'm with you."

"Good," he whispered, drawing her closer. "Because neither do I."

***

Edward's hand found the small box in his pocket for what felt like the hundredth time that morning. The ring inside wasn't what society would expect for a Hartwell—no massive diamond, no ancestral heirloom. Just a simple silver band set with a small emerald—green like the Georgia forests where they'd fallen in love.

"Just breathe," Beatrice said from behind her desk, watching him pace. She straightened an already-perfect stack of papers, a nervous tic even she didn't seem aware of.

Edward paused, sweat beading at his temples despite the cool air. "You're sure about this? Helping me? After everything with your father two weeks ago..."

Beatrice's jaw tightened. The memory burned fresh.

She'd walked into their father's study to find Edward standing ramrod straight, his face unreadable while Randolph Hartwell delivered his verdict.

"Let me be perfectly clear, Mr. Stuart," Randolph had said, his accent sharpening every syllable. "You may have temporarily turned my daughter's head, but you are not—nor will you ever be—worthy of a Hartwell."

Edward had held his silence, military discipline anchoring his posture.

"I've heard rumors," Randolph continued. "But I dismissed them. My daughter would never lower herself to your... level."

"Daddy!" Beatrice had cut in from the doorway, her shock quickly hardening into fury.

Randolph barely glanced at her. "You. I expected better. Enabling this... whatever it is? Did you think I wouldn't find out?"

Edward had finally spoken, voice steady despite the storm. "I came here out of respect—to ask for your daughter's hand in marriage."

"Marriage?" Randolph's laugh had been cruel. "You're a security contractor. One phone call from me, and not only do you lose your job, you become unhirable in this city."

Beatrice had stepped forward, her voice iron-clad. "You can't do this. Abbie loves him."

"Love," he sneered. "Is that what this rebellion is?" Then, coldly: "This ends now."

Now, in her office, Beatrice stood and adjusted Edward's collar, her touch precise, deliberate.

"Edward," she said, meeting his eyes. "You came to me first. You asked for my blessing. That alone tells me everything I need to know."

She exhaled, her gaze hardening. "My father doesn't get to decide who Abbie loves. Family is about bloodlines, yes, but also about who shows up, who stays, who fights."

"He'll make good on his threats." Edward's hand drifted to his side—where his weapon would normally rest. A combat reflex surfacing under pressure. "Your career, your relationship with him..."

"Let him try." Her smile held quiet steel. "I didn't become Atlanta's top M&A lawyer and earn a purple belt by backing down from bullies—even when they're family."

—

An hour later, Abbie's voice drifted through the parking lot outside Big Joe's BBQ. "You're still not telling me why we're here? It's closed on Mondays."

"Usually." Edward stepped out and opened her door with a dramatic bow. "Joe owed me a favor."

He glanced toward the back, where Beatrice's car was hidden. Through the window, her thumbs-up flashed like a green light.

Inside, their usual booth had been transformed. Fairy lights twinkled overhead, casting a warm glow. A vase of wildflowers—the kind that lined their favorite trails—sat on the table.

Abbie stopped short, breath catching. "Edward…"

"Sit with me?" He guided her to the booth where they'd first connected, where stolen fries and shared laughter built something real.

Abbie sank into the seat, her eyes already glassy. "You did all this?"

"Joe helped." Edward reached into his coat and pulled out a familiar sketchbook—her original one, from the gala. The binding creaked as he opened it.

"I had some inspiration."

She took it carefully, her fingers trembling. Inside, beside the original portrait she'd drawn of him, were new sketches—her, laughing over fries. Her, brow furrowed in concentration. Her, looking up with unguarded joy.

"When did you—?"

"I've been working with a certain artist for months." His voice roughened. "I'll never match your technique, but I wanted to show you how I see you."

Tears slid down her cheeks as she turned the pages. "These are all moments..."

"Moments I fell more in love with you." He slid out of the booth and dropped to one knee. The box in his pocket was suddenly heavy.

"Moments that showed me exactly who I want to spend my life with."

From the kitchen, Beatrice watched quietly through the serving window. Behind her, Roderick gently kneaded the tension from her shoulders.

Edward took Abbie's paint-stained hand in his. His heart pounded so loud, he was certain she could hear it.

"Abigail Hartwell," he said. "You see the truth in people—the beauty, the flaws, what they hide and what they hope. You saw past my walls. Past everything I thought I knew about love, and life, and happiness."

Abbie's fingers rose to her silver necklace, catching the echo of her own words.

"I know it won't be easy," Edward said. "I spoke to your father."

Her eyes widened. "You did?"

He nodded. "He made his position clear." He didn't elaborate—she didn't need that weight. "I know he'll fight this. That society will whisper. That we're breaking every rule."

He opened the box, revealing the emerald ring. "But you're worth it. We're worth it. Marry me, Abs. Let's build a life where we never have to hide who we are."

For a breathless moment, Abbie just stared. Then she slid out of the booth and knelt with him on the scuffed linoleum.

"It's perfect," she whispered, fingers brushing the emerald. "It looks like..."

"Our forests." His voice cracked. "Where a society princess and a security guard found something real."

"Yes." Her smile lit the room.

"Yes to the ring?"

She laughed, tears falling freely. "Yes to everything. The ring. The life. The love. Yes to breaking rules and making our own. Yes to you, Edward Stuart. Forever and always."

He slipped the ring onto her finger, and from the kitchen, Beatrice emerged carrying champagne and peach cobbler. Roderick followed with glasses, his smile warm and easy.

"Welcome to the family," Beatrice said, her voice a perfect blend of warmth and authority. "Officially, this time."

Abbie launched herself into her sister's arms, nearly upending the tray. "You knew! You helped plan this!"

"Of course I did, sugar." Beatrice steadied the tray and pulled her in. "You think I'd miss your big moment? I wasn't about to let you get engaged to this guy without being here."

"Hey now," Edward grinned. "That's brother to you."

Beatrice winked. "I'm so happy for you guys."

They crowded into the booth, sharing cobbler and champagne. Abbie sketched as they talked, her ring glinting under the lights. Edward couldn't stop watching her—the joy in her eyes, the smudge of peach on her chin, the way she paused to admire the ring like she couldn't believe it was real.

"What are you thinking?" Beatrice asked, watching them both.

"That Mom would've loved this," Abbie said, reaching across the table to squeeze her sister's hand. "All of it."

"She'd have loved him," Beatrice agreed, squeezing Edward's hand. "Almost as much as we do."

Edward kissed Abbie's temple. "I can't wait to see what you draw next," he whispered. "We've got a lifetime of moments to capture."

"And I'll be here to help tell your story," Beatrice added, her silver bracelet catching the light. "Every messy, beautiful, perfect chapter."

Abbie raised her glass. "To breaking rules and making our own."

"To family," Roderick added, clinking his glass.

"To love worth fighting for," Edward said, eyes locked on Abbie.

Beatrice's sharp gaze softened. "Dad's not going to know what hit him," she said, a confident smile curling her lips. "But don't worry. I've been preparing for this moment my entire career."

"We all have," Abbie said, squeezing Edward's hand.

Edward lifted her hand and kissed the ring. "Let him bring his worst," he murmured. "We've got something stronger."

***

The Hartwell mansion seemed to loom differently now. Its grandeur felt more like prison walls than luxury. Edward tightened his grip on Abbie's trembling hand as they walked up the familiar path. Her emerald ring caught the afternoon light, casting green reflections across their joined fingers. Beside them, Beatrice's heels clicked steadily—a comfort and a shield.

"We don't have to do this today," Edward murmured, catching the quickening of her breath.

"Yes, we do." Her voice carried the lingering buoyancy of their engagement, even as her hand shook. "Besides, I don't think it'll be that bad. I think Daddy will understand now."

Beatrice and Edward exchanged a look—the kind forged over countless brunches and late-night strategy sessions. They both knew better.

Edward squared his shoulders, scanning the property with habitual precision—sightlines, exit points. Beatrice moved closer, her voice low.

"Whatever happens, we face it as a family."

—

Inside, Randolph greeted his youngest daughter with a hug. His salt-and-pepper hair gleamed under the windows' light, suit immaculate as always. He smiled, but it tightened the moment he spotted Edward.

"Daddy, I have some exciting news," Abbie began, her voice pitched high with nerves.

Randolph kept his smile—barely—as Edward stepped into view. His posture shifted: father to adversary in a breath.

Abbie turned, reached for Edward's hand, and blurted, "We're getting married!"

Randolph's gaze sharpened, eyes cold and hawk-like. "So. You chose to ignore my warning, Stuart. After our discussion two weeks ago, I thought I was clear."

"Sir, I—"

"What discussion?" Abbie cut in, the light dimming in her expression. "What warning?"

Randolph's smile didn't waver. "How dare you propose after I told you to stay away?" He turned sharply. "And you, Beatrice—how long have you been enabling this?"

"Stay away?" Abbie echoed, her fingers tightening around Edward's. Her eyes darted between them as the truth clicked into place.

Randolph's voice iced over. "I don't know how you've manipulated her, but—"

"He hasn't manipulated anyone," Abbie said, barely above a whisper. Her pulse beat fast beneath Edward's thumb. "We're in love. We're getting married."

"The hell you are." Randolph's voice dropped, soft and dangerous. "I didn't spend all these years protecting you, giving you everything, so you could throw it all away on a security guard."

"Daddy," Beatrice said, her tone calm but firm. "They love each other."

He turned on her, jaw tightening. "So that's it—you've chosen your side."

"There are no sides here," Beatrice said. "Just family."

"Family?" Randolph barked a brittle laugh. "Is that what this betrayal is?"

Abbie froze beside Edward, her face pale. Each word from her father landed like a strike.

Edward stepped forward. "Mr. Hartwell, I understand this is hard, but—"

"Understand?" Randolph snapped. "You know nothing about my family. About our world. You were hired to protect her—not to court her."

"Stop it!" Abbie sobbed. "You don't know him. Edward is the most honorable man I've ever met. He loves me for who I am."

"And what is that, exactly?" Randolph sneered. "A trust fund? The Hartwell name? That's what's at stake."

"Just like you made Mom's family disappear?" Beatrice's words landed like stones in still water. "All those relationships, erased because they weren't 'suitable'?"

Randolph went still. The vein in his temple pulsed. "Don't you dare—"

"Why not?" Beatrice pressed. "Mom died believing she'd destroyed her family. But she didn't—you did."

Edward moved subtly in front of Abbie.

"I don't want your money," he said. "Never have."

"No?" Randolph closed the distance, voice silk over steel. "Then sign a contract. Renounce all claims to the Hartwell fortune. Of course, that means you can't give her the life she deserves."

"The life I deserve?" Abbie laughed bitterly, tears streaking her cheeks. "You mean Mom's life? All the galas and perfection—while she was dying inside?"

"Don't you dare bring your mother into this." Randolph jabbed the air between them.

"She'd be standing right here," Beatrice said, her voice shaking. "Right now. With Abbie."

"Enough!" Randolph slammed his hand on a side table. The crystal decanter rattled. "Your mother was a dreamer. And now look—my daughter engaged to a bodyguard."

Abbie flinched like she'd been slapped. Her shoulders curled inward, and Edward held her tighter.

"Mr. Hartwell," Edward said evenly, tamping down fury. "Maybe we should finish this later—"

"There won't be a later," Randolph said, voice smooth again. "This discussion is over. Abigail, go to your room. We'll speak when you've regained your senses."

"Daddy, please—" Her voice broke.

"Now, Abigail."

Edward watched in disbelief as Abbie's posture shifted—years of command taking hold. Her shoulders slumped, chin lowering as she turned to him.

"I…" She looked up at Edward, eyes clouded. "I need to…"

"Abs, we can leave together." He reached for her, palm up. "You don't have to stay."

Randolph's voice sliced through. "You are no longer welcome here, Mr. Stuart. Leave."

"Abbie," Edward said gently, trying to reach her. But she stepped back, torn between instinct and freedom.

"I need time," she whispered. "Please."

The words cut deep. Edward lowered his hand. "Of course. Whatever you need."

"Go to your room, Abigail," Randolph said again, voice gentler now—manipulation she'd known all her life. "We'll sort this out."

Abbie turned and fled, her sobs echoing through the hall. The sound of her door slamming reverberated through the house.

"You've failed, Stuart," Randolph said, satisfaction lacing every word. "She'll come to her senses—she always does."

Edward's fists clenched at his sides. "This isn't over."

Randolph adjusted his cuffs. "My daughter may be confused, but she knows where she belongs. Now get out of my house."

"You really think manipulating her is the answer?" Beatrice asked, her voice cutting.

For a moment, something flickered in Randolph's face—regret? Doubt? But it vanished.

"I'm protecting her," he said, cold again. "Now go."

Beatrice stepped forward, her voice calm but burning. "This isn't one of your mergers. This is your daughter."

"You're wrong," Randolph replied, settling behind his desk. "It's the most important one."

He turned to his computer, dismissing them.

Edward hesitated, torn. *His training screamed not to leave a team member behind.* But Abbie had asked.

Beatrice's hand on his arm steadied him.

"I'll stay with her," she said quietly. "Give her time."

"Bea, I can't—"

"Trust me."

—

The walk back to the car felt like a retreat. Each step dragged like a loss. Edward's chest ached—like something vital had been carved out and left behind.

"Edward," Beatrice said, catching up as he reached the door. "She loves you. But she loves him too."

"I know." His voice was hollow.

"This is round one." She glanced back at the house. "Daddy will use everything—guilt, legacy, fear. He'll paint a future of regret if she chooses you."

"Maybe he's right." Edward's throat tightened. "Maybe I can't give her what she needs."

"Don't you dare." Beatrice's eyes flared. "That's what he wants—for you to doubt yourself, to walk away. But you've seen the real Abbie. Fight for her."

Edward swallowed hard. "Tell her…"

"I will." She squeezed his arm. "And I'll call tonight. This isn't over."

***

Abbie sat in her childhood bedroom, a familiar space rendered foreign. Sunlight filtered through lace curtains, sketching delicate patterns across a duvet she hadn't used since high school. Her phone lay silent on the nightstand—five missed calls from Edward yesterday. None today.

A soft knock interrupted her thoughts.

"Miss Abigail?" Martha, their housekeeper of twenty years, stood in the doorway. Her usual warmth was replaced by formal restraint. "Your father requests your presence for dinner. Seven o'clock sharp."

"Thank you, Martha." Abbie offered a hollow smile. "Is he in his study?"

"Yes, miss. But he asked not to be disturbed."

Of course he did. Three days of strategic silence—close enough to impose his presence, far enough to withhold approval.

After Martha left, Abbie typed a message to Edward: *I need more time. Please understand.*

She deleted it. What could she say that wouldn't hurt him more?

Instead, she called Beatrice.

"How's the prisoner of Buckhead?" her sister asked, her brightness brittle.

"Dying slowly." Abbie twisted the emerald ring on her finger, watching it catch the light. "How's Edward?"

A pause. "Struggling. Jax called him—Daddy already pulled the Hartwell contracts from Claremont."

"Oh God." Nausea rose in her throat. "That quickly?"

"Daddy doesn't waste time making a point." Beatrice's voice softened. "Edward didn't want me to tell you. He didn't want you to feel pressured."

"But I should." Anger flared in her chest. "People are losing jobs because I couldn't walk away from my father."

"This isn't your fault. It's Daddy's. He's the one weaponizing his influence."

Abbie's eyes drifted toward her dresser, where her sketchbook was hidden beneath cashmere sweaters. "Has he said anything about me?"

"He thinks you're 'coming to your senses.' He's convinced this is just rebellion. Temporary."

A rebellion. Her laugh was dry. "That's what love is to him."

"How are you holding up?"

Abbie hesitated. How could she explain the storm inside her? The child desperate for approval battling the woman who loved a man her father despised.

"I feel like I'm drowning," she whispered. "Every time he looks at me with disappointment, I'm ten again. Then I remember Edward's face when I stayed behind, and I hate myself for being so weak."

"You're not weak. You're trying to reconcile two definitions of love."

"Have you seen him?"

"He's at my place. Sleeping on the couch—refuses the guest room. He's looking for work outside Atlanta."

The words landed like a blow. Her chest tightened.

"Because of me."

"Because of Daddy," Beatrice corrected. "Roderick and I are taking him to dinner tomorrow. Come with us. Neutral ground."

"I don't know if I can face him yet. Not until I'm sure."

"Just think about it."

After they hung up, Abbie pulled out her sketchbook. The binding creaked softly. On the newest page, Edward's face stared back—devastated, hollow—drawn from memory. Tears blurred the lines as she pressed the book to her chest and wept.

—

Dinner that evening was a masterclass in control. Abbie's favorite dishes. Her preferred wine. Casual conversation about charity events—as if Edward had never existed.

"The Whitmores were asking about you," Randolph said, swirling his wine. "James is back from London. Investment banking. Harvard Business."

Abbie set down her fork. The silver clinked. "Are you matchmaking?"

"Just mentioning a suitable young man." He smiled thinly. "Someone who understands your world."

My world. She tasted the words. They rang hollow. "And what exactly is that?"

"This." He gestured at the room—crystal, antique furniture, curated legacy. "Responsibility. Privilege. The Hartwell name."

"Was that Mother's world too?"

His expression hardened. His signet ring tapped against his glass. "Your mother understood sacrifice."

"Did she? Or did she sacrifice herself for your expectations?"

"That's enough, Abigail."

"No. It's not." Courage rose. "You've been pretending everything's normal—like throwing Harvard boys at me will make me forget Edward."

He set down his glass. "That man cost me two major contracts. He pursued you knowing it would drive a wedge between us."

"He resigned so I wouldn't be used as leverage. He's leaving Atlanta because you've made it impossible for him to stay."

"If he truly cared, he'd have walked away."

"He gave me the choice," she said, her voice rising. "You didn't."

"I want what's best for you."

"You want what's best for the Hartwell name."

"To me, they're the same."

She saw then the futility of the argument. They spoke different languages.

"I'd like to be excused."

"Of course." His voice softened to fatherly concern. "Take your time, princess. Just remember who was there before this... distraction. And who will be there when it ends."

———

Edward paced Beatrice's living room, phone in hand. Two weeks of silence had hollowed him out. Every tick of the clock dragged.

"Wearing a hole in my carpet won't make her call faster," Beatrice said, entering in a court-worn suit.

"Randolph's blacklisted me. Pulled every Hartwell contract this morning."

"I know. Roderick's looking into a firm in Columbia. Solid, reputable."

Edward stilled. "Columbia."

"It's an option. Not a sentence."

He sank onto the couch, head in his hands. "I replay that day constantly. If I'd said something else, followed her, not proposed—"

"Don't. Daddy's tactics were surgical. Emotional warfare."

"I've been in war zones less calculated."

Beatrice's phone buzzed. She answered, voice softening. "Yes, he's here. Dinner tomorrow? Let me check."

She covered the mic. "Roderick wants to take us out. He has news."

Edward nodded.

"We're in," she told the caller. A pause. "Really? That's... surprising. I'll tell him."

She hung up. "Daddy's removing Abbie's name from every patron list in Atlanta."

Edward's jaw clenched. His hand went to his hip, reaching for a weapon that wasn't there.

"He's erasing her."

"It's his scorched earth policy," Beatrice said, old pain darkening her voice. "It's what he did to Mom's family. Destroy the support system until he's the only option."

"We need to get her out."

"We need her to choose to leave."

Edward's phone buzzed. Unknown number. His heart stopped:

Edward. It's me. Using Martha's phone. Can you meet tomorrow? I need to see you.

———

The next afternoon, they sat in a quiet café outside the city. Abbie clasped her coffee cup to steady her hands. Edward looked thinner, haunted. Guilt gripped her.

"Thank you for coming," she said.

"I'd go anywhere for you."

Silence stretched between them, heavy with all the words unsaid.

"Beatrice says you're looking at Columbia."

"Nothing's final."

"Because of my father."

"Because I need work. He made sure I wouldn't find it here."

Tears welled. "I'm so sorry. This is all because I—"

"No." His tone was gentle but firm. "This is on him."

"I don't know what to do. I look at him and see the man who held my hand at Mom's funeral. But then he talks about you like you're nothing, and I don't know who he is."

Edward reached across the table, palm up. She hesitated—then placed her hand in his. Warmth rushed through her.

"I love you," he said. "Enough to wait. Enough to walk away if that's what you truly want."

"Walk away?" Her voice cracked. "That would kill me."

"If your father's approval means more than what we have, I'll respect it. But if you choose me, we build something—together."

She looked at their hands—hers pale, his darker—an image her father would never accept.

"I need a few more days."

He nodded, the effort it took visible in every line of his face. "Take what you need."

When he walked her to her car, he kissed her forehead gently, and tears spilled down her cheeks.

"Whatever you decide," he whispered, "loving you has been the greatest privilege of my life."

—

Three days later, Abbie stood in her father's study, the ancestral eyes of Hartwells watching her from leather-bound volumes.

"I've been thinking about what you said," she began. "About legacy."

Randolph looked up. "I'm glad."

"The Hartwell name opens doors. Creates opportunity."

"Exactly."

"And our responsibility?"

"To protect and elevate it."

"I visited the Symphony Board. Spoke with Mrs. Whitmore."

Surprise flickered. "Did you?"

"She said my name was removed. On your instruction. As were the Junior League, the Arts Foundation, and the hospital board."

He stiffened. "Temporary measures."

"I've been learning what legacy means. What your legacy is."

"You're twisting this."

"No, Daddy. You're erasing me. Just like you erased Mom's family. Anyone who doesn't conform, gone."

"I'm protecting you."

"By isolating me?"

He turned to the window, shadowed. "You're young. Infatuated. Edward filled your head with romantic delusions."

She laughed, hollow. "Do you even know me?"

"Of course I do."

"Then tell me—what medium do I prefer for landscapes? Which gallery gave me my first show? Who was my professor that submitted my work?"

Silence.

"You never asked."

"Abigail—"

"Edward knows. Oils for landscapes. Charcoal for portraits. Blue Door Gallery. Professor Stevens—the one you tried to bribe."

His head snapped up. "Who told you that?"

"It doesn't matter. It's true."

She stood. "I love you. I always will. But your ideal daughter and who I am—aren't the same."

"You're making a terrible mistake."

"You're right. He can't give me the life you think I deserve. But he gives me something better—freedom."

She walked to the door, then paused. "I think Mom would've told me to run toward love with both arms open. That's who she was. That's who she raised us to be."

She left him standing there, his figure silhouetted in the window.

The mansion no longer loomed. It echoed. She retrieved her packed bags and stepped into the light.

—

Edward answered on the first ring. "Abbie? What's wrong?"

"Nothing's wrong," she said—and meant it. "I've made my decision."

He held his breath.

She placed her suitcase in the trunk, her fingers brushing the emerald ring. "I want you. I'm coming home."

Silence. Then—

"If you still want me."

"Forever, Abs. I will always want you."

Her smile bloomed—like the first stroke on a blank canvas. "I love you too."

For the first time in nearly a month, the light reached her eyes.

***

The weeks after she faced her father felt like a bruise—tender, slow to heal, dark at the edges. Abbie sat in Beatrice's breakfast nook, watching rain streak the windows. Her coffee cooled, untouched. Her phone lay silent beside her, the screen flaring now and then as she checked it, hoping.

"He's not going to call," Beatrice said gently, sliding into the chair across from her. Dark circles shadowed her eyes— evidence of late nights spent juggling merger briefs and sisterly duties.

"I know." Abbie traced the rim of her cup. "I just thought... maybe if I explained it differently. If I could make him understand—"

"Oh, sugar." Beatrice reached over, covering her hand. "You can't reason with someone who refuses to see."

The sound of Edward's truck in the driveway brought a fleeting smile to Abbie's lips—one that vanished as quickly as it came. He'd been staying nearby, sleeping on Beatrice's couch. He never used the guest room—he didn't want her waking up alone.

"I went by the house today," Abbie said quietly as Edward stepped in, rain clinging to his jacket. "Martha wouldn't even look at me. Twenty-one years of cooking my breakfast, bandaging my knees... and now she won't meet my eyes." She swallowed. "They've already cleared my room."

Edward moved behind her and laid his hands on her shoulders, thumbs working gentle circles. "We'll build something new. Something that's ours."

"But it shouldn't have to be either-or," she cried, tears finally spilling. "Why can't he love me and accept you? Why can't he see I'm not a little girl anymore?"

Beatrice and Edward shared a look over her head. They'd known this storm was coming—the heartbreak delayed by Abbie's need to fix what couldn't be fixed.

"I wrote him a letter," Abbie said, pulling a crumpled envelope from her pocket. "Told him everything. How Edward makes me feel safe. How Mom always said true love was worth any sacrifice." Her voice wavered. "Will you give it to him? He still talks to you."

"Barely," Beatrice said. "But yes. I will."

Three days later, the letter returned unopened—accompanied by a formal document from Randolph's lawyers. Beatrice read it in her office, hands trembling. The legal jargon was clear: Abigail Claire Hartwell was disinherited. Trust funds frozen. Patronage positions erased.

She found Abbie sorting art supplies, brushes spread in neat rows. An old coping mechanism—controlling what could be controlled.

"He sent it back," Beatrice said, sitting beside her. "And... other things too."

Abbie's hand stilled. A charcoal pencil rolled from her fingers, smudging the coffee table. "He really means it."

"He does."

"Did you read it?"

"He's making it official. The money, the boards—he's even having your name removed from the Symphony's spring patron list."

A bitter laugh escaped. "Always thorough." She set the pencils down harder than intended.

Her voice softened. "What hurts the most... isn't the money or society. It's that he'd rather have no daughter than one who chose her own path."

A quiet moment passed. Then Edward appeared at the threshold—rested but hollow, framed by hallway shadows.

He watched them as he moved, determination set in his features. When he knelt beside Abbie, her tears splintered his chest.

"Marry me," he said quietly. "Now."

Abbie flinched in surprise, uncertainty flickering in her eyes.

"What?"

She swallowed, tears shining.

"I can't wait. Not someday—now," he said, offering more than a promise. "I've accepted a job in Columbia. We leave. We start fresh—together."

Beatrice watched as the room stilled. Abbie's smile came slowly, blooming like dawn. "Yes," she said, voice steady.

Edward exhaled relief. "Yes?"

"Yes. Yes to all of it."

He pulled her into a fierce hug.

"Let's build our own life," he whispered.

She laughed through tears. "Let's choose happiness."

Edward pulled out his phone. "I know a little chapel outside Charleston..."

That night, after Edward took the guest room and Abbie finally slept, Beatrice sat at her desk. Letters, contracts, legal briefs—they all blurred together. She drafted a message to their father. About courage, choice, and the difference between wealth and worth. About love that broke rules.

Her fingers hovered over the send button.

She didn't press it.

Instead, she made calls—to the chapel, to Columbia real estate agents, to her bank. If Randolph wanted a war of influence, fine. Beatrice had weapons of her own.

A week later, she helped Abbie pack. The silver necklace caught the light as Abbie folded a sweater—each item a quiet decision about what to carry forward, and what to leave behind.

Abbie paused.

"Bea," she said softly. "Thanks for everything."

Beatrice tucked a strand of hair behind her ear. "I love you, sugar. I'm always here."

Abbie wrapped her in a tight embrace—and for the first time in weeks, it didn't feel like goodbye.

Chapter 4

The Edge of Everything

THE LITTLE CHAPEL outside Charleston had seen better days. Coastal winds and time had peeled away its white paint. Abbie stood at the bridal room window, fingering her mother's pearls as she watched each car turn onto the chapel's winding drive. Part of her still watched for her father's Mercedes to appear through the morning mist.

"Sugar?" Beatrice's voice pulled her back. "Let me help you with that veil."

She turned, managing a smile. The delicate lace veil, hand-selected from a French boutique during their weekend shopping trip, was simple by choice—nothing like the custom gown she'd commissioned from a designer for the wedding she once imagined.

"It's perfect," she said, meaning it despite the ache in her chest.

"Hold still now," Beatrice said, adjusting the jewelry at her neck. "There. Mom would be so proud of you, sugar."

A gentle knock at the door preceded Roderick's appearance, his tall frame filling the doorway. "Everything okay in here? The minister's getting a bit anxious."

"Just finishing up," Beatrice replied.

Roderick approached with a small box. "I thought you might need this." He opened it to reveal a delicate silver bracelet. "It was my grandmother's. Something borrowed."

"Roderick, it's beautiful," Abbie whispered as he fastened it around her wrist.

"I keep thinking about Mom's wedding photos," she said as Roderick stepped back, her brow furrowed as she fought back tears. "How happy Daddy looked, back when love mattered more than status."

Beatrice's hands stilled on the veil. "He'll come around, sugar. Just give him time."

"What if he doesn't?" Abbie's voice wavered. "What if—" She stopped as another car turned into the drive, but it was just the pianist arriving.

"Then he's the one missing out," Beatrice said firmly.

"And you'll still have quite the family cheering you on," Roderick added with a reassuring smile.

Beatrice turned her sister to face the mirror. "Look at you. Mom would be over the moon seeing you now."

The reflection showed a different bride than Atlanta society expected—no designer gown, no professional makeup, just Abbie in a simple white dress chosen specifically for its elegance and comfort, her honey-blonde hair crowned with wildflowers. She smiled through tears.

Another knock revealed Edward in his dress uniform, the only trace of military precision in their deliberately intimate ceremony. He stopped short at the sight of her: "God, you're beautiful."

"You clean up pretty nice yourself, soldier." Her smile brightened, though her eyes still darted to the window.

"The minister's ready," he said, offering his arm to Beatrice. Then, softer, to Abbie: "Are you sure about this? We can wait…"

"No." Abbie squared her shoulders, a gesture so like her mother's that it caught Beatrice's breath. "I want to marry you today. Here. Now."

The ceremony was simple, witnessed by Beatrice and Roderick, with the elderly chapel pianist they'd hired for the occasion. There was no string quartet, no society photographers—only the soft strains of the pianist and the scent of jasmine on the breeze. The warm Carolina air drifted through open windows, and distant waves kept time with their heartbeats.

During the vows, Abbie kept her eyes fixed on Edward, drawing strength from his steady gaze. But when the minister asked who gave this woman in marriage, the pause felt heavy with absence.

"I do," Beatrice said, her voice steady with all the love and protection she'd given since their mother's death.

Abbie squeezed her hand, gratitude and grief mingling in her eyes.

"I, Edward Devline Stuart, take you, Abigail Claire Hartwell…"

As Edward recited his vows, Beatrice watched her sister's face. She saw the joy there—real and pure—but also caught the moments when Abbie's eyes drifted to the chapel doors, that flicker of hope not quite extinguished.

Later, over champagne and cake from an exclusive Charleston bakery, Edward revealed a surprise. "I found the perfect cottage just outside Columbia," he said, sliding a photograph across the table. "Three bedrooms, incredible natural light, and a garden space that's practically begging for your touch."

Abbie gasped, picking up the photo. "It's beautiful! When did you—"

"Roderick helped," Edward admitted. "We've been watching the listings for months. The owners just accepted our offer yesterday."

Roderick raised his glass with a wink. "The studio potential alone made it worth the search."

"Our first real home," Abbie whispered, tracing the cottage's outline in the photograph.

"Though," Edward added, glancing at Beatrice, "we expect frequent visits from our favorite sister."

"You better believe it." Beatrice raised her glass. "To new beginnings."

"To love," Abbie added, her smile bright with something hard-won.

"To family," Edward finished. "The kind we choose."

"And to good legal counsel when selecting real estate," Roderick quipped, drawing laughter that softened the day's weight.

That evening, helping them load the last boxes into Edward's truck, Beatrice noticed Abbie's hand lingering on her phone.

"Still nothing?" she asked gently.

Abbie shook her head. "I just thought... it's my wedding day, Bea. Even if he's angry—even if he disapproves—I'm still his daughter."

Roderick carried the last box to the truck. "Sometimes people need time to realize what truly matters," he said, his voice gentle. "Your father's a prideful man."

"You've got the emergency numbers?" Beatrice asked, falling back on old habits to distract her sister from the pain.

"Yes," Abbie said with a watery laugh. "And your spare key, and directions to every hospital between here and Columbia."

"And my promise to take care of her," Edward added softly, embracing his new sister-in-law. "Always."

"And my legal expertise whenever you need it," Roderick added, joining the embrace.

Beatrice watched them—these people who had chosen one another despite everything.

"Be happy," she whispered, watching the truck's headlights flicker on. "Be free."

Edward helped Abbie into the passenger seat, then turned back to Beatrice and Roderick. "We'll call when we arrive."

"You better," Beatrice replied, her voice catching. "And Edward? Remember what I told you. No matter what my father does next, you're family now."

"Eccentric, but legally recognized," Roderick added, his hand finding Beatrice's as they watched the truck pull away.

As their taillights disappeared around the bend, Beatrice and Roderick stood in the gathering dusk. The Carolina moon cast silver light across the chapel grounds.

Back in Atlanta, Randolph Hartwell sat alone in his study, a glass of bourbon untouched, the ice long melted. On his desk lay a wedding invitation torn precisely in half.

"Sir?" Martha appeared in the doorway. "Will you be needing anything else tonight?"

"No," he said, not looking up from the torn invitation. "Nothing else."

His hand hovered over it a moment longer, then pulled back.

In their new home, Abbie and Edward Stuart unpacked boxes by lamplight. Wedding bands caught the glow as they hung art, arranged books, and transformed the space with touches of their new shared life.

Abbie placed a box on the highest closet shelf, her fingers lingering on its lid—childhood photos, mementos from her father's house, pieces of a past she couldn't quite let go.

Edward wrapped his arms around her waist from behind. "We can unpack that one later," he murmured against her hair. "Whenever you're ready."

"What if I'm never ready?" she asked, leaning back against his chest.

"Then we'll make new memories," he said, turning her to face him. "Better ones."

Abbie smiled as she reached up to trace the scar along his jaw. "Promise?"

"With everything I am," he whispered, his kiss a quiet promise of home.

Two years into their life in Columbia, Abbie and Edward had found their own rhythm. The stone cottage vibrated with life—her paintings leaning against walls, waiting to be hung; his running shoes lined up neatly by the door; coffee mugs left on the porch railing after their morning rituals. The honeysuckle Abbie had planted that first spring now climbed the trellis Edward had built, its scent drifting through open windows. But nothing about that morning felt routine.

Abbie sat on the bathroom floor, cool tiles pressed against her legs. The porcelain sink dug into her shoulder as she leaned back against it. Ginger ale fizzed in the glass beside her, the soft pop marking the rhythm of her shallow breaths.

Beatrice's weekly video call lit up her phone screen.

"Don't say a word," Abbie warned, a dimple flickering despite the pallor. "I haven't even told Edward yet."

"Told Edward what?" Beatrice's innocent tone fooled neither of them. Two years of weekly calls had only strengthened their connection, making Beatrice's feigned ignorance almost comical.

"Bea…"

"Fine, but when you do tell him, I want video evidence." Her professional mask slipped, her eyes bright with excitement. "I'm going to spoil this baby rotten."

Abbie touched her silver necklace, the metal cool against flushed skin. "I've been thinking that after two years, maybe…"

"Daddy might have softened?" Beatrice supplied, raising an eyebrow.

"Is it stupid? After all this time?" Abbie's hand drifted to her still-flat stomach. "The last time I tried was Christmas. He wouldn't even open the card."

"It's not stupid. It's hope," Beatrice said, aligning papers on her desk with habitual precision. "And hope's never wrong."

Even when it hurts—especially then.

That evening, Abbie arranged the dining table, her hands trembling. Candlelight flickered across the walls of their home, casting dancing shadows on the artwork they'd collected. She'd recreated their first meal together—his "world-famous" grilled cheese—though the smell now triggered a wave of nausea.

Edward entered and paused, scanning the room with that quick military assessment she knew so well.

"Abs?" His eyes moved from the table to her face. "What's going on? Everything okay?"

"I..." Her necklace caught the candlelight. "We're going to need a bigger place."

Edward's brow furrowed, then cleared. "Are you...?"

Her dimple answered before she nodded. "Yes."

The grilled cheese went cold as Edward swept her into his arms, spinning her until she laughingly protested. His eyes, always alert for threats, now shone with wonder.

Later, curled together on their worn couch, they began to dream aloud. The ceiling fan's rhythmic creaking kept time with their whispered plans.

"Columbia's been good to us," Abbie said carefully, tracing patterns on Edward's arm. "But I've been thinking..."

Edward's hand stilled where it had been drawing circles on her shoulder. "About Atlanta?"

About second chances—olive branches—and doors not quite closed.

"The medical care is better there," she said instead. "And Beatrice..."

"And maybe after two years," he finished, "your father might be ready?"

"Am I being naive?" Her voice carried the weight of every ignored letter and missed birthday.

"No, love." He kissed her temple. "You're being you. It's one of the reasons I fell in love with you."

The decision to return wasn't simple. Edward was due for a promotion. Abbie had exhibitions lined up. But when Beatrice mentioned a security position opening at a prestigious Atlanta firm and a small house just outside the city, it felt like fate.

"It's perfect," Abbie breathed, walking through the single-story ranch just outside the city the following weekend.

Sunlight streamed through windows that would make ideal studio space. The garden reminded her of helping her mother tend roses—a memory so sharp it caught in her throat. The kitchen's worn countertops held character—something the marble in her father's mansion never did.

"The commute's not bad," Edward said, already running numbers in his head.

"And it's only fifteen minutes from my place," Beatrice added, watching her sister's face glow.

It was close enough for emergencies, far enough for independence.

They moved in the spring, when Georgia's dogwoods exploded in white bloom. Beatrice had already stocked the kitchen with basics and filled the nursery with essentials, her excitement showing in her practical way.

"The best obstetrician in Atlanta," she announced, handing Abbie a thick folder, neatly tabbed and highlighted.

"Of course you have." Abbie hugged her, both pretending not to notice how pregnancy hormones amplified every emotion.

The familiar scent of Beatrice's perfume mingled with the fresh paint smell of their new home. Outside, the hum of cicadas and distant traffic replaced Columbia's hush.

Their first week back brought the appointment with Dr. Reynolds. Her office smelled of antiseptic and artificial lavender.

"Your blood pressure's a little elevated—140 over 90," the doctor said, frowning slightly at the chart. "And there's a trace of protein in your urine. Nothing alarming yet, but it's something to watch."

Edward and Abbie exchanged a glance, concern flickering behind their eyes.

"Should we be worried?" he asked.

Dr. Reynolds offered a reassuring smile, though her voice held weight. "Not if we stay ahead of it. With plenty of rest and limited stress, we should remain on track." She turned toward the monitor. "Let's check on baby, shall we?"

Abbie reached for Edward's hand without looking away from the screen. He laced his fingers with hers, his thumb brushing gently across her knuckles.

"We're okay," she whispered—more to herself than to him.

"We will be," Edward said, though his grip told her he wasn't sure.

"Would you like to know the sex?" she asked, the ultrasound wand gliding across Abbie's belly.

Edward squeezed her hand.

"Yes," they answered together.

"It's a girl," Dr. Reynolds said, pointing to the screen. "Everything looks perfect."

Abbie's eyes filled with tears. A daughter. A little girl who might inherit her mother's artistic passion—or her father's quiet strength. Or both.

That night, Abbie woke drenched in sweat, her heart pounding. The shadows of their new bedroom loomed unfamiliar.

Edward stirred beside her, alert in an instant. "What's wrong?"

"Nothing," she said too fast. "Just warm."

His eyes narrowed. "You sure? You've been tossing all night."

"Just adjusting to the new space," she said, twisting the sheet in her fingers.

But Edward noticed—how she fumbled the coffee pot, winced at morning light, and braced herself when she thought he wasn't watching. He cataloged each moment with the precision that had kept him alive in warzones.

He hadn't yet spoken of his worry, but Beatrice saw it anyway—in Abbie's face, her silences.

Since the move back, she'd sensed Abbie's longing to reach out to their father. But after so much rejection, hesitation had taken root. Beatrice knew it was eating her alive. So she suggested sending the baby announcement, hoping it might ease the weight Abbie carried.

"Just the facts," she said, smoothing the envelope. "No pressure. No expectations. Two years is a long time to hold onto anger."

"Even for Randolph Hartwell?" Edward asked, jaw tightening.

Beatrice didn't answer. She didn't need to.

Like the others, the envelope came back unopened. Abbie stared at it, then crushed it in her hand. Edward noticed the pallor, the clenched jaw, the way her eyes shut against the pain.

"Headache again?" he asked, casual.

"Just tired."

"That's the third this week," he said, moving closer. "You didn't have these in Columbia."

"It's nothing," she insisted. "Just adjusting to Atlanta's air quality."

Or to another rejection—another door closed.

Over the next week, Edward watched her mask fatigue with half-smiles. She'd pause mid-sentence, grip chair backs when dizzy. Each moment tightened the knot in his chest.

That night, he found her in the nursery, organizing tiny clothes with almost obsessive care. A habit she'd picked up from him—bringing order to manage stress.

"He's missing out," Edward said, wrapping his arms around her from behind. "On you. On these two years. On our daughter. On everything that matters."

"I know." She leaned into him as he lifted the weight from her belly with his hands. A soft moan escaped—brief, involuntary, full of relief. "I just thought... maybe time and a granddaughter... might be enough."

She turned. Her eyes lost focus. Her hand reached blindly—Edward caught her.

"That's it," he said. "I'm calling Dr. Reynolds."

"Edward, it's nothing—"

"It's not nothing," he cut in, guiding her to the rocker. "Not when it happens daily. Not when you're carrying our daughter."

"It's the stress. The move."

"Exactly," he said, already dialing. "And we shouldn't have rushed it."

If he hadn't rejected every olive branch...

Dr. Reynolds saw them the next morning. She asked sharp questions. Edward answered when Abbie minimized symptoms, filling in things even she hadn't realized he'd observed.

"Your blood pressure's elevated," the doctor said, removing the cuff. "Not dangerously so, but enough to be concerned—especially given your symptoms."

"What does that mean?" Abbie asked, hand finding Edward's.

"Rest," the doctor said. "Reduced stress. No heavy lifting, no prolonged standing." She looked at Edward. "She needs support. Rigorously."

"I'll see to it," he said, his military bearing returning.

A week later, a package arrived—from Randolph's office. Not from Sheila, who'd known Abbie since childhood, but from a new assistant. Inside: a check with many zeros and a cold note about "providing for the child's future."

No congratulations. No acknowledgment.

Abbie stared at it, her hand resting on her belly. The paper felt sterile. She'd hoped—naively, maybe—but still hoped.

"This move was a mistake," Edward said from the doorway, watching her press fingers to her temple.

"Don't." Her voice cracked. "This was my choice too."

"Your blood pressure was perfect in Columbia," he said, guiding her to the couch. "The stress of hoping he'd change..."

"I need to stop expecting anything from him." Tears welled. "I thought a grandchild might soften him."

"But he's Randolph Hartwell," Edward said. "And Randolph Hartwell doesn't bend."

Abbie shifted, her head in his lap. She shut her eyes tightly as his fingers pressed her temples.

Edward pushed damp curls from her skin. "Headache's back?"

"Just a twinge." Her voice trembled. "Drawing usually helps... but the lines keep blurring."

He ran his fingers through her hair. His presence was her anchor.

She cupped his cheek. "I dragged you into all this."

"No, Abs." His jaw clenched under her palm.

It's not your fault he can't see past himself.

Despite the pain, her dimple surfaced. "Our daughter will never question her worth." Her fingers found the silver chain at her neck. "She'll never wonder if she's loved. She'll know."

The Georgia sunset bathed their home in warm light.

Downtown, Randolph Hartwell sat alone in his marble office. A grandmother's silver rattle—still boxed—sat in his drawer. Two years of stubbornness had aged him, but not softened him.

"Have you finished the quarterly projections?" he asked his intercom, eyes fixed on his screen.

"Yes, sir," came the reply. "And Ms. Whitmore called again about their son James attending the charity auction with Miss Abigail."

"Inform them my daughter won't be available." He closed the drawer on the rattle. "Some matters require personal attention."

His signet ring tapped the desk—three sharp clicks in the silence.

In the nursery, Abbie hung her latest sketch—three generations of women: her mother's smile, her own freckles, and the promise of new life. A legacy of love.

Another spell of dizziness washed over her.

Edward was there instantly, his arm around her waist. "You're supposed to be resting."

"Come feel this first," she said, guiding his hand to her belly. "Already dancing."

"Or sparring," he said, eyes shining despite concern. "Either way, this kid's got good taste in parents."

The baby kicked again, stronger. Abbie winced.

"Bed," Edward said, steering her toward it. "Doctor's orders."

She didn't protest. And that worried him most.

As she sank into the pillows, Edward watched her—his hand resting protectively on the curve of her belly—and wondered if Atlanta's return had cost them more than they could afford.

✳✳✳

The third trimester had brought changes to Abbie's routine. Her afternoon walks grew shorter, painting sessions less frequent. Her doctor had been clear at her last appointment: "Your blood pressure concerns me. More rest, less stress."

Today, however, as Beatrice's car pulled into the familiar circular drive of the Hartwell mansion, Abbie's heart raced despite every promise she'd made to stay calm.

"We can still turn around," Beatrice said, killing the engine, though she made no move to exit. "He doesn't even know we're coming."

Abbie placed her hand over her swollen belly, feeling Abbeline's reassuring movements. The name still made her smile, remembering the baby shower just a month ago.

"Remember that ridiculous name game at the shower?" Abbie asked, grateful for the distraction. "When everyone had to combine mine and Edward's names to come up with something unique for the baby?"

Beatrice laughed, the tension cracking just for a moment. "God, yes. 'Edwigail' was the worst."

"And 'Abbward,'" Abbie groaned. "Or Sara's suggestion—'Stabbie.'"

"I still can't believe she didn't realize how that sounded," Beatrice said, shaking her head. "Thank goodness Roderick saved the day with 'Abbeline.' Combining your nickname, Abbie, with the end of Edward's middle name, Devline, was inspired."

"Abbeline Lena Stuart," Abbie whispered, stroking her belly. "I'm so grateful we didn't end up with 'Edwabbie.'"

Her smile faded as she looked up at the imposing mansion. "Ugh."

"We don't have to do this," Beatrice said, hoping she'd change her mind.

"No, Bea. This is ridiculous. Three years of silence and returned letters—I need to look him in the eye before she's born."

"Edward's going to be furious when he finds out."

"That's why you promised not to tell him," Abbie reminded her, reaching for the door handle. "This is between me and Daddy."

The familiar weight of the mansion pressed down as they entered. Everything remained unchanged—the gleaming marble floors, the portraits of stern-faced Hartwells, the subtle scent of lemon polish and old money. Martha's face registered shock when she saw them, her eyes darting to Abbie's pronounced belly.

"Miss Abigail," she gasped. "I didn't... we weren't expecting..."

"Is he in his study?" Abbie asked gently.

Martha nodded, her eyes filling with tears she quickly blinked away. "He's reviewing quarterly reports. Shall I announce you?"

"No need," Beatrice said, squeezing Martha's arm as they passed. "We know the way."

Their father didn't look up when they entered, his attention fixed on the computer screen. Afternoon light cast his profile in stark relief, highlighting new lines around his mouth—a weariness that hadn't been there three years ago.

"Martha, I asked not to be disturbed," he said without looking up.

"It's not Martha, Daddy," Abbie said.

His fingers froze over the keyboard. For a moment, the only sound was the soft ticking of the antique clock on the mantel—the one that had timed so many silent dinners, so many carefully measured conversations.

"Abigail," he said finally, slowly turning his chair. His eyes flickered briefly to her stomach before returning to her face with practiced detachment. "This is unexpected."

"You wouldn't accept my calls or open my letters," she said. "I didn't see another option."

"So you decided to ambush me." He glanced at Beatrice. "And you assisted in this... confrontation."

"Don't blame Bea," Abbie said. "This was my idea. I wanted to see you before your granddaughter arrives."

Randolph's jaw tightened at the word "granddaughter," but he gestured toward the chairs. "Sit," he said. "You shouldn't be standing in your condition."

Abbie lowered herself into the familiar leather chair, suddenly exhausted. The baby kicked—sharper, more insistent than before—as if sensing her tension. Beatrice remained standing, one hand on her sister's shoulder.

"I received your check," Abbie said after a moment of silence.

"Good. It should cover the child's immediate needs." His voice was all business, as if discussing a corporate acquisition.

"That's not why I came." She leaned forward slightly. "Money isn't what she needs from you, Daddy."

"What she needs," Randolph replied, "is security, proper connections, and a place in the right circles. All of which I'm prepared to provide."

"What about love?" Abbie asked. "What about accepting her parents and the life we built?"

Randolph's sigh held years of stubborn certainty. "You've made your choices, Abigail. I've made mine."

"That's it? After three years, that's all you have to say to me?"

He turned back to his screen, shoulders rigid. "I have a board meeting in thirty minutes. Was there something specific you needed?"

The coldness stunned her more than any insult might have. Abbie felt tears building but refused to let them fall. This indifference was worse than anger.

"I love you, Daddy," she said, voice steady now. "I've always loved you. But I won't apologize for loving Edward too—for building a life with him."

"No one's asking you to apologize." He still wouldn't look at her. "I'm simply suggesting we acknowledge the reality of our situation."

"And what reality is that?"

"That some divisions cannot be bridged. That some choices carry permanent consequences."

Beatrice stepped forward, her patience snapping. "For God's sake, Daddy, look at her. Really look at your daughter. She's carrying your grandchild, and you can't even ask how she's feeling?"

Randolph glanced up. Something flickered—a brief flash of uncertainty, or maybe pain—but it vanished just as quickly. "I assume her health is being properly monitored. The check should cover any medical expenses."

"I don't want your money," Abbie said quietly. "I want my father back."

"The father you remember wouldn't have allowed his daughter to throw away her future on... inappropriate attachments."

The room swayed slightly. Abbie pressed her hand against her temple. A dull throb had been building behind her eyes, and the baby kicked harder than before.

"You're right," she said, rising with effort despite Beatrice's steadying hand. "The father I remember wanted my happiness, even if it didn't match his plans. I don't know who you are anymore."

Randolph finally turned fully toward her—a gesture so familiar it made her heart ache. "I will ensure your daughter has every advantage, Abigail. That is my commitment."

"But not a grandfather who loves her," she said. "Not a family united instead of divided by pride."

"I have a meeting to prepare for." He adjusted his cuffs—a gesture so familiar it made her heart ache. "Martha will see you out."

Beatrice helped Abbie to the door. In the foyer, Abbie paused, one hand at her lower back. The baby had gone still.

"Are you okay?" Beatrice asked, concern rising.

"Just tired," Abbie lied. "Take me home."

By the time they reached Abbie's house, her limbs felt like lead. She sank onto the sofa, her body finally registering the toll.

"I should never have let you do this," Beatrice said, pacing. "The doctor said to avoid stress."

"It was my choice, Bea."

"A choice that could harm you and my niece!" Beatrice ran her hand through her hair, undoing her neat chignon. "Edward's going to kill me when he finds out."

"When I find out what?" Edward's voice cut through the room. He crossed the floor in three strides, eyes scanning Abbie's face. "What happened?"

"I went to see Daddy," she said.

Edward went pale. "You did what?"

"I had to try one more time. For her." She placed both hands on her belly. "So she'd know I did everything possible."

"Damn it, Abbie!" His voice rose, sharp with panic. "Dr. Reynolds told you to avoid stress. Your blood pressure—"

"I know what she said," Abbie interrupted. "But this was important."

Beatrice moved toward the door. "I should go."

"No, you shouldn't," Edward said, turning to her. "You drove her there? Knowing her condition?"

"Edward, don't blame Bea," Abbie said quickly. "If she hadn't taken me, I would've gone alone."

"That's supposed to make it better?" He paced, sharp and controlled. "Three months of careful monitoring, and you risk it all for him? For a man who's made it clear we mean nothing?"

"For our daughter," Abbie said. "So she wouldn't have to wonder why I didn't try harder."

"Our daughter needs her mother healthy!" The fear beneath his anger cracked his voice. "She needs you, Abs. I need you."

Abbie struggled to stand. Beatrice and Edward reached her simultaneously.

"You should rest," Beatrice said. "I'll call Dr. Reynolds, see if she wants to check in."

"I'm fine," Abbie insisted, though the pounding behind her eyes made her wince.

"I'll make sure she rests," Edward said, gentler now. "And I'm sorry for snapping."

"Don't be," Beatrice replied. "You were right." She kissed Abbie's cheek. "Call me later, okay?"

After she left, Edward helped Abbie to bed. His movements were careful, the set of his jaw tense.

"I'm sorry," she said. "I should have told you."

"You should have." He sat beside her, taking her hand. "But I understand why."

"He didn't even ask about the baby," she whispered. "His own granddaughter."

Edward's expression darkened. "He doesn't deserve you."

That night, Abbie woke to find Edward's side of the bed empty. The clock read 2:17 a.m.

"Edward?" she called softly. No reply.

The next morning, he was quiet over breakfast, his shoulders tense.

"Where did you go last night?" she asked.

He hesitated. "I needed to clear my head."

"You went to see him, didn't you?"

Edward set down his coffee. "Someone needed to make him understand the damage he's doing."

"Edward, no..." Her stomach dropped. "What happened?"

"I said what needed saying." His jaw ticked. "He needs to know what he's doing. What it's costing."

"Did he listen?"

"People like your father don't listen. They dictate." He softened slightly, reaching for her hand. "But I had to try. For you. For our daughter."

The day passed quietly. By evening, her headache had dulled.

"Go to the gym," she urged. "You need a break."

"I don't want to leave you."

"I'm okay now," she said. "And I'll be asleep before you're out the door."

Reluctantly, Edward agreed. He kissed her goodnight. "I'll have my phone."

He had just grabbed his bag when a low groan stopped him.

Abbie stood in the hallway, gripping her belly, tears streaking her face. She thrust the phone toward him, hands shaking.

"Dr. Reynolds," she gasped. "Something's wrong."

Edward took the phone, listening as the doctor's voice sharpened: "Get her to Atlanta General immediately."

As he helped her to the car, he sent a quick text to Beatrice. Her reply came at once: On our way. Roderick and I just left the charity event.

Edward's hands stayed steady on the wheel despite the panic flooding his chest. In the passenger seat, Abbie's eyes were closed, her breathing shallow.

"Stay with me, Abs," he whispered. "Both of you—stay with me."

Beatrice's final text chimed: I've told Daddy too.

***

The hall outside the maternity operating wing was a corridor of purgatory. Fluorescent lights buzzed overhead, cold and unrelenting. Vending machines blinked like unmoved sentries.

Edward paced its length with fists clenched, the sterile air scraping at every breath.

Preeclampsia. Emergency C-section. Internal bleeding.

Each phrase had landed like a bullet—controlled, clinical, deadly.

"Edward!" Beatrice's voice snapped him from the loop. She appeared in the corridor like something torn from another world, evening gown still clinging to the shimmer of the gala. Roderick followed, tension etched in every line of his jaw.

"They said it's critical," Edward said, his voice frayed. "Her blood pressure was... it spiked in the car. They couldn't wait."

"Where is she?"

"In surgery. They rushed her in. I couldn't—" He looked at his hands as if only now noticing their trembling. "I couldn't follow."

Roderick stepped forward, grounding a hand on Edward's shoulder. He had no words.

Edward's focus remained locked on the doors, as if will alone could hold them open and pull Abbie back.

"We never should've come back here," he whispered. "Everything got worse the second we did."

"No one knew this would happen," Beatrice said. "This is not your fault."

The doors opened. A nurse in scrubs and surgical cap appeared, her face taut with measured calm.

"Mr. Stuart. She's asking for you."

Edward followed her into a maze of antiseptic hallways and low, humming machines. When he entered the room, the breath left his body.

Abbie lay small beneath a tangle of monitors and IVs. Pale. Eyes closed. Only the soft rise and fall of her chest, shallow and hesitant, told him she was still fighting.

"Hey, soldier," she murmured as he approached. Her lips barely moved, but her voice still held that dry, defiant humor.

"Hey, baby." He took her hand. It felt like holding tissue paper.

She opened her eyes fully, finding his. "If something happens..."

"Don't—"

"If something happens," she repeated, clearer now, "don't ever let her wonder."

"I won't. I swear it."

"Tell her everything. How much I love her. How much I wanted her." Her fingers clutched his. "Promise me, Edward."

"I promise." He leaned in, forehead to hers. "But you'll tell her yourself."

A smile ghosted her lips. Then—something shifted.

Her breath hitched.

The monitors began to scream.

"Abbie?"

She looked at him, wide-eyed, lips forming one last message he knew without sound—I love you—before her grip went slack.

A voice called, "Code blue," and hands pulled him back. The curtain of bodies closed around her.

He stumbled into the hallway, where Beatrice caught him as his knees buckled.

Her voice echoed in his mind—soft, determined, unfinished. Tell her everything.

Time lost meaning. Minutes blurred. There were voices. Dr. Reynolds. Beatrice. The throb of fluorescent lights overhead.

"It was HELLP syndrome," someone said—quietly, almost apologetically. "It progressed too fast. We tried everything."

None of it mattered. The only thing that made sense— Abbie—was gone.

And Edward shattered.

Edward didn't even know how long it was, or how he made it to the hospital nursery, but there he sat cradling their daughter beneath soft yellow light. She was impossibly small, impossibly alive. His hands shook as he held her, as if his body didn't know whether to break or protect.

"Abbeline Lena Stuart," he whispered, his throat raw. "You made it. She didn't, but... you did." A tear dropped onto the blanket. Then another. He blinked fast, trying to steady his breath. "She would've loved you so much."

The door opened behind him.

He didn't turn.

The scent of expensive cologne arrived first—sharp, sterile, misplaced. Edward's jaw flexed. He adjusted his grip on Abbeline, steadying the blanket with fingers that refused to stop trembling.

Randolph Hartwell entered, posture impeccable, grief hidden beneath tailoring and decades of control.

"So. It's true."

Edward said nothing. His throat burned. The room still smelled of sterile plastic, formula, and loss.

Behind them, Beatrice entered quietly. She had been just down the hall handling arrangements. Her eyes, raw and red, darted between both men.

Randolph moved closer, gaze falling—briefly, and perhaps not entirely by choice—on the baby. A flicker passed across his face. But whatever it was, it vanished before it could settle.

"This changes things," he said, adjusting his cufflinks.

"She belongs with her family," he added, as if clarifying a contract. "With us."

Edward tightened his hold on Abbeline.

He didn't look up. Didn't speak.

But his silence was sharp enough to wound.

Beatrice blinked hard, stunned. "Her family? Daddy, do you even hear yourself?"

She stepped forward. "That's her father."

"Him?" Randolph said. "A man with no influence, no name, no—"

"None of that mattered to Abbie," she cut in. "It still doesn't."

Edward shifted, tucking Abbeline's cap a little lower against the light. He kissed her forehead—steadying her, steadying himself.

"My daughter made a mistake," Randolph snapped, voice rising. "One that cost her everything."

Beatrice's voice dropped, brittle. "This is too far, even for you, Randolph Hartwell. You'd take a daughter from her father?"

Randolph's tone cooled, more dangerous now. "The courts will decide."

Edward stood. The motion was stiff—anchored in protection. Abbeline stirred, and he adjusted her again, shielding her from the overhead light.

He stepped forward. Not threatening, just closer.

"And nothing you do—no lawyer, no threat—will take her from me."

They stood like that for a long moment. Two men bound by loss, staring over the ruins of love and legacy.

One unyielding in performance. The other—cracked open, but still standing.

A nurse appeared in the doorway, her voice gentle. "Mr. Stuart? The pediatrician's ready."

Edward took one last look at Randolph.

Then he walked past him, never looking back.

***

The harassment started with phone calls. At first, just breathing on the line—then cryptic references to Kandahar that made Edward's hands shake. He silenced another private number—just static and his own panic—before tossing the phone across the room. Unknown numbers lit up his screen at all hours—during Abbeline's feedings, interviews, even the rare moments she finally slept.

"You can't protect her," one caller whispered. "Not from us, not from the truth."

What in the world?

"How's the job search?" another would ask, then laugh. "Oh, wait..."

Then Randolph himself began calling—each conversation a curated blend of veiled threats and false concern. "Just looking out for my granddaughter's welfare," he'd say before casually mentioning another company that had suddenly filled its security position.

Three months after Abbeline's birth, the letter from Sterling Guards arrived—termination effective immediately. During the exit interview, Edward rose from the table, shoulders bowed, bracing for another blow.

"It's not right, but Randolph Hartwell sits on half the boards in Atlanta. One phone call, and our biggest clients were threatening to pull contracts."

By month five, Edward screened every call. Telemarketers, private numbers—even Beatrice's voice sometimes made him freeze.

The harassment escalated: canceled credit cards, anonymous HOA complaints, and then—a sudden visit from Child Protective Services.

His sleepless nights carved hollows beneath his eyes. His military posture, once ramrod straight, now slumped in corners where no one was watching.

But Edward fought back at night. After Abbeline slept, he'd meet Roderick in dim diners or under streetlamps. Over coffee and scattered papers, the guardianship plan took shape.

"We file these now," Roderick said. "You grant Beatrice temporary guardianship. What looks like surrender is actually a shield."

Edward nodded. "If he tries later…"

"He'll have to prove why Beatrice—legally fit—should be unfit. Hard to do."

By evening, Edward recorded lullabies and stories:

"Your mama had this laugh—it started in her eyes, like sunshine bursting—just like yours."

He filled cassette tapes with Abbie's voice, with promises, with love for a daughter who deserved both.

Beatrice's presence became constant. She'd taken leave from work—to the shock of her partners—to help. Weekends at her condo gave Edward sleep. Weekdays, she brought food and diapers, moving seamlessly from briefs to baby bottles.

"You need to go to your tournament," Edward protested when she canceled.

"Abbeline needs me here," she said.

"And you need something that's yours," he replied, voice cracking. "At least one of us should keep fighting."

Guardianship papers sat in Beatrice's drawer—waiting.

***

That Wednesday evening, the bell chimed. Beatrice entered with groceries, head bowed.

Edward stood over Abbeline's crib—silent, shoulders slumped, his jaw working through unseen battles.

"I brought dinner... and the shampoo you like."

He didn't turn right away. "Thanks," was all he said—his voice as hollow as the house felt.

She watched his jaw tighten and release. "You need to eat," she said. "I'll stay with her."

Before he could answer, headlights swept the nursery wall.

Edward exited. Randolph stood on their porch—sharp in a tailored suit, impossibly calm.

Edward stared back—exhausted, furious, broken. *What now?*

"Your stubbornness is hurting her already," Randolph began. "No job, no prospects, mounting bills... How long before you're selling that house in Columbia? Living on military pension in some cramped apartment?"

"You're orchestrating this harassment," Edward said quietly, his voice steadier than he felt. He nearly flinched when his nightmares—Kandahar, civilian blood—flared behind his eyes. "The calls, the job losses, the CPS visit—it's all you."

"I'm ensuring she has the life Abigail would've wanted."

"Do you even hear yourself? Abbie ran from that life," Edward's voice cracked. The dark circles beneath his eyes matched the grief pooling in his chest. "She wanted her daughter to be free. She made me promise—"

"To protect her?" Randolph interrupted, pulling out a manila folder. "Operation Shadowpoint. Tell me—does that name ring a bell?"

Edward's blood ran cold. Weeks of veiled threats had led to this.

"Marcus Chen," Randolph said. "Young lieutenant—trusted you. That checkpoint. The civilian casualties, the review, the breakdown."

"Stop." Edward's hands curled into fists. He could feel it—guilt, shame, trauma, all rising.

"I have friends in powerful places," Randolph continued. "I can ensure every detail becomes public. Georgia newspapers would love a decorated veteran's tragic mistake, questions of judgment, PTSD. Imagine Abbeline growing up with that shadow."

Abbeline's cry shattered the moment.

Edward flinched. He closed his eyes.

"You'd destroy your granddaughter's life to win?"

"No." Randolph's voice softened—a calculated mercy. "I'm giving you a choice. Walk away. Let her have the Hartwell name. A future unmared by scandal."

Inside, Abbeline's cries grew louder.

"Twenty-four hours," Randolph said. "Say goodbye and—"

Chapter 5

The Unmaking of Self

"TWENTY-FOUR HOURS," Randolph said. "Say your goodbyes and—"

"Stop," Abbeline's voice cracked like glass. She stood so fast, her teacup toppled, its contents blooming dark and ominous across Beatrice's coffee table.

"I can't—I can't hear anymore."

Her hands clutched her temples, fingers trembling. The room pitched sideways, Beatrice's face blurred through tears Abbeline hadn't realized were falling.

"Bella, sweetheart—"

Beatrice reached for her, but Abbeline stepped back.

"He gave my father twenty-four hours to disappear?" The words sliced her throat on the way out—jagged, ragged. "My grandfather, who I've spent my whole life trying to impress, who I moved into his house to be closer to, threatened my father into abandoning me?"

"We managed to extend it to seventy-two hours," Beatrice said gently.

"Seventy-two," Abbeline echoed. The number was meaningless, empty. Three days. Three days to say goodbye to his daughter. To memorize everything about her before vanishing.

The walls spun. Her stomach turned. Without warning, she bolted, barely registering the doorframe catching her shoulder as she staggered into the bathroom. She dropped hard to her knees, the cold tile jolting her spine as her body convulsed, purging grief before she could name it.

Beatrice appeared seconds later, her hands steady. One gathered Abbeline's hair back, the other moved in slow circles along her spine, offering no words, only presence. Anchoring her.

When there was nothing left—only dry heaves and trembling silence—Abbeline slumped sideways, her cheek against the bathtub's cool porcelain. Her designer blouse clung to her, soaked in tea, tears, and shame.

"I thought—" Her voice was brittle. "I thought he didn't want me enough to stay."

Beatrice sat beside her on the floor, her designer skirt forgotten, her own grief carefully restrained. "Your father would've moved mountains to stay with you."

"But he couldn't fight Grandfather." Not a question. Just truth—terrible and inescapable.

"No. If he had, the fallout would've followed you everywhere: school, friends, internships, job interviews. Edward didn't leave to protect himself, Bella. He left to protect you."

Abbeline clutched her mother's silver necklace. The cool metal pressed against her skin, sharp and real. A lifeline. Her fingers curled around it, desperate as a prayer.

"All these years, I hated him," she whispered. "I thought he'd just... left. But I was living in the house of the man who stole him from me."

"You didn't know."

"But I should have." The words surged with sudden clarity. "All those times he changed the subject when I asked about my parents. How he'd distract me with gifts whenever I showed interest in art, or even said Mom's name."

She struggled to her feet. Beatrice followed, ready to catch her, but Abbeline stood—shaky but upright.

"I need air," she said, already moving.

"Bella, wait—"

She didn't. Her hands shook so violently that she dropped her keys once, then again, before gripping them tight enough to hurt.

"You shouldn't drive like this," Beatrice said, close behind. "It's nearly midnight."

"I can't just sit here and talk about this like it's... normal, like it's just another story we tell over wine."

Her reflection in the entryway mirror caught her—pale, red-eyed, mascara-streaked. She barely recognized herself. Or maybe this was the first time she truly saw herself.

"Then let me drive you," Beatrice offered. "Wherever you need to go."

"I need to be alone." The keys dug into her palm, the pain sharp and grounding. "Just for a little while."

Beatrice hesitated, then nodded. "Promise me you'll call if you need anything."

"I promise."

Outside, the garden gleamed under moonlight—perfect rows of flowers, colors curated with ruthless precision. It looked fake now, a lie, like everything else.

So was she.

She got in her car and drove with no destination, only the need to escape the shattering truth she couldn't outrun. Her fingers twisted the necklace again and again, a physical mantra. Seventy-two hours. That was all he'd had. Three days to say goodbye. Three days to love her for a lifetime.

She ended up in a park she didn't recognize. Killed the engine. Let the silence press in.

And screamed.

It was primal—hoarse, cracked, not even human. But it tore from her anyway, as if her body knew what her mind couldn't articulate.

Randolph Hartwell had shaped her life, one rule, one compliment, one carefully chosen punishment at a time. He had stolen her father, controlled her mother's memory, and twisted love into performance.

She bent forward, forehead pressed against the steering wheel. Sobs racked her. Years of betrayal flooding her all at once.

Her phone buzzed from inside her purse, screen lighting up in the dark. Without thinking, she looked.

Missed calls. Messages from Madison. A text from Randolph: *Hope you're over whatever bug Beatrice mentioned.*

And three quiet pings from Chance:

Hope you're okay.

Let me know if you need anything.

No pressure. Just checking in.

She turned the phone face down.

———

Back at home, Beatrice paced the living room. Her phone was silent in her palm; she'd already texted Roderick. The spilled tea still untouched on the table. A dark Rorschach of a moment she couldn't take back.

She'd thought she was protecting Abbeline. Preserving her childhood. Giving her peace. But now the silence had become its own form of violence.

Roderick's reply had come quickly: *Fifteen minutes. I'm coming.*

Beatrice stared at the door. She should've done it differently. Should've told her sooner, told her softer. But how do you soften that truth?

She pressed a hand to her mouth, biting back a sob. The secrets she'd kept to protect Abbeline were the same ones tearing her apart now.

The grandfather clock chimed midnight.

In the quiet that followed, Beatrice closed her eyes and sent up a prayer—to God—for the strength to help her niece survive what came next.

***

Abbeline didn't remember the drive back to Beatrice's house. The journey blurred, like watercolors in rain—each street bleeding into the next. She parked crookedly in the driveway, tires scraping the curb. The house lights glowed in warm rectangles against the night, a silent confirmation that Beatrice was awake, likely with Roderick beside her, both of them ready with comfort Abbeline couldn't bear to receive.

She slipped around to the back garden, avoiding the front door.

The garden studio—once a shed, transformed by Beatrice years ago—stood quiet and forgotten. The key still waited beneath the stone angel. Her fingers found it by instinct, grief and memory guiding her movements.

Inside, the air was thick with dust and the scent of linseed oil and turpentine. Drop cloths draped over old shapes—her childhood easel, a broken drafting table, forgotten canvases. The space smelled like the past—unfiltered and real. Like something untouched and honest.

She switched on the light and winced. The studio blinked awake, a long-forgotten memory stirring. In the corner, a box labeled *Bella's Art Supplies* waited. She dragged it into the center, tearing off the brittle tape with shaking hands.

Inside: charcoal sticks wrapped in faded paper, brushes gone stiff with neglect, sketchbooks full of life before Randolph's influence redirected her toward "suitable" pursuits.

A larger canvas leaned against the wall, cloaked beneath an old bedsheet. A memory surfaced—fifteen years old, sobbing over failed proportions and a crooked smile. Beatrice had sat beside her, murmuring, "Just cover it for now. Sometimes you need distance to see clearly."

Abbeline yanked the sheet away.

A half-finished portrait of her mother looked back. Unpolished, raw—but vibrant. The smile caught mid-laugh, freckles scattered without symmetry, curls in wild rebellion. Not the curated version framed in Randolph's halls, but her mother, real and imperfect.

"You tried to tell me," Abbeline whispered. Her fingertips hovered over the painted cheek. "Through Beatrice. Through this."

In the window's reflection, her own face came into view—smudged makeup, tear tracks, curls beginning to reclaim their natural shape as her carefully maintained facade unraveled.

He shaped me. Trimmed me. Remade me. All the talks about posture, speech, "appropriate" hobbies. All the subtle digs at her hair needing to be "tamed." He hadn't just raised her—he'd redesigned her.

Rage surged. She grabbed a palette knife. Its weight was reassuring. One clean slice through the canvas ripped the silence, a gasp of release. Again, and again. Pristine surfaces torn in protest.

When her fury burned out, only her reflection remained. The curls were still held in place by fading product. With a fierce sound—half sob, half groan—she plunged her head under the tap in the corner sink, scrubbing until water streamed down her back and her blouse clung to her skin.

She straightened, dripping, curls fully released.

She looked like her mother—and her father.

A box of acrylics caught her eye—surprisingly usable. She squeezed a violent streak of crimson onto a torn canvas. Then cobalt. Then cadmium red. Her hands replaced brushes. She pressed, smeared, scraped.

Hours disappeared into raw sensation. She painted fear in jagged black on midnight blue. She painted betrayal as shattered faces—Randolph's image fragmented and reassembled in grotesque patterns. She poured grief in rivers of violet and indigo.

At dawn, surrounded by the chaos she'd unleashed, Abbeline stood still. Paint streaked her hands, her face, her clothes. The Hartwell heiress had vanished.

A soft knock barely registered. Then a second.

"Bella?" Beatrice's voice was gentle. "I saw the light. Can I come in?"

Abbeline looked at her hands—red, blue, yellow. Chaos incarnate.

"I need more time," she called back, her voice hoarse.

A pause. "Roderick brought breakfast. And coffee. Should I leave them outside?"

"Please."

"Bella…" Beatrice hesitated. "You don't have to face this alone."

"I know." Abbeline stared at her stained palms. "But right now, I need to figure out who I am without him in my head."

Silence. Then footsteps retreating. A soft clink of dishes being set down outside.

She turned back to her work, not blindly now, but with purpose.

On a fresh canvas—the last she could find intact—she began a self-portrait. Not society's version. Not Randolph's.

Her own.

Who am I beneath this performance?

Not Abbeline Hartwell.

Abbeline Stuart. That's who I should have been.

Twenty years of pretending.

Now, I begin again.

Each brushstroke reclaimed a piece of herself. Her mother's eyes. Her father's jaw. The intensity in her brow— shared by both. Truth bled through every line.

When her phone buzzed somewhere under a drop cloth, she ignored it. Beatrice returned at noon with lunch. She accepted the sandwich through the door but didn't speak.

The day became another storm of color and memory.

By nightfall, the studio swelled with the scent of turpentine and rebirth. Canvases bore witness to her pain, rage, and slowly—her clarity.

At one point, she heard Beatrice's muffled voice: "Madison and Chance stopped by. They're worried."

It barely registered.

She couldn't explain this metamorphosis yet—not to them.

By the second night, her phone battery died. She let it.

By dawn of the third day, something inside her had changed. The wild color attacks calmed into intention. The chaos had hardened into something sharper—a kind of focus.

I need to face him.

Not in anger. Not in sorrow. In truth.

He needs to see what he destroyed.

The family she should've had. The person she might've been.

She wanted him to say it—clearly. That he'd threatened Edward. That he'd erased her life's foundation with careful lies. She needed those words. Only then could she start to rebuild.

When Beatrice knocked that morning, Abbeline opened the door.

Paint streaked her skin. Her curls hung loose. Her eyes, shadowed by fatigue, were clear and steady.

"I need to see him," she said.

Beatrice's eyes widened. "Your grandfather?"

"Yes." Her fists curled, still stained in defiant color. "I want to hear him say it. To my face."

"Are you sure?"

Abbeline nodded. "I've spent twenty years believing his version of my life. It's time I hear the truth from his own mouth."

Beatrice stepped forward and placed a hand on her shoulder. "Then rest first. Shower. Eat something. Face him with clear eyes."

Abbeline looked down at her clothes—ruined and paint-slick. "Tomorrow morning," she agreed. "Will you and Roderick come with me?"

"Of course," Beatrice said softly. "We'll be right beside you."

As Abbeline stepped outside, morning light touched her face. Behind her, the studio glowed, canvases humming with pain, rage, and the beginnings of resolve.

"I don't know who I am yet," she said quietly, gesturing at herself. "But I know who I'm not. And that's a start."

Beatrice's voice broke. "You're your mother's daughter. And your father's. That's who you've always been, Bella."

Something inside Abbeline loosened. Not happiness. Not yet. But something solid. The beginning of self.

***

Morning came quickly, its light was too bright for what she was about to do. They drove in silence, the Hartwell estate rising like a monument to a life she was ready to leave behind.

The Hartwell mansion loomed against the morning sky—its grandeur now more oppressive than impressive. Abbeline sat in the passenger seat of Beatrice's car, twisting her mother's silver necklace as they pulled into the circular drive. Her natural curls framed her face, her clothes simple—jeans and a soft blue blouse. No designer labels, no mask.

"He's expecting us," Beatrice said quietly, killing the engine but not moving. "I told him two days ago."

Abbeline glanced at her. "How did he take it?"

Beatrice's eyes darkened. "As you'd expect. Denial. Anger. Then this strange calm—that worried me more than the shouting."

Two days earlier, Beatrice had stood in her father's study.

"You had no right," he'd said, low and sharp.

"She deserved the truth," Beatrice had replied. "I warned you. You built this family on a lie. And now, it's crumbling."

He'd gone pale then. His signet ring had tapped out his old distress rhythm on the desk—tick, tick, tick.

Now, in the car, Roderick leaned forward. "We're right here with you, Abbeline. Every step."

"I'm ready." Her voice was steadier than her heartbeat. She let go of the necklace and squared her shoulders. "Let's do this."

Martha answered the door, her eyes softening at the sight of Abbeline. The marble floor, the towering chandelier—once symbols of power, now just stage props in a life she'd outgrown.

"Miss Bella," she said gently. "He's in the study. He hasn't left much since Beatrice told him."

Of course he hadn't. Randolph Hartwell faced crises from behind his desk.

"Thank you, Martha," Abbeline said, already walking. The house felt unfamiliar—a memory misremembered.

I came to make him hurt: to feel what I've carried all these years. So why does the thought of his pain make me sick?

Beatrice and Roderick flanked her—silent, solid sentinels.

At the heavy oak door, she didn't knock. She pushed it open.

The smell hit her—leather, lemon polish, and whiskey, though it was barely 10 a.m. The room was dim, curtains half-drawn. Papers lay scattered across the desk. Randolph Hartwell sat behind it, smaller than she remembered. His suit hung loose, his hair slightly disheveled. The breakfast tray beside him sat untouched.

He looked up, hope flickering for one beat in his eyes. Then it vanished behind familiar restraint.

"Abbeline." His voice was composed, controlled. "Good morning."

"I imagine it is." She stepped inside. "I've been busy learning about the past."

His gaze flicked to Beatrice, then back to her. Slowly, he set his reading glasses down. "I see."

"Do you?" Her hands trembled, but her voice held. "Do you really see what you've done?"

"Perhaps you should sit."

"I'll stand." She folded her arms, trying to still the shaking. "I know what you did to my father."

The air tightened. Randolph's posture shifted slightly—not much, but enough.

His ring tapped the desk once. Twice. A pause.

"I did what was necessary to protect you," he said, the edge sharper than usual. "To give you every advantage."

"Advantage?" She laughed, bitter and soft. "Growing up without my father was your idea of protection?"

"Growing up without scandal was."

"You painted it as scandal. He made a mistake. He was cleared." Her voice cracked slightly, but she didn't stop. "You threatened him. You made him leave."

"I gave him a choice." Randolph rose, walked to the window. Sunlight etched new silver in his hair. "He could fight and taint your future... or step away and allow you to grow up untouched by controversy."

Abbeline watched him—less titan, more man. Fragile. Fallible.

"Untouched?" she whispered. "Is that what you call it? You erased my father. You scrubbed every piece of my mother that didn't fit."

He turned back, mask slipping. His expression tried to soften—tried to explain.

"Everything I did was for your benefit," he said. But the words, this time, carried hesitation.

"If by benefit you mean cutting pieces of me away until I fit your script. If you mean silencing my grief, my art, my voice—then yes. Beneficial indeed."

His jaw twitched. "Your mother rejected stability. She—"

"She chose love over your control," Abbeline said, stepping forward. "And you punished her for it. You punished all of us."

Randolph looked to Beatrice. "So this is the story now. I'm the villain."

"Don't." Abbeline's tone cut the air. "Don't you dare turn this on her. This is not Aunt Bea's fault."

His composure faltered again. "Then whose fault is it?" He spread his hands. "Edward Stuart's, for having a past that could hurt you? Your mother's, for leaving you without a parent? Mine, for stepping in to protect what was left of my family?"

"Yes." The word landed heavy. "Your fault. You disowned your daughter. You drove my father away. And for years, I believed I wasn't worth staying for. That I killed my mother."

"Oh, sugar," Beatrice gasped softly, stepping forward.

Abbeline's voice broke, her vision blurring through unshed tears. "Do you know what that does to a child? To think you're the reason no one stayed? To spend your life afraid one wrong move will make the last person you love disappear too?"

Randolph recoiled as if struck. His hand gripped the desk edge, whitened at the knuckles.

"You thought…" His voice broke mid-sentence. He sank into his chair, shoulders folding inward. The mask was gone.

"I never meant—" he tried, but the words crumbled.

His hand shook. The signet ring dulled in the light. Not power now—just weight.

Part of Abbeline ached to comfort him. She remembered stories read aloud during storms. Bike lessons. Her first recital.

He looks so lost.

But she remembered Edward—and Abbie.

Beatrice moved beside her, clasping her hand. "I will never leave you, sugar. Never."

Randolph stared at them, then at the family photos lining the wall. His gaze landed on a picture of young Abbie, laughing among flowers.

"I told myself I was protecting you," he said, voice faint. "I did the same with your mother. Believed I knew better. I was wrong then. And now."

For a moment, the silence was immense.

"No," Abbeline said quietly. "You did what was easy. What protected you. Not me."

"I gave you every—"

"Every limitation. Every lie. You didn't protect me. You controlled me."

"That's not true," he insisted. "I love you, Abbeline."

She snapped. "Then you should have let me be myself. You should have let me know him. I don't want love that comes with conditions."

The words struck deep. His mouth opened—but nothing came.

"What do you want me to say?" he asked finally, broken. "That I regret it?"

"I want you to see it. I want you to stop calling this love."

Randolph sat hollow in his chair. The room had never felt so empty.

Abbeline turned toward the door—then paused.

She crossed to the sideboard, lifting the photo of her mother. Abbie, laughing, alive.

"This belongs with someone who loved her as she was," she said.

Randolph didn't stop her. His hand twitched, but dropped. The ring flashed, then dimmed again.

"Abbeline." His voice cracked. "What happens now?"

She paused, hand on the knob.

"I don't know," she said. "But it won't involve you."

His face crumpled. No words came.

Then, softly—barely audible through the heavy door—

"…Bella."

That name. The one that had once meant safety.

Her hand hovered.

I could go back. Forgive. Understand.

But some betrayals cut too deep.

She let her hand fall and walked away.

In the hallway, Beatrice touched her arm.

"You okay?"

"No," Abbeline whispered. "But I will be."

She stepped into the morning light, her mother's photograph under her arm. For the first time, she walked not as a Hartwell, but as herself. A Stuart.

***

The drive back from the Hartwell mansion passed in silence. Abbeline stared out the window, her mother's photograph clutched to her chest, each breath was a deliberate act. She felt scraped hollow—excavated, raw at the edges.

He called me Bella.

After everything… he still called me Bella.

"Should we stop somewhere?" Beatrice asked gently as they wound through Buckhead's tree-lined streets. "Get some lunch maybe?"

Abbeline shook her head. Even the thought of food made her stomach twist. "I just want to go home."

Home. Not the mansion with its polished marble and curated art, but Beatrice's place—worn hardwood floors, mismatched furniture, and rooms where truth had always belonged.

When they arrived, she headed straight for the studio. The space had become her sanctuary over the past few days, a place where emotion had found shape and color. But now, with clarity returning, the studio revealed itself for what it really was.

"God," she muttered, stepping inside. "What the hell happened in here?"

Turpentine and dust thickened the air, paint splatters coating nearly every surface. Torn canvases lay crumpled like fallen soldiers. Empty tubes rolled underfoot, dried brushes leaned in grim resignation, and violet paint had congealed into a sticky puddle on the floor.

Cobwebs clung to the ceiling corners. A spider skittered across a drop cloth, and she yelped, stepping back reflexively. Part inherited neglect, part emotional combustion—all of it hers now.

"Where's Martha when you need her?" she muttered, brushing a spot on the windowsill with her sleeve before giving up halfway through.

There wasn't a clean surface anywhere. After a pause, she gently propped the photograph of her mother against the least grimy stretch of the window frame. Her mother's eyes sparkled with the freedom that had been denied to both of them.

She'd have known what to do. Roll up her sleeves. Turn the mess into something beautiful.

Abbeline reached up to sweep away a cobweb and ended up with sticky strands on her fingers. She wiped them on her jeans, then just stood there, overwhelmed.

A chime cut through the silence. She jumped, turning toward the sound—her phone, glowing faintly on the couch where someone—probably Beatrice—had plugged it in.

For three days, she'd ignored the outside world. And now, suddenly, it was waiting for her.

She hesitated, then picked up the phone. Dozens of missed calls and texts flooded the screen. Madison. Professors. Messages from her grandfather, which she didn't open.

And then: Chance Bianchi.

Friday night: *Hey, missed you at dinner. Everything ok?*

Saturday morning: *Stopped by your aunt's place. She said family stuff.*

Sunday: *Please let me know you're okay. People are worried.*

Monday: *If you need someone to talk to, I'm here.*

Today: *I promise this is my last text. Just want you to know someone's thinking about you.*

She stared at the screen.

Chance was… peripheral. A familiar face from the same glittering circles she'd grown up in. Kind, polite. But they'd never been more than acquaintances. She didn't know why. But for the first time in days, she wanted to answer.

I'm okay. Just going through some family stuff. Thank you for checking.

His reply came almost instantly.

Thank God. Was getting worried. No pressure to talk about it, but I'm here.

She sat on the couch, the room still an emotional battlefield around her. Somehow, that last message—a gentle reassurance with no pressure—landed exactly right.

Actually, talking might help. Just not sure where to start.

Start anywhere. I'm a good listener.

Her thumb hovered over the keyboard. Then, without fully deciding, she hit Call.

He picked up on the first ring, without hesitation.

"Hey," he said, surprised but warm. "Didn't expect a call."

"Texting felt too small," she said, curling into the corner of the couch. "I hope that's okay."

"More than okay," he replied, a soft rustling on his end suggesting he was settling in. "I'm all ears."

The words came slowly at first. Shaky, unfinished. But Chance never interrupted. He gave her silence, space, encouragement. And so she spoke—the attic discovery, the hidden letters, the confrontation with Randolph just hours ago.

She held back the military details. Her father's trauma. But she gave him enough.

"So basically, my whole life's been scripted by someone else," she finished. "Right down to how I wore my hair."

"That's... a lot," he said. Understatement. It made her laugh—for the first time in days.

"Yeah. And then I exploded in this studio—paint everywhere, canvases torn to shreds, ruined brushes, a total disaster. I tried to clean earlier, but I honestly had no idea where to start. Three years at my grandfather's and I forgot how to function like a normal person."

"Well," he said, a smile audible in his voice, "that sounds exactly like what you needed."

"Maybe." She looked around. "But now it's just a mess. I'm going to need help just figuring out where to begin."

"Would you…" he hesitated, nervous for the first time, "Would you want help? I'm pretty handy. My Aunt Margo raised me right."

"You'd help clean this disaster?"

"I'd be honored," he said lightly. "Besides, I have a cousin who'd disown me if I ever acted too good to clean. Big Italian family—chores are mandatory."

She smiled, warmth curling in her chest. "That's… surprisingly refreshing."

"Not much about me is society-approved. But I'm good with a mop."

The conversation wandered—classes, restaurants, shared acquaintances. The sun shifted. Beatrice peeked in once, then quietly left them alone.

Eventually, Chance said, "It's getting late. I should let you rest."

"Yeah," she said, surprised she didn't want it to end. "Thank you. For listening."

"I'm glad you called," he said. "I was starting to feel like a stalker."

She laughed. "Why'd you keep trying?"

A pause. Then: "I've always noticed you. Not just the Hartwell version—but the girl sketching during speeches, chatting with staff like they mattered, zoning out like she was dreaming of somewhere better. I wanted to know that girl."

Heat rushed to her cheeks. "Oh."

"Too much?" he asked softly.

"No," she said quickly. "Just… unexpected."

"Would it be more unexpected if I asked to bring coffee tomorrow? Maybe help you tackle that mess?"

Abbeline looked at the studio again—ruined, chaotic, overwhelming. She touched her mother's photo gently.

Today, she'd confronted the man who shaped her life. Tomorrow... she could choose something different.

"I'd like that," she said. "Coffee and reinforcements."

"Deal," he said. "We'll figure it out."

After they hung up, she sat quietly. The sharp pain hadn't disappeared, but something else stirred beneath it—a thread of connection, of healing.

The studio around her was a wreck. Like her life: messy, layered, in need of care—but not beyond hope.

A soft scuttle from the corner made her jump. Another spider. The metaphor shattered. The spell broke.

"Okay, nope. Not tonight."

She stood, careful not to touch anything sticky, and moved to the door. Her gaze settled on her mother's photo, still propped on the windowsill. The smile on her mother's face seemed to echo her own—small, tentative, but real.

She shook her head, exhaling.

"Yeah, we'll deal with you tomorrow."

She flipped off the light, leaving the room to its dust and ghosts. Tomorrow would bring coffee. And Chance. And maybe a broom.

Tonight? She just wanted a hot bath and clean sheets. After everything... that felt like luxury.

***

Light streamed through the bedroom window, warming Abbeline's face and gently pulling her from sleep. For a moment, she blinked up at the unfamiliar ceiling, disoriented.

Then she remembered—not Randolph's ornate moldings, but the simple crown of her old room at Beatrice's house. The air smelled of wood polish and morning coffee.

She checked the clock—eight hours of uninterrupted sleep. No nightmares. No spirals.

The bath the night before had helped, washing away more than just paint and dust. The confrontation with Randolph had been brutal, but it had flushed something toxic from her system. And the phone call with Chance... unexpected, grounding. He had listened. And somehow, understood.

Her phone buzzed on the nightstand.

Still on for coffee? I can be there in 20.

A flutter stirred in her chest. It was just coffee. Just someone kind. She typed a reply:

Looking forward to it. See you soon.

She paused before getting ready. Nothing here bore the designer labels from Randolph's closets. Those clothes belonged to a curated version of herself. Instead, she chose jeans and a faded yellow infographic T-shirt—they were clothes from a quieter time. The face in the mirror surprised her: natural curls wild around her face, her mother's eyes, her father's cheekbones. Real. Unmasked.

People used to say she looked like a young Halle Berry. She'd never believed them—she'd been too polished, too controlled. But now, with her freckles visible and no styling product weighing her down, she could almost see it. Not the glamour, but the essence—something open and honest.

Downstairs, Beatrice was already working through legal briefs, coffee in hand.

"Good morning, sugar," she said without looking up. "Sleep okay?"

"Better than I have in days," Abbeline said, pouring herself a glass of water. "I think... everything finally cracked open."

"And talking with Chance?"

"Helped more than I expected."

Beatrice nodded, her expression carefully neutral, but her eyes curious. "He's been persistent. Madison gave up faster."

"I needed the space."

"And you took it," Beatrice said simply, turning back to her notes.

Fifteen minutes later, a car pulled into the driveway. Abbeline glanced out and saw Chance, walking up the porch steps with coffee and a bakery bag. At 6'2", he was casually handsome. Athletic build, dark brown hair slightly tousled. Eyes that looked both serious and kind.

As she opened the door, his gaze caught on her curls and plain clothes. His smile widened.

"You look different," he said, then winced. "I mean... good different."

"Thanks," she said, tucking a curl behind her ear. "This is more me than I've looked in years."

He nodded, and his smile shifted from cautious to something warmer. "I like her already."

They settled in the sunroom, the late-morning light streaming through the windows. Birds danced in Beatrice's rose bushes. The scent of almond and chocolate filled the air as she opened the bag.

"You said you hadn't been eating," he said, nudging the bag toward her. "Figured I'd bring reinforcements."

The gesture caught her off guard—thoughtful, not performative or expected.

"Thank you," she said, taking a bite of croissant. The buttery flakes melted on her tongue. "That's... incredible."

"You sound surprised," he teased gently.

"I'm just not used to this."

"To what?"

"Kindness without strings."

He didn't press, just sipped his coffee and nodded. "Happy to be an exception."

They chatted easily. She found herself leaning into his presence. Comfortable. No masks. No games.

Beatrice passed through, keys jangling as she headed for the door. "Off to meet Roderick. There's leftover pasta in the fridge if you get hungry later." She nodded politely to Chance. "Nice to see you again."

"You too, Ms. Hartwell."

"Beatrice, please. 'Ms. Hartwell' makes me feel ancient."

Chance laughed, ducking his head slightly. "My grandmother and Aunt Margo would have my backside if they heard me being so informal with someone I respect. How about 'Aunt Bea'? That's what my Italian cousins would say."

Beatrice's eyebrows rose, but her lips curved in amusement. "Aunt Bea works fine. Back by one, Bella."

When they were alone again, Chance leaned back. "So, what's on the agenda today? Studio exorcism?"

Abbeline laughed. "Something like that. I want to clean up enough to bring down my parents' things from the attic."

"Want help?"

"You sure?" she asked, raising a brow. "You haven't seen it yet."

He grinned. "Bring it on."

The walk to the studio was quiet. Morning dew still clung to the garden path. The shed door stood ajar. As they stepped inside, the full scope hit him—paint-streaked walls, shredded canvases, ruined brushes, layered with years of dust and cobwebs.

Chance blinked. "Okay. That's... a lot."

"Told you," she said, oddly relieved.

He pulled out his phone. "I'm calling backup."

"Seriously?"

"My cousin Marco. Georgia Tech. He owes me one."

She tensed at the thought of another stranger seeing her like this.

"He's good people," Chance added gently. "No pressure."

A few texts later, Chance rolled up his sleeves and they got to work. Trash out, surfaces cleared, brushes sorted.

"How are you actually doing?" he asked as they scrubbed side by side.

Abbeline stilled. No one had asked her that.

"I'm... angry. Wrecked. Relieved."

Chance nodded. "That last part's the trickiest, huh? Feeling lighter, even though everything's blown up."

She looked at him, startled. "Exactly."

"I get it," he said simply.

He hummed as they worked. She noticed his ease—the lack of posturing.

Then the door opened. A young man stepped in—stockier, darker, with a thick New York accent.

"Yo," he said, clapping Chance's shoulder. "You didn't say we were helping a dime."

"Marco," Chance warned.

Abbeline smiled despite herself. "Abbeline Stuart."

"Well, Ms. Stuart," Marco said with a grin, "let's get this place back to life."

They fell into a rhythm. Banter, laughter, elbows bumped, dust flew, and music played from someone's phone.

Later, Roderick and Beatrice arrived with sandwiches and drinks. Roderick rolled up his sleeves without question. Beatrice took pictures.

"For posterity," she said.

By sunset, the studio was clean. Functional. Alive.

Abbeline stood at the center, overwhelmed. "I can't believe you stayed this long."

Chance leaned in the doorway. "Worth it."

She smiled. "I need supplies. And then... I need to find my father."

He nodded. "One step at a time."

"I'm not going back to classes."

"You shouldn't. Not yet."

The understanding in his voice undid something in her.

"Thank you," she said. "For seeing me."

Chance looked at her, quiet and sincere. "That's the only you I was ever interested in."

Their eyes held. The air between them felt warmer.

"I should go," he said gently. "But text me tomorrow?"

"I will. After I start the attic search."

"Perfect."

At his car, he turned. "Goodnight, Abbeline Stuart."

"Goodnight, Chance Bianchi."

Back inside the studio, she ran her fingers over a clean table. Dust gone. Clutter cleared.

Through the window, stars winked into view.

She opened a fresh sketchbook and began to draw—not rage, not pain. Just stillness. And something open, as if a doorway had appeared where none had been.

The first honest line of a new beginning.

***

Three weeks had passed since the confrontation with Randolph. Three weeks of sorting through memories and letters with Chance's quiet help, of beginning the slow, uneven work of becoming someone new.

The kitchen glowed with soft evening light, dishes from dinner stacked neatly in the sink. Outside the window, fireflies blinked across Beatrice's garden—random, luminous patterns that somehow made sense together. Abbeline sat at the table, a mug of chamomile tea warming her hands, her gaze fixed on the small plastic card resting between her fingers.

ABBELINE STUART.

The court had declared it, but this card proved it—she wasn't just someone's legacy anymore. The photo captured her natural curls, her mother's dimples, a tentative smile she barely recognized—yet one that looked more familiar than anything from her years as the polished Hartwell heiress.

It looked right. It felt right.

So why did it still ache?

"Social Security card should come tomorrow," Beatrice said, sitting across from her. "Passport will take a little longer, but Roderick's contact in D.C. promised a rush on it."

Abbeline set the license on the table. "I still can't believe how fast all this happened. Roderick made it sound like it'd take months."

"Judge Halvorsen owed him a favor," Beatrice said with a small smile, though something unreadable flickered in her eyes.

What Abbeline didn't know was that the judge had quietly reached out to Randolph. Expecting a battle, he'd been surprised, when the old man gave immediate consent. *She wants to be a Stuart. I won't stand in her way. Not anymore.*

Beatrice reached out, squeezing her hand gently. "How does it feel? Really."

Abbeline glanced down at the card again. "Right," she said softly. "Like something finally fits."

She hesitated.

"But also... strange. Like I've lost something I didn't even know I'd grown attached to."

Beatrice nodded slowly. "You wore the Hartwell name for twenty years. It's okay to feel its absence, even if you never asked for it."

Abbeline looked away, shame and confusion rising in equal measure. Her voicemail still showed twenty-three missed calls from Randolph—his messages reduced to polite brevity. The last had simply read: *I understand your choice. I'm proud of you.*

She deleted it, but the words stayed with her.

"I keep thinking about him," she admitted. "Sitting in that huge, empty house. Alone with his pride and whatever's left of his guilt."

"He made his choices," Beatrice said, not unkindly. "Same as you're making yours."

The grandfather clock chimed nine times, its deep tone stretching through the house. Abbeline felt a quiet hum building in her chest—a need, persistent and sharp, like a page she hadn't yet turned.

"Any word from those firms in Portland?" she asked, shifting toward something she could act on.

"Not yet," Beatrice said, sipping her tea. "But Chance said he had some leads he wants to run by us tomorrow."

Every afternoon, Chance showed up—with coffee, with ideas, with calm. His presence had become something stable. Not urgent. Not overwhelming. Just there.

Beatrice raised a brow. "That boy's smitten. You know that, right?"

Abbeline flushed. "He's just... being kind."

Beatrice arched an eyebrow. "Uh-huh. And you just like his spreadsheet skills."

Abbeline smiled despite herself, but her tone sobered. "It's complicated. I need time to stop being who I was told to be before I decide who I want to become... I can't exactly offer much more than that right now."

"Life's always complicated," Beatrice said gently. "Doesn't mean you have to put everything on pause."

Abbeline ran her thumb along the edge of the license, cool plastic grounding her.

"Aunt Bea," she said suddenly. "I think I'm ready."

Beatrice tilted her head. "For what?"

"To hear the rest. About my father. About what happened after Grandfather gave him that ultimatum." She hesitated. "I've been avoiding it. But I need to know."

Beatrice was quiet for a long moment, then rose and set the kettle on the stove. "Are you sure?"

Abbeline nodded. "Yes. I need to understand."

When Beatrice returned to the table, her fingers traced faint patterns on the wood. Abbeline watched, realizing with a jolt that she'd picked up the same habit—quietly creating order when emotions threatened to overwhelm.

"After the ultimatum," Beatrice began, "Edward had seventy-two hours. Three days to say goodbye. Three days to hold you, memorize your face, record messages... to make peace with the impossible."

Abbeline closed her eyes briefly, picturing the man from the photos holding an infant version of her, grief already shadowing his face.

"He spent the first day fighting," Beatrice said. "Lawyers. Military contacts. Desperate options. But your grandfather had already moved too many pieces. There was no winning."

Abbeline's throat tightened.

"So he shifted," Beatrice continued. "He read you storybooks into a recorder. Wrote letters for birthdays. Set up a trust with everything he had left. Not much, but enough to hope."

Abbeline's eyes stung. "The recordings. I've listened to some of them. I didn't know..."

"The day before he left, he and Roderick moved you into my condo. The guardianship papers were ready—he'd drafted them weeks before, in case. He had everything planned."

Beatrice's voice faltered.

"And the last day?"

Beatrice swallowed hard. "He held you for hours. Kissed your forehead. Whispered something to you. I don't know what. Then I walked him out. We stood in the parking lot. He got in the car. And as he drove away, you started wailing. You cried all night."

Silence settled around them.

"We stayed in contact," she added quietly. "Through Roderick. I sent photos. Updates. He sent letters. Gifts. The sketchbook when you were fourteen. The horse figurine. All his ways of staying close."

Abbeline nodded, tears tracing silently down her cheeks. "And all this time, I thought he had just... left."

"He never stopped loving you, Bella. Never."

Abbeline looked at her aunt. "Then why didn't you tell me?"

Beatrice's face darkened as she leaned back, hands folding together tightly.

"Because I wasn't allowed to. The day I filed those guardianship papers, your grandfather called in every favor he had. Judge Baker—his old Harvard buddy—warned me off. He said if I ever told you the truth, I'd lose custody. And probably my license."

Abbeline's breath caught. "You stayed silent to protect me."

"I hated it," Beatrice whispered. "Every time you asked about him, every birthday you asked if he'd call... I hated it. But I couldn't lose you."

Another pause. Then Beatrice said, "He left another voice-mail today."

Abbeline stiffened, knowing she meant her grandfather.

"Just asked how you were. If you needed anything. He sounded... subdued."

She nodded, staring at her name on the license: STUART. Her father's name. Her mother's choice. Her own now.

"I can't talk to him yet," she said quietly. "Maybe someday. But not now."

Beatrice squeezed her hand. "That's okay, sugar."

They sat in silence, the night stretching around them. Finally, Abbeline rose and carried their mugs to the sink. The ordinary act grounded her.

"Tomorrow," she said softly, "we'll chase those leads. We start looking."

"One step at a time," Beatrice replied.

Abbeline paused at the kitchen window. In the distance, she could see the outline of the studio—clean now, quiet, waiting. And she knew Chance would arrive in the morning, coffee in hand, ready to search again.

She thought of Edward's voice on those recordings. Of Beatrice's sacrifices. Of Chance's quiet presence and unshakable patience.

Sometimes, the people who walk beside you are the ones who become your home.

She touched the edge of the license—a page finally ready to turn.

STUART.

"Aunt Bea?" she said.

"Yes, sugar?"

"I'm ready for whatever comes next."

Beatrice's smile was soft and certain. "I know you are, baby. I've always known."

Chapter 6

Tracking the Invisible

MORNING SUNLIGHT FILTERED through the studio windows, casting golden stripes on Abbeline's cluttered worktable. Maps, printed emails, handwritten notes, and photographs formed an intricate mosaic—pieces of a puzzle they were only beginning to assemble. In the center lay a leather-bound notebook, its pages filled with Abbeline's careful documentation of every clue, every memory, every breadcrumb that might lead to Edward Stuart.

"Alright," Chance said, arranging color-coded pushpins beside a map of the Pacific Northwest, "let's look at what we know for certain."

Abbeline nodded, eyes flicking to the notebook she'd filled over the past few days. That morning, she had listened to one of her father's earliest recordings—his voice deep, steady, carrying a faint Virginia lilt. It had been both familiar and heartbreakingly foreign. She had to stop more than once, overwhelmed by the realization: this man she barely remembered had never stopped speaking to her.

"We know he went to Seattle first," she said, pointing to the blue pin on the map. "The earliest letters to Beatrice were postmarked there. And he mentions Mount Rainier in the first recording."

Chance pressed the pin in. "Then Portland in 2006, from the return address on your tenth birthday letter."

"Right." Abbeline added a green pin. "And in a 2011 recording, he talks about a 'small town outside Boise.' But no name."

Roderick entered from the house carrying mugs of coffee. Since joining their search, his early mornings were spent digging through veteran databases and making quiet inquiries. He brought a steadying calm to the room.

"I might have something new," he said, setting the mugs on a clear corner of the table. "A colleague in veteran services mentioned an Edward S. working with a wilderness therapy program for combat veterans in Montana. Around 2016. Age, background—both line up. But no current address. He left a few years ago."

Abbeline placed another pin, yellow, on the map. The constellation was growing—each point a story of movement, silence, a man slipping between places and time.

She stared at the pin. He kept moving. Still running, even now?

"What about security firms in those areas?" Chance asked, scrolling through a shared document on his tablet. "He might have stayed in the field."

"Beatrice has contacts digging, but so far nothing solid," Roderick replied. "If he's working, he's off grid."

Abbeline's gaze fell to a photograph—her father at his wedding, eyes shining with a joy he couldn't have known was fleeting. She tried to age him in her mind: softer jaw, graying temples, something quieter behind the eyes.

Would I even recognize him now? Would he recognize me?

The studio had changed around them. Once a chaos of old paint and rage, it now bore the structure of intention. One wall held their timeline: maps, photos, pinned notes. What once was chaos now held purpose. Her grief had become a composition.

"What about Ranger networks?" Chance asked. "They stay in touch, don't they?"

"We'd risk triggering alerts through Randolph's channels," Roderick warned. "He still has eyes in those spaces."

Abbeline's head snapped up. "I thought he backed off. He didn't contest the name change."

Chance and Roderick exchanged a look—quiet, practiced.

"What?" she asked. "What aren't you telling me?"

Roderick sighed. "He's been asking around. Through intermediaries. Nothing overt, just... keeping tabs."

Her chest tightened. *Still watching. Still reaching.*

"That's control."

Roderick didn't flinch. "It's monitoring. There's a difference. And... it may not be what you think."

"What does that mean?"

Chance leaned in, voice low. "Maybe he's worried. In his own... warped way."

Abbeline's fingers brushed her mother's silver necklace. A few weeks ago, she would've shouted. Now, a cooler sort of grief settled in. Not forgiveness. Not peace. But something closer to understanding.

Let him watch. It changes nothing.

"Either way," she said, voice firm, "we keep looking. If Grandfather finds out, so be it. I'm not waiting anymore."

Chance nodded. "So we have Seattle, Portland, Boise area, and possibly Montana. He's drifting north to east."

"But it's a cold trail," Roderick added. "Everything we have is years old."

Abbeline picked up a cassette, its label written in careful handwriting: Abbeline – 16th Birthday. She hadn't listened to it yet. Hadn't felt ready. A part of her still wondered why he'd stuck with tapes—why not CDs, or something digital? Even in 2011, it felt like a relic. But maybe that was the point. He'd chosen something tactile, something that demanded time and attention. Like a ritual. Like memory.

"I need to go through the rest," she said quietly. "There could be names, places, hints he didn't mean to leave."

"Good idea," Chance said. "And I'll follow up on the VA lead."

"I'll call in on my way to court," Roderick said, checking his watch. "Back by five."

After he left, the silence was companionable. They worked across the table, sorting photographs, logging documents, chasing fragments. Occasionally, their hands brushed. A look passed between them—a wordless acknowledgment that something unspoken was taking root.

Then Chance said, almost to himself, "There's something we haven't considered."

She glanced up. "What's that?"

"Maybe he's looking for you, too."

The thought stopped her. She had been chasing ghosts, trying to stitch the past into something solid. But the idea that her father was reaching for her—that somewhere, Edward Stuart might be trying to find a way back—unsettled something long sealed.

"Why do you think that?" she whispered.

Chance gestured to the table. "A man doesn't send eighteen years of letters and tapes if he's done. These aren't memories. They're promises."

Abbeline reached for another tape—For Abbeline, When You Ask Why. The label was slightly faded, the edges crisp. Not worn, but waiting. Preserved, like something meant to last.

"I've been afraid," she said. "Afraid of what I'll hear. Of who he was. Of what it means for me."

Chance didn't push, just watched her with something quiet and steady in his eyes.

"And now?"

She looked at him. "Now, I need to know. All of it."

He started gathering his notes. "Then I'll give you space."

"No," she said quickly. "Stay. Please. I don't want to do this alone."

He paused, then gave a small nod. "As long as you need."

They crossed to the corner where Beatrice had placed an old cassette deck. The air smelled like paper, old plastic, and a trace of rain through the open window.

Abbeline's hands trembled slightly as she slid the tape into place. Her thumb hovered over the play button. Then, with a click, the machine whirred to life. The deck itself felt like a museum piece—plastic faded, buttons soft with age. It wheezed to life like something remembering how to work.

Her father's voice filled the room.

"My darling Abbeline. If you're listening to this, it means you know the truth. About me. About why I left. And you probably have questions—so many questions that no recording could possibly answer. But I'm going to try, sweetheart. I'm going to try to explain why a father would ever walk away from his child..."

Abbeline closed her eyes, her father's steady voice guiding her through the shadowed paths of her life. Beside her, Chance didn't move—just stayed, solid and quiet, a lifeline in the dark.

Outside, life went on—cars hummed by, birds called, neighbors shuffled through their morning routines. But inside the studio, time bent. The past breathed into the present. Loss reached toward possibility.

The search for Edward Stuart had truly begun.

***

Six weeks into the search

Abbeline's hand ached. For three hours, she'd been transcribing details from her father's recordings—locations, names, and landscapes that might hold clues to his whereabouts. The yellow legal pad beside her was filled with her careful handwriting, arrows linking names to places, question marks marking the unknown.

The cassette player sat silent now, Edward's voice stilled after hours of pouring his heart across time. She had listened to five recordings in succession, each one revealing another piece of the man who had given her life and then disappeared to protect it.

Chance returned from a coffee run, the familiar scent of lattes preceding him into the studio. He set one cup on the side table near Abbeline, careful not to disturb her notes.

"How's it going?" he asked, settling onto the wooden stool they'd salvaged during their studio renovation.

"It's..." She paused, searching for the right word. "Overwhelming. But good, I think."

"Find anything useful?"

She nodded, tapping her pen against a section of notes. "He worked for Vista Security in Portland for almost three years—the longest he stayed anywhere. A woman named Janet Barnes was his supervisor. He mentions hiking at Silver Falls State Park on weekends."

Chance made a note on his phone. "I'll add Janet Barnes to our contact list. What about the wilderness therapy program?"

"He mentions it in the 2016 recording. Says he was working with veterans outside of Missoula for about eighteen months." She flipped to another page. "He doesn't name colleagues, but he talks about the healing that comes from guiding others through trauma."

"That's something to follow up on," Chance said. "I can reach out to some veterans' organizations in Montana, see if anyone remembers him."

She rose from the paint-spattered couch they'd dragged into the studio, stretching muscles stiff from sitting too long. Outside, the afternoon had deepened toward evening, shadows lengthening across Beatrice's manicured lawn. She moved to the window, watching a cardinal flit between branches of the old oak tree.

"These recordings," she said quietly, "they're not what I expected."

Chance joined her at the window, his reflection beside hers in the glass. "In what way?"

"I thought they'd be... I don't know, explanations. Justifications. But they're not that at all." She turned to face him. "They're love letters, Chance. Eighteen years of a father loving his daughter from afar, telling me about his day, his hopes, his memories of my mother. Making sure I'd know who he was, even if we never met."

Something caught in her throat. She looked away quickly, blinking back sudden moisture. Chance's hand found hers, a gentle pressure that anchored rather than intruded.

"That fits everything we know about him," he said softly.

When she'd regained her composure, Abbeline returned to the couch where several yellowed envelopes lay beside the cassette player.

"I haven't opened his written letters yet. I've been saving them."

"Want me to give you some privacy?"

She considered this, then shook her head. "No. Stay. Please."

The first envelope was addressed in a strong, precise hand: For Abbeline, on her 8th birthday. To be opened when Beatrice thinks appropriate. The paper had aged to a soft cream color, the corners slightly worn from years of careful storage. With trembling fingers, Abbeline broke the seal.

Inside, a single sheet of stationery held her father's thoughts from twelve years in the past. His handwriting was methodical, each letter carefully formed as if each word carried its own weight.

My darling daughter,

Today you are eight years old. I wonder what you look like now. Do you still have your mother's dimples? Has your hair darkened or stayed that beautiful honey-blonde? Are you short for your age like your mother was, or taking after my side of the family?

I imagine you starting third grade, learning multiplication tables, perhaps playing an instrument or joining soccer. I wonder if you've discovered your passion yet, or if you're still sampling all the world has to offer, as children should.

Eight is a magical age. Old enough for real conversations but young enough to believe in possibilities. I hope you're having adventures, making messes, asking impossible questions that make the adults in your life think harder about their answers.

I've sent along a small wooden horse with this letter. I carved it myself from cedar wood found near a cabin where I'm staying. Your mother loved to ride—did you know that? She said it was the closest thing to flying without leaving the ground. I hope someday you'll understand that freedom she described.

Remember that you are loved, Abbeline. Not just by those who have the privilege of seeing you grow, but by a father who carries you in his heart every single day.

With endless love,

Your Dad

Abbeline ran her fingers over the words, feeling the slight indentations where his pen had pressed against paper. In the margins, he'd sketched a small horse in mid-gallop, its mane flowing behind it. The wooden horse itself sat on her dresser in Beatrice's house—a treasure she'd found in the attic trunk, its cedar scent still faintly detectable after all these years.

"He carved this," she whispered, more to herself than to Chance. "With his own hands."

She opened the next letter, dated for her twelfth birthday. This one described a sunset over the Columbia River, how it reminded him of the way light used to catch in her mother's hair. He'd included a pressed wildflower—a paintbrush lily—saying its color matched Abbie's favorite lipstick.

Letter after letter revealed Edward Stuart not just as a father, but as an observer, an appreciator of beauty—a man who processed his grief and love through the natural world around him. He wrote of mountain hikes where he'd imagined holding her hand at steep sections, of seeing father-daughter pairs at local diners and how his heart would simultaneously warm and break, of how autumn always reminded him of Abbie's favorite season—and of the quiet agony of the 72 hours he was given to disappear from his daughter's life.

"He wasn't just existing all these years," Abbeline said, carefully refolding the most recent letter—from her eighteenth birthday. "He was deliberately creating a record. Making sure I'd have this piece of him, even if we never met."

"A legacy," Chance agreed, his voice soft in the dimming light. "Something no one could take away."

Abbeline glanced at the timeline pinned across the far wall—threaded maps, photographs, sticky notes faded from sunlight. So many places. So many gaps. But tonight, she could let it rest, just for a little while.

Chance glanced at his watch. "It's getting late. We should probably take a break."

"You go ahead. I want to keep working a bit longer."

"You've been at this all day," he said gently. "Maybe we could both use a change of scenery, clear our heads."

She looked up, surprised by the suggestion. "What did you have in mind?"

"There's a small art exhibition opening tonight at the Westside Gallery. Nothing fancy, just some local artists. Might be good to step away from all this for a couple of hours." He gestured to the investigation board. "Sometimes taking a break is the best way to gain perspective."

Abbeline hesitated, guilt rising at the thought of stepping away—but it was thin, outmatched by the quiet fatigue in her chest. After six weeks of constant focus, even she had to admit they were hitting walls.

"Okay," she said finally. "But just for a little while."

Ninety minutes later, they stood in the small gallery, plastic cups of mediocre wine in hand, surrounded by the works of emerging Atlanta artists. The space hummed with quiet conversation, the crowd a mix of art students, young professionals, and a few curious passersby.

"What do you think?" Chance asked, nodding toward a large abstract canvas.

Abbeline tilted her head, studying the controlled chaos of color and form. "It's interesting. There's a rawness to it that feels honest—like the artist wasn't trying to impress anyone, just expressing something genuine."

Chance smiled. "That's exactly what caught my eye."

They moved through the gallery slowly, pausing before pieces that drew their attention. For the first time in weeks, Abbeline felt her mind shifting away from maps and timelines, allowing the visual feast to awaken parts of herself that had been dormant.

She paused before a collage of torn paper layered over faded ink. "It's like memory," she murmured. "You think you know the shape of it, and then it changes."

"I haven't been to a gallery opening since... well, since before the attic," she said aloud.

"Do you miss it? The art world?"

She considered this, surprised by her own answer. "Yes and no. I miss creating. I miss losing myself in a painting. But I don't miss the society openings, the networking, the performance of it all." She nodded toward the space around them—simple, unassuming. "This feels more real."

As they moved to the next room, Chance's hand lightly touched the small of her back, guiding her through a congested doorway. The casual contact sent a ripple of awareness through her, reminding her how comfortable they'd become with each other.

"What about you?" she asked, taking a sip of wine. "What did you do before getting pulled into my family drama?"

Chance laughed. "The usual finance major stuff. Classes, internship at my dad's firm, occasional parties with people I've known since prep school." He shrugged. "Nothing particularly exciting."

"And yet you dropped everything to help a virtual stranger search for her long-lost father." She studied his face. "Why?"

Something vulnerable flickered in his expression before he answered. "Maybe I needed a break from the usual, too." He held her gaze. "Or maybe I saw someone brave enough to look—and I wanted to be part of that."

The moment stretched between them, charged with possibilities neither was ready to explore. Abbeline looked away first, her attention caught by a series of small ink drawings.

"These are beautiful," she said, moving closer to examine the intricate linework.

As they continued through the exhibition, their conversation shifted to childhood memories, favorite books, dreams for the future—topics unrelated to the search but revealing in other ways. Abbeline shared stories of her early art lessons, while Chance spoke of summers spent with his Italian relatives in New York, learning that wealth didn't define capability.

When they finally left the gallery two hours later, Abbeline felt lighter somehow, as if stepping away had cleared mental cobwebs she hadn't known were there.

"Thank you for suggesting this," she said as they walked back to the car. "I needed it more than I realized."

"Sometimes the best way forward is to step sideways for a bit," Chance replied. "My grandmother always says that."

The drive back to Beatrice's was easy, filled with casual conversation and soft laughter. As they pulled into the driveway, Abbeline found herself reluctant for the evening to end.

"I had a good time tonight," she said, unbuckling her seatbelt.

"Me too." Chance turned toward her, his expression serious now. "For what it's worth, I think we're going to find him, Abbeline. Your father. The patterns are starting to emerge from all these fragments."

She nodded, hope and determination replacing the temporary lightness of the evening. "We're close. I can feel it."

As they walked back to the studio to retrieve her notes, Abbeline realized something had shifted during their night away from the search. A new clarity had formed—not just about finding Edward, but about what might come after.

Not just reunion. Not just answers.

Possibility.

***

Two months into the search

The candle atop the cupcake flickered, casting a soft glow across Abbeline's face. She was twenty-one years old today. She drew a deep breath and closed her eyes briefly before blowing out the solitary flame.

"Happy birthday, sugar," Beatrice said, squeezing her niece's shoulder as a small cheer went up around the kitchen table.

Unlike the elaborate birthday galas Randolph had orchestrated throughout her adolescence, this celebration was intimate—just Beatrice, Roderick, Chance, and Marco gathered around Beatrice's well-worn kitchen table. No champagne flutes, no string quartets, no society photographers chronicling the Hartwell heiress's every milestone. Just people who cared about her, sharing cake on mismatched plates.

"Thanks for this," Abbeline said, glancing around at the small group. "It's perfect."

"Wait till you taste my cousin's cupcakes," Chance said, grinning as he pushed the plate closer to her. "Family recipe. Worth the sugar hangover."

"He's not exaggerating," Marco added. "Our Nonna would smack me if I got it wrong."

Abbeline took a bite and closed her eyes in appreciation. "Oh my God."

"Told you," Chance said with satisfaction.

As they ate, conversation flowed naturally—updates on the search, stories from their respective weeks. Marco shared an amusing tale about his engineering professor, while Roderick and Beatrice exchanged looks that suggested they were holding back news of their own.

"Okay, what's going on with you two?" Abbeline asked, catching another significant glance between them.

Beatrice reached for Roderick's hand, a smile spreading across her face. "We were going to wait until later tonight, but...She held out her left hand, where a vintage sapphire ring now adorned her finger.

"You're engaged?" Abbeline gasped, launching out of her chair to hug her aunt. "When did this happen?"

"Last night," Roderick admitted, looking both proud and slightly embarrassed by the attention. "At the restaurant where we had our first real date, more than twenty years ago."

"Twenty years?" Marco whistled. "Man, you two know how to take things slow."

"We prefer 'thorough,'" Beatrice countered, though her smile betrayed her joy. "It was worth the wait."

"This calls for champagne," Chance announced, retrieving the bottle they'd chilled earlier. He poured for everyone, then raised his glass. "To new beginnings. And," he added, with a pointed look at Abbeline, "to finding the missing pieces."

She met his eyes over the rim of her glass, warmth spreading through her that had nothing to do with the champagne. These past two months of working together had created a connection she couldn't quite name—deeper than friendship, yet cautiously held in check while they focused on the search.

The celebration continued into the evening, a welcome respite from the intensity of their investigation. Around ten, Marco announced it was time for him to head back to campus.

"Some of us still have finals to pass," he said, giving Abbeline a brief hug. "Happy birthday. Let me know if you need more muscle for the search."

After Marco left, Roderick and Beatrice retreated to the living room with coffee, leaving Abbeline and Chance to clean up the kitchen.

"Your first birthday as Abbeline Stuart," Chance observed, stacking plates. "How does it feel?"

"Different. Good different." She wiped down the countertop, thinking. "I've never had a birthday this simple before. Grandfather always made such productions out of them."

"Too much?"

"Always." She smiled ruefully. "For my sixteenth, he flew in a Parisian designer to make a custom gown. The party cost more than some people's homes."

"And yet here you are, looking happier over cupcakes in Beatrice's kitchen."

"Because this is real," she said. "You all actually know me."

Even as she said it, a part of her drifted to the unopened message they'd been waiting on—the commander. The strongest lead. It hadn't come yet, but tonight, she pushed it aside.

They worked in companionable silence for a few minutes before Chance spoke again.

"Marco likes you, you know."

Something in his tone made her look up. "Does that bother you?"

"Should it?" He kept his focus on rinsing glasses, but his shoulders tensed slightly.

"No," she said softly. "It shouldn't."

The moment hung between them, charged with unspoken possibility. Then Beatrice called for coffee from the other room, and it passed.

"Thanks again," Abbeline said, drying her hands on a towel. "Tonight meant a lot."

"I'm glad I was part of it."

He paused. "I'll stop by tomorrow after the gym."

"Good. Roderick's contact is supposed to call."

"Right," he said. "The search continues."

But when morning came, so did crushing disappointment. The former commanding officer who might have had information about Edward's unit had passed away three years earlier. His records, which might have contained contact information for squad members, had been destroyed in an office fire.

"It's a dead end," Abbeline said, pacing the studio floor. "Two months of tracking him down, and it's a complete dead end."

The map on the wall stared back at her, its pins now just scattered points instead of a coherent trail. Emails to Vista Security had gone unanswered. The wilderness therapy program had changed management twice in recent years, with records from Edward's time there incomplete at best.

"We'll find another way," Chance insisted. "This isn't over, Abbeline."

"Isn't it?" Frustration sharpened her voice. "Every lead dries up, every connection goes nowhere. What if he doesn't want to be found? What if all this"—she gestured to their research wall—"is just me refusing to accept reality?"

"That's not true. You've heard his recordings. Read his letters. Those aren't the actions of a man who wants to stay lost forever."

"Then why is he so damn good at it?" She grabbed her jacket from the back of a chair. "I need some air."

Before Chance could respond, she was out the door, striding across Beatrice's back garden toward the small wooded area bordering the property. Her eyes burned, but she wouldn't cry. Crying felt like surrender—and despite her outburst, she wasn't ready to give up.

The path through the trees was barely visible, overgrown from disuse. Branches caught at her clothing as she pushed deeper into the woods, their resistance mirroring the emotional barriers she kept hitting in the search.

She didn't stop until she reached the small clearing with its ancient oak. As a child, she'd come here with Beatrice to picnic and read stories. Later, as a teenager, it had been her retreat when Randolph's expectations became too heavy to bear.

Abbeline sank onto a fallen log, burying her face in her hands. The commander had been their strongest lead in weeks. With his death, they were back to guesswork and hope.

She wasn't sure how long she sat there before sensing a presence. Looking up, she saw Chance standing at the edge of the clearing, hesitant to intrude.

"I followed your footprints," he explained. "Pretty easy with those fancy boots crushing everything in their path."

She laughed quietly. "Not exactly built for the woods."

"Mind if I join you?"

She patted the log beside her, and he crossed the clearing to sit down, leaving a respectful distance between them.

"I'm sorry about the commander," he said after a moment.

"Me too." She picked up a twig, breaking it methodically into smaller pieces. "I really thought this was it."

"I know." He watched her hands work. "But we still have other avenues. The recordings, the letters—there are more clues we haven't fully explored yet."

"What if it's not enough?" The question escaped before she could stop it, giving voice to the fear that had been growing with each failed lead.

Chance turned toward her fully. "Then we try something else. And if that doesn't work, we try again." His conviction was unwavering. He paused, then added gently, "I think we need a day off."

"A day off?" She looked at him skeptically. "While my father is still out there somewhere?"

"One day, Abbeline. To clear our heads, to step back and see what we might be missing because we're too close to it." He held her gaze. "Meet me for breakfast tomorrow. Nine o'clock.

No maps, no recordings, no talk about the search. Just breakfast."

She started to protest, but found herself reconsidering. The past two months had devoured her—five hours of sleep at best, meals taken only when Beatrice or Chance insisted, her mind consumed by the search.

"Just breakfast?" she asked.

"Just breakfast," he confirmed. "And maybe a walk afterward if you feel like it."

Abbeline looked around the clearing—at the sunlight filtering through leaves, at the undemanding simplicity of nature continuing its cycles regardless of human quests or disappointments.

"Okay," she agreed finally. "One day off."

Chance smiled, relief evident in his expression. "I'll pick you up at nine."

As they walked back toward the house, Abbeline felt something shifting inside her—not resignation, but a different kind of resolve. Perhaps Chance was right. Perhaps taking a step back was exactly what they needed to move forward.

Tomorrow wouldn't be about maps or leads. It would be about breath, stillness—the kind of discovery that only comes when you finally stop chasing.

***

Three months into the search

The studio pulsed with quiet energy as dusk settled against the windows. Abbeline stood before the investigation board, tracking the lines of red string that now spiderwebbed across the wall. What had begun as a careful system of logic had evolved into something more abstract—chaotic, even beautiful, like one of her own canvases in progress.

The door opened, bringing in a gust of cool air and the scent of pad thai.

"Food has arrived," Chance announced, balancing a takeout bag and his messenger bag. Still in a button-down and slacks from his late finance class, his sleeves were rolled to the elbow.

"You're a lifesaver," Abbeline said, only now realizing how hungry she was. The only thing she'd eaten all day was the apple Beatrice had handed her that morning.

"Professor Wilson still thinks I'm destined for hedge funds," Chance said as he unpacked containers, steam rising in fragrant plumes. "Didn't have the heart to tell him I might have other plans."

"Like what?" she asked, grabbing two bottles of water from the mini-fridge.

He passed her a set of chopsticks, hesitating just a second. "Impact investing, maybe. Or sustainable development. Something more meaningful." He gave a self-conscious shrug. "Sounds kind of idealistic when I say it out loud."

"It doesn't," she said, settling beside him. "It sounds like someone trying to matter."

They ate in comfortable silence. Over the months, the studio had changed shape—not just a sanctuary for art, but a command center for the search. Shelves now held files beside paint jars, and a new seating area bore the imprint of late-night strategy sessions and quiet exhaustion.

"I've been thinking," Chance said, setting aside his container, "we've been digging through Edward's old security contacts and job records, but... nothing's moving."

"Because he probably doesn't exist in those systems anymore," Abbeline said. The sting of recent dead ends hadn't faded.

"Exactly. So maybe we shift focus, try a different angle." He opened his laptop and turned it toward her. "What if we look for his woodworking?"

She froze, chopsticks halfway to her mouth. "You mean... the carvings?"

"He sent them to you all the time, right? The horse, the turtle... they weren't random. That kind of craftsmanship—it's not just a hobby. And if he's off grid, maybe he's found a quiet way to support himself—like selling at craft fairs."

He clicked open a list of artisan shows across the Pacific Northwest.

"These are juried fairs—woodworkers, metal artists, that kind of thing. Some have archived exhibitor lists going back years."

Abbeline felt something spark. The wooden horse from her childhood was still on her dresser, its surface worn but deeply familiar. Each carved curve had carried more than skill—it had carried love.

"That's actually brilliant," she said, sliding her stool closer. "We've been tracking like detectives. Maybe we should've been tracking like artists."

"I like the sound of that," he said, smiling modestly. "Even if I still don't know the difference between birch and basswood."

She smiled and took another bite.

They spent the next hour compiling lists of shows near Edward's last known locations. Chance built a spreadsheet, while Abbeline drafted emails to organizers.

The door opened again, and Marco stepped in, backpack over one shoulder.

"Knew I'd find you two still at it," he said. "Got something for you."

Abbeline glanced up. "More takeout?"

"Better." He dropped his bag and reached for the pad thai leftovers. "My roommate's dad runs a veterans' network through his church. I mentioned the search—kept it vague, like you said. He gave me a list of organizations that help vets who want to stay off-grid."

Abbeline straightened. "Off grid how?"

"Guys dealing with PTSD, legal stuff, or just wanting peace. They help with housing, work, even medical care—but no paper trails. Totally quiet."

Chance leaned in. "You think Edward might've found one?"

"Wouldn't be surprised," Marco said. "Especially after what you told me about Kandahar."

He pulled a folded paper from his pocket and handed it over. "Most of these don't even have websites, but they're real. Grassroots stuff."

Abbeline scanned the names, heart thudding. "How do we contact them without triggering alarms?"

"Carefully," Marco said. "Be honest about who you are, but don't mention Randolph or family money. They're suspicious of institutions."

Chance nodded. "This is big. These groups could've helped him disappear by design."

Abbeline looked up from the list. "This changes everything." She smiled at Marco. "Thanks."

He shrugged.

As they ate, Marco launched into a story about a failed engineering lab experiment. The studio warmed with laughter. For a few moments, the gravity of the search lifted, replaced by the familiar comfort of camaraderie.

When Marco eventually left, Chance stayed behind to help reorganize the board.

"Your cousin's full of surprises," Abbeline said, pinning up a note about the veterans' groups.

"He's a walking resource. My family believes in knowing everyone—plumbers, bakers, priests. Just in case."

"I like that he just shows up. No pretense. Just shows up."

"That's Marco."

He leaned back, watching her quietly. "You look wiped. We can call it."

She shook her head. "Let me finish this. I want the new timeline in place."

He moved beside her, helping untangle threads and re-pin new connections. Their movements were practiced now, a rhythm built from months of shared purpose.

"I've been thinking about what Marco said," she said after a pause. "About being honest."

Chance glanced over. "What about it?"

"We've been tiptoeing around the Hartwell name, afraid we'll set off alarms... but what if that's been limiting us? What if I need to be fully transparent—Abbeline Stuart, yes, but also formerly Hartwell. Daughter of Abbie, granddaughter of Randolph."

Chance hesitated. "It's a risk. If Randolph finds out..."

"Let him," she said, voice low but steady. "I'm twenty-one. I've changed my name. I've left his house. What else is he going to take from me?"

He studied her for a moment, reading the quiet fire behind her eyes.

"If we do this," he said, "we do it on your terms. Not as Randolph's granddaughter looking for scandal, but as a daughter looking for peace."

She nodded. "No more hiding."

Later, after Chance had gone, Abbeline crossed the studio to her easel. The canvas had evolved over weeks—layer by layer, shaped by emotion, memory, and uncertainty. She dipped her brush into a rich blue and made a single, decisive sweep across the surface, linking separate shapes into something new.

As she painted, she reflected on the shift they'd made—not just in tactics, but in truth. Edward wasn't just a former soldier. He was an artist, a father. A man who had disappeared not out of carelessness, but for survival.

The image on the canvas wasn't finished. But something in it had changed—lines that once drifted apart now found cohesion. Like her. Like this search.

Tomorrow would bring more calls, more questions, more risk. But tonight, in the quiet company of her paints and memories, Abbeline found a kind of clarity.

A sense that she was not only searching for her father.

She was beginning to find herself.

***

Six months into the search

"I've triple-checked the timing," Chance said, zipping his weekend bag closed. "My flight lands at LaGuardia at 6:38, and my uncle is picking me up. I'll call once I'm settled at my grandmother's."

Abbeline nodded, leaning in the doorway of her studio. The morning light caught the strands of gold now threaded through her curls, subtle markers of time passed. "Two weeks feels longer than it should."

"It's her hundredth birthday," he reminded her, though his fingers lingered a moment too long on the zipper. "If I skip, my Italian relatives will never forgive me."

"And we can't have that." She smiled, but it flickered. "Give her my best."

"I will." He hesitated. "You'll keep working the leads?"

"Yes. Roderick's helping draft letters to the veteran groups Marco found. And I've got new craft shows to investigate." She gestured behind her at the growing constellation of red pins on the studio wall.

Their goodbye was casual—just a hug and a promise to check in—but as Chance's car disappeared down the driveway, a sudden stillness crept into the studio, leaving hollow the space he'd helped fill.

She drifted back inside, taking in what their shared work had built: maps, timelines, cabinets full of correspondence, each detail painstakingly compiled. She eased into Chance's usual chair, her fingers grazing a stack of craft fair programs. They'd shifted their focus months ago to Edward's artistry, and this stack represented hours of combing through obscure fair websites and vendor rosters.

Her phone buzzed. Beatrice.

"Morning, Aunt Bea."

"Did Chance get off okay?" Beatrice asked, clearly juggling a second task.

"Just now. What about you?"

"Henderson deposition prep. Roderick's bringing lunch. Join us?"

"Thanks, but I've got a lot to work through." Something in her tone must have caught Beatrice's attention.

"You sound a little off. Everything okay?"

Abbeline hesitated. "It's strange. I didn't expect to miss him this fast."

Beatrice chuckled warmly. "He's been your shadow for half a year. It makes sense."

"It's more than that." The words came without filter.

"I know," Beatrice said gently. "And I think he does too."

Abbeline didn't answer. Her eyes had landed on a photograph in the fair program. A display of carved wooden animals, each rendered in smooth, flowing lines that captured more than anatomy—they conveyed spirit. Her breath caught. She knew this style.

"Aunt Bea, I need to go. I think I've found something."

She ended the call, heart pounding, and studied the booth's listing: E.S. Woodcraft. The same fluid design as the horse Edward had sent her as a child. Her hands trembled as she grabbed her laptop and searched for more.

The fair had taken place in Oregon, two years ago. No contact info—just a booth number.

She snapped a photo and texted Chance:

Found this. E.S. Woodcraft. What do you think?

His reply came almost instantly:

Holy crap. That's him. Has to be. Same style as the horse.

Does the program list contact info?

No, just a booth number. I'll call the organizers when they open.

As she waited, she flipped through more programs and found two more listings—Washington, Portland. A pattern. Real. Close.

At 10 a.m. Pacific, she called the Oregon fair office.

"I'm trying to reach a former exhibitor—E.S. Woodcraft, from 2022."

"I'm sorry, we don't share contact info," the administrator said.

"I understand," Abbeline said, steadying her voice. "But... I think he's my father. We've been separated for a long time. I just want to send him a message—if you'd be willing to forward it?"

A pause. Then, "Let me check with my manager. Can I call you back?"

Abbeline agreed, passed along her number, and texted Chance an update. His reply buzzed in while she reheated soup on the stove:

Smart. Even if the email's outdated, it's a real trail. Fingers crossed.

The call came two hours later. The manager had agreed to forward a message to the email on file—though they warned it might be out of date.

Abbeline spent the next hour crafting the message: her name, age, the discovery of his letters and recordings, her legal name change to Stuart. She offered her phone number, email, Beatrice's address. Just enough for him to know she was real.

That evening, she video called Chance. He looked travel-worn but animated.

"This is it, Abbeline. Even if that email's dead, he's out there, showing his work. That's proof."

"I've started compiling a list of other fairs. I won't stop now."

His smile was warm. "Wish I was there."

"Me too. It's quiet without you."

His eyes softened. "Two weeks will fly by. And I'm just a call away."

After they ended the call, she turned to her easel. Her brush moved with quiet urgency, color and form pouring from the emotional churn beneath the surface. She painted deep into the night.

No reply came the next morning. She didn't expect one. Still, she expanded their reach, contacting other fairs, following Marco's veterans' network leads. The days were filled with effort, the hope sparked by E.S. Woodcraft lighting every step.

Her nightly calls with Chance became an anchor. She learned about his grandmother's stories, his childhood rituals, the pressure and pride that came with his family. Through him, she saw another kind of legacy—messy, loving, and deeply alive.

During their sixth call, he said, "My grandmother asked about you. Apparently, I talk about you a lot."

"What did you tell her?"

"That you're the most determined person I've ever met." He paused. "And that I miss you more than I expected."

The air between them quieted. Neither filled the space.

Then, the breakthrough came. Ten days into Chance's absence, a call from a wilderness therapy program administrator.

"I don't have current info," she said, "but Edward listed a Marcus Chen as his emergency contact. San Francisco address."

Abbeline froze, wrote it down carefully, her hands unsteady.

She called Chance immediately. "We have a name. Marcus Chen. Afghanistan. Emergency contact."

"That's huge. Have you reached out?"

"Not yet. We need a plan. He's protective. If he knows about Kandahar, he might not trust a Hartwell connection."

"Then we go in person. Show him the letters. Let him see who you really are."

"Exactly. But you stay. Your grandmother's birthday is in three days. I'll start prepping. We'll hit the ground running when you're back."

"Are you sure?"

"I'm sure. This whole search has been about family. You taught me that."

That night, Abbeline researched Chen: head of a respected security firm, veteran advocate, conference speaker. Clearly guarded. Clearly loyal.

She gathered information meticulously, preparing for their approach. Each night, she updated Chance, and each call wandered further into personal ground—her painting, his stories, the spaces between them narrowing despite the miles.

On the eve of his return, Chance said, "I've been thinking."

"About what?"

"About what happens after we find your father. About us."

The words hovered, delicate but undeniable.

"We'll talk when you get back," she said.

"We will."

His smile was soft, and certain.

Afterward, Abbeline lingered at her desk, eyes on the investigation board—a web of threads now leading somewhere real. Six months ago, she had only wanted to find her father. But the journey had offered her more: connection, strength, a future reshaped by every step.

Marcus Chen was their best lead yet. But even before she reached him, she understood something quietly, fully.

The search hadn't just been about finding someone lost.

It had helped her discover who she was becoming.

Chapter 7

The Turning Point

Seven months into the search

A morning breeze stirred the scent of Beatrice's heirloom roses through the open studio windows as Abbeline pinned a printed photo of Lieutenant Marcus Chen to their investigation board. His military portrait showed a man with sharp eyes and a composed expression that revealed little.

"All this time," she murmured, stepping back to survey the board. "This is our strongest lead yet."

Chance stood beside her, his shoulder almost brushing hers. Since his return from New York three weeks ago, something between them had shifted. The conversation he'd promised about "us" lingered, postponed by this new lead but present in each glance and every subtle brush of contact.

"Chen's background is impressive." He scanned the notes. "Two tours in Afghanistan, Bronze Star recipient, commanded your father's unit during the Kandahar incident. Now runs a private security firm for major tech companies."

Abbeline nodded, tapping her pen—a habit from months of record digging. "If anyone knows where my father is, it's him."

The board—once chaotic—now formed a focused map. Red string linked Chen to Edward through the wilderness therapy program and military service. Their pattern of movement—Seattle to Portland to Idaho to Montana—now arched back toward the coast.

Roderick arrived with a leather portfolio and a tray of coffee. His morning visits had become routine, grounding their search in quiet ritual. "I pulled everything I could find on Chen's company," he said, passing out mugs. "He's carved out a solid niche in corporate security."

Chance flipped through the folder and stilled at a page. "Chen's firm covers several tech companies in Silicon Valley," he said slowly. "One of them is TechAdvance Industries."

Abbeline looked up. "Is that significant?"

"TechAdvance is owned by Alex Patel," Chance said, his voice sharpening. "My dad's college roommate. I've known him all my life—he's like an uncle. If Chen works with TechAdvance, I might have a way in."

"You think you can get him to talk without tipping him off?" Roderick asked.

"I can get a meeting. Whether he opens up depends on how carefully we approach it."

Abbeline's thoughts spun. After months of dead ends, here was someone who might know her father's whereabouts.

Someone with history and loyalty—but also someone who might not want to be found.

"When can we go to San Francisco?" she asked.

"We?" Beatrice asked, entering with a plate of muffins and a raised eyebrow.

"I'm not staying behind," Abbeline said firmly. "This is my father."

Beatrice set the plate down and looked between them. "Then let's plan this right. If Chen's as disciplined as his record suggests, he'll be wary. We have one chance to make the right impression."

"She's right," Roderick added. "He'll respond better in person. Bring the letters, the recordings—anything that proves your identity."

Chance reached for his phone. "I'll call Alex this morning—frame it as a favor, nothing more."

They spent the morning assembling a portfolio: carefully selected letters, photographs, Abbeline's name change documents, and the wooden horse carving—a symbol of Edward's artistry and love.

Beatrice examined each item with a lawyer's precision. "If Chen's protective, sentiment won't sway him unless it feels real. You need to make him believe Edward would want you to find him."

When Chance returned from his call, his cautious optimism spoke volumes.

"Tuesday at 2 PM. Alex can set the meeting, but Chen's curious—not hostile."

Abbeline felt a mix of nerves and anticipation. "That's less than a week."

"Alex says to manage expectations. Chen is loyal and private."

"It's enough," she said, opening her laptop. "We'll be ready."

As they finalized the travel plans, Beatrice pulled Abbeline aside.

"You're doing well," she said quietly. "But be careful. People like Chen—they guard more than secrets. They guard pain."

"I know," Abbeline said. "But I'm not going to flinch from it."

That evening, the setting sun bathed the studio in warm light. Alone, Abbeline studied the board. Her fingers brushed the red thread connecting Chen to her father, then the carved horse beside his photo.

Chance's footsteps echoed as he returned from dinner with Marco. He paused in the doorway, then stepped beside her.

"Penny for your thoughts?"

"I've been thinking about what to say to Chen," she said. "What if he knows where my father is but won't tell us?"

Chance didn't hesitate. "Then we're no worse off than now—just one piece of truth closer."

His presence steadied her.

"Marco sends his best," he added, softening. "Still hates his engineering professor. But he's invested—said he's all in for 'Operation Mystery Dad.'"

Abbeline smiled. "I'm glad he's coming. Three perspectives might help."

"He also wants to see the Golden Gate Bridge."

They laughed, tension easing.

"We should rest," she said. "Big week ahead."

Chance nodded but didn't move. In the golden hush of twilight, with seven months behind them and a meeting ahead, something shifted.

"Chance," she said quietly.

"I know," he replied, equally quiet. "Me too."

It was enough. Soon, they would fly west. Tonight, they stood in quiet acknowledgment of all they'd risked and all they still might gain.

Chen's photo watched them in silence: the first direct link to Edward Stuart. The path was finally narrowing.

***

Eight months into the search

The June heat pressed down on the San Francisco sidewalk as Abbeline and Chance exited the gleaming glass headquarters of Chen Security Consulting. The California sunshine felt too bright, too cheerful—mismatched with the cold knot forming in Abbeline's chest. She slipped on her sunglasses, grateful for the protection they offered from both the sunlight and Chance's searching glance. Marco had to back out last minute—an unexpected family emergency had called him back to New York.

"I really thought he would help us," she said at last, breaking the silence that had followed them since leaving Marcus Chen's office. "He served with my father. They reconnected after Kandahar. I thought that would mean something."

Chance led her across the street to a small park, finding a shaded bench beneath a blooming cherry tree. Pale petals drifted to the ground like soft confetti, untouched by the urgency tightening in her chest.

"He was being careful, not dismissive," Chance said, sitting beside her. "There's a difference."

"'I can neither confirm nor deny any knowledge of Edward Stuart's current whereabouts,'" Abbeline quoted bitterly. "That's corporate speak for 'go away.'"

"That's military speak for 'I'm protecting someone who trusted me,'" he replied gently. "Your father spent two decades staying hidden, probably for a reason. Chen wasn't stonewalling—he was shielding."

She pulled off her sunglasses and rubbed the bridge of her nose. Three days in San Francisco, and all they had to show for it were hotel receipts and not-quite-answers.

"But he kept watching me," she said. "Like he saw something... like he knew."

"I saw it too." Chance leaned forward, resting his elbows on his knees. "He was weighing you—deciding if you were the kind of person he could trust with something bigger than yourself."

A breeze stirred the petals at their feet. Abbeline watched a woman in designer heels step neatly over the fallen blossoms, her phone conversation unbroken. Everyone here moved forward, with somewhere to go. Someone waiting for them.

"I keep wondering if this is a sign," she murmured. "That maybe I should stop pushing. If my father wanted to be found, wouldn't he have made it clearer? Maybe he built a new life that doesn't have room for me."

"Do you really believe that?" Chance asked. "After everything we've read? After listening to his voice in those recordings?"

"I don't know what to believe anymore," she admitted, her voice breaking at the edges.

Chance's phone chimed. He checked it, and his eyebrows lifted.

"What is it?"

"Alex. He wants to meet for coffee. Says he has something that might help with our project."

Hope flickered—timid, wary. "Or he's just being polite. Connections only get us so far."

"Maybe," Chance replied, already responding. "But Alex doesn't do small talk. If he says it matters, I trust him."

Twenty minutes later, they sat at a corner table in a café near Union Square. The place buzzed with midafternoon chatter. Alex Patel arrived with an easy stride, placing a small paper bag on the table before greeting them.

"Good to see you again, Chance," he said warmly, then turned to Abbeline. "Ms. Stuart, a pleasure to meet you properly. Yesterday's consultation didn't leave much time for introductions."

"Thank you for meeting us," she said, eyeing the paper bag. "Chance said you might have information?"

Alex glanced around and leaned in slightly. "Marcus called me after your meeting. Said your visit left an impression."

"An impression," Abbeline repeated. "He didn't act impressed."

"He's a soldier. And a protector—which means he doesn't reveal what he knows until he's sure it's safe." Alex sat, pushing the bag toward her. "He asked me to give you this. Said you'd know what it meant."

Inside, nestled in brown paper, was a small, carved wooden fox. Abbeline's breath caught. The lines, the details—everything about it echoed the wooden horse from her eighth birthday.

A folded note lay beneath it:

The craftsman frequents Pike Place Market on Saturday mornings. Booth 37. He appreciates honesty and recognizes his own work.

She held the fox in her palm, her fingers trembling. The craftsmanship was unmistakable—too familiar to doubt. Her father had carved this. Her vision blurred as the room seemed to quiet around her.

"This is his," she whispered. "My father made this."

"So it would seem," Alex said, watching her closely. "Marcus wanted you to have it."

"Pike Place," Chance read, taking the note from Abbeline's hand. "That's Seattle."

"The first place he went after Atlanta," Abbeline added softly. "A return to the beginning."

Alex rose. "I've got meetings all afternoon. But Ms. Stuart"—his voice softened, his practiced tech-world confidence giving way to something quieter—"I hope you find what you're looking for."

Four hours later, they were thirty thousand feet above the Pacific Northwest. Abbeline held the carved fox like a compass, tracing its curves as the sky darkened outside the plane window.

"What if he's not there?" she asked suddenly. "What if this is another breadcrumb that leads nowhere?"

"Then we keep going," Chance said, without hesitation.

"Just like that? After all this?"

"Just like that," he repeated. "Abbeline, you've spent eight months rebuilding who you are. You've faced Randolph. You've claimed your truth. Do you really think a missed connection is going to undo that?"

She turned toward him. "It's not just the fear of another dead end. It's..." Her voice faltered. "What if he doesn't want to be found? What if I ruin something he's finally managed to rebuild?"

"Then at least you'll know," Chance said quietly. "Better than living the rest of your life wondering."

Their Seattle hotel overlooked the waterfront. From the window, Pike Place Market was a scatter of lights and awnings just a few blocks away.

Chance spread a map across the desk. "Booth 37. Crafts section. Opens at nine. I think I should go ahead first—see if he's there."

"No." Abbeline's voice was firm. "I need to see him with my own eyes. Even if I don't speak right away."

Chance studied her, then nodded. "Okay. Together."

She stood at the window, watching the ferries slip across Puget Sound.

"I keep practicing what I'll say," she whispered. "But nothing feels right. Twenty-one years is a long time."

"Maybe start with something simple," Chance said, joining her. "Hello. I've been looking for you."

She nodded, her voice barely audible. "I'm scared."

"I know." He took her hand gently. "But you're brave too. And tomorrow, one way or another, you'll have the truth."

Later, in the dark, Abbeline lay in bed, unable to sleep. The fox rested on the nightstand beside her, its silhouette barely visible in the city glow.

"Chance?" she called softly.

"Mmm?"

"Thank you. For not giving up."

He shifted on the pullout couch. "You're not alone in this, Abbeline. Not anymore."

She held the fox close as sleep finally came, filled with restless dreams—market stalls, wooden animals, and a face she might finally see.

***

Morning light filtered through Seattle's cloud-softened sky, casting a silvery hue over Pike Place Market. By eight-thirty, the historic marketplace was already humming—vendors arranging produce, fishmongers prepping for the day's spectacle, and early tourists meandering with steaming coffee in hand.

Abbeline and Chance moved through the growing crowd, her heart pounding so hard it echoed off the brick walls. They'd arrived early and staked out a quiet alcove with a clear view of Booth 37, still hidden beneath a blue tarp.

"Over there," Chance said, nodding toward their vantage point. "We can wait here."

Abbeline only nodded, too keyed up for words. She'd agonized over what to wear—an absurd concern, maybe, but deeply human. In the end, she chose a simple charcoal top that matched her gray eyes, fitted jeans, and her mother's silver necklace that rested just above her collarbone. She needed to be seen as herself—Abbeline Stuart. Not just a name on a birth certificate. Not a Hartwell legacy. The daughter Edward had loved from afar.

"Nine o'clock," Chance murmured as the market bells chimed. "Booth should open any minute."

Moments later, a tall figure appeared, carrying a folding stool and a wooden crate. From their spot, she couldn't make out his face—just the broad-shouldered silhouette of a man in his fifties, setting out wooden carvings with deliberate care.

"Is it him?" Chance asked quietly.

Abbeline squinted, tension blooming in her chest. "I can't tell," she whispered. "Maybe it is."

"Watch how he scans the crowd," Chance added. "That's muscle memory. Military."

She nodded, breath shallow. Her hands curled at her sides. *What if it's him? What if it's not? What if I ruin everything?*

Then Chance's hand found hers, steady and warm. "Now," he said softly, "you go talk to him. I'll be nearby, but this moment belongs to you."

Panic flickered.

What if he doesn't want to see me? What if... he doesn't remember?

"No more what-ifs," Chance said, reading her perfectly. "You're ready."

His certainty anchored her.

She stepped from the alcove and into the flow of the market, the crowd dissolving into background noise. Her pulse thundered in her ears. Booth 37 came into sharp focus—a man arranging foxes, owls, horses, and birds with the precision of someone who still needed order in a world that had offered little of it.

Abbeline stopped a few feet from the booth, her throat suddenly dry. Twenty-one years of separation, of wondering, of imagining what this moment might be—and now that it had arrived, the words deserted her.

He turned as if sensing her. For a heartbeat—an eternity—they stared at each other.

His face was weathered by time, his hair more gray than not, but the eyes were unmistakable. Her eyes. Alert. Deep. Searching. Her breath caught.

Recognition flickered in them, widening into shock—then something deeper, older. His hands, midway through arranging a small wooden owl, froze in place.

"Abbeline?" he said. His voice was rough, uncertain, barely audible above the hum of the market.

The sound of her name, in his voice, cracked something wide open inside her.

Tears surged. Her throat clenched. But she found the words.

"I got your messages," she said, voice trembling. "All of them."

His expression shifted—shock to awe, disbelief to absolute recognition. His hand hovered above the owl, as though afraid even a movement might shatter the moment. He looked like a man who'd been holding his breath for twenty-one years and had only now remembered how to exhale.

"How did you—" He stopped, glancing around the market with sudden wariness. "Is he—"

"No. Grandfather doesn't know," she said quickly. "This is my search. My choice."

Emotion fractured the last of his composure. "You look just like your mother," he whispered.

A sob escaped her—raw and irrepressible. Two decades of absence collapsed into this single moment of recognition, anchoring her to the truth: she belonged here, in front of the man who had loved her enough to let her go.

She rounded the booth slowly. He stepped from behind it with equal caution, tentative—as if she might vanish if he moved too fast.

"I've been looking for you," she said, her voice steadier now. "We followed your trail—Seattle, Portland, Montana. Marcus Chen gave us the last piece."

"Marcus," Edward echoed, comprehension dawning. "He asked questions a few days ago—subtle ones. I never imagined he was... preparing me."

They stood two feet apart, decades distant. Neither of them knew how to bridge the final space between them.

"Can I..." His voice faltered, uncertainty in every line of his face. "Would it be all right if I hugged you?"

Her only answer was to step into his arms.

He held her as if she were something sacred—gently, reverently—but with the quiet strength of a man who had imagined this moment in countless shapes and had never dared to believe in any of them.

"I'm sorry," he whispered. "For everything. For missing everything."

"You were there," she said fiercely. "Your letters, your voice—they were with me. Aunt Bea kept them safe."

Edward pulled her closer for a heartbeat, then slowly let go, wiping his eyes. He seemed unable to stop looking at her—studying every feature with quiet, disbelieving awe.

"Your eyes," he said again, barely audible.

"They're yours," she replied. "I always wondered."

The market churned around them, but inside the moment, time stilled.

"We shouldn't stay out here," Edward said at last. "There's a café just around the corner. It's quieter."

He glanced past her and spotted Chance, standing respectfully nearby.

"Your friend should come too."

"That's Chance," she said. "I wouldn't have found you without him."

Edward nodded. "Then I owe him more than I can say."

Ten minutes later, in the warm cocoon of the café, they sat in a quiet corner. Chance chose the counter, giving them space but remaining nearby.

"I don't even know where to begin," Edward said. "There's so much I need to explain."

Abbeline met his eyes. "I understand why you left. Aunt Bea told me everything—Grandfather's threats, the custody ultimatum. You didn't abandon me. You protected me."

Relief broke across his face like light through storm clouds.

"I've questioned that decision every day for twenty-one years," he admitted. "Wondered if there could've been another way."

"There wasn't," she said simply. "Not then. But there is now. I've legally changed my name to Stuart. I left the mansion. I'm rebuilding my life—starting with you."

His hand trembled as he took hers.

"You claimed my name," he said, voice thick. "Even when you didn't know if I'd still be here."

"It's mine too," she replied. "It always was."

His eyes welled, one drop escaping before he could stop it. He didn't brush it away.

They spoke for over an hour. Abbeline shared her discovery in Beatrice's attic, the unraveling of the Hartwell illusion, the cross-country search. Edward told her about his years on the move, the therapy program, the woodworking that became his lifeline.

"The wilderness program was faith-based," he said. "Founded by a chaplain who served in combat. He taught me that healing doesn't mean erasing pain—it means learning to live with it and still having hope."

Abbeline nodded slowly. "Did it help? Faith, I mean?"

Edward's eyes met hers. "I don't always get it right. But it's why I kept sending messages. Kept believing you might find me."

"You did everything you could," she said. "And I found you."

He glanced toward the counter. "And Chance—where does he fit into all this?"

Abbeline's cheeks warmed. "He's… been more than I expected. He saw me when everything else fell apart. Helped me keep going."

Edward smiled. "Sounds like I owe him a lot." He glanced toward Chance and gave a nod. Chance nodded back.

They made plans for the next day—a visit to Edward's cabin and workshop an hour north.

"I have something for you," Edward said as they stood to leave. He reached into his coat pocket and placed a small carving in her palm.

A hummingbird in flight.

"Your mother loved hummingbirds," he said. "Said they reminded her that small things could have the fiercest hearts."

Abbeline held the carving to her chest. "Thank you."

Outside, the sun broke through the clouds.

As they walked back toward the hotel, Abbeline turned to Chance.

"He's exactly who I imagined," she said. "Strong, observant... kind."

"He has your eyes," Chance replied. "Or maybe it's the other way around."

At the corner, she stopped him.

"I couldn't have done this without you," she said. "When everything crumbled, you didn't. You believed in this search—even when I didn't."

"I believed in you," he corrected gently. "Still do."

The simple statement, delivered with such quiet certainty, broke something open inside her. All the emotions she'd been carefully managing—the joy of finding her father, the relief after months of searching, and the growing feelings for the man standing before her—surged past her defenses.

She didn't want to wait another day. Not for this. Not anymore.

Without a word, Abbeline wrapped her arms around Chance, pressing her face against his chest. He stiffened in surprise for just a moment before his arms encircled her, one hand cradling the back of her head, the other drawing her closer. The embrace was different from any they'd shared before—not a quick hug of celebration or a gesture of comfort, but something deeper, more complete.

When they finally pulled apart, they remained close, neither willing to fully break the connection. Abbeline looked up to find Chance watching her with an intensity that made her heart race. The unspoken thing between them, carefully sidestepped for months, suddenly filled the space between them—impossible to ignore.

Before she could second-guess herself, Abbeline slid her hand around the back of his neck and rose up on her toes. Their lips met in a kiss that started gentle but quickly deepened as Chance's arms tightened around her waist, lifting her slightly. The Seattle street faded away—the pedestrians, the traffic noise, everything beyond this moment slipped from focus.

When they finally parted, breathless, no words came. None were needed. Chance's smile—surprised and joyful—told her everything. As they resumed walking toward the hotel, their bodies naturally shifted together—her arm around his waist, his draped over her shoulder, keeping her close against his side.

Abbeline's mind raced with a thousand thoughts, her pulse still hammering in her ears. Eight months of searching had ended in two life-changing discoveries in a single day—the father she'd been seeking and the relationship she hadn't known she wanted.

The hummingbird nestled in her pocket. The market behind them. The future ahead.

For the first time since opening that attic box, Abbeline felt not just found—but whole.

Tomorrow would bring more. But tonight, she walked into it with both her history and her heart intact.

***

Abbeline woke to sunlight filtering through the hotel curtains, momentarily disoriented before yesterday's events came rushing back—finding her father, the wooden hummingbird, kissing Chance on a Seattle sidewalk.

The memory made her heart flutter. She rolled onto her side to find Chance already awake on the pullout couch, watching her with a smile that felt both familiar and thrillingly new.

"Good morning," he said softly.

"Morning." She sat up, suddenly shy despite the ease that had existed between them last night. "Did you sleep okay?"

"Better than okay." He stood, stretching. "So... yesterday happened."

"Which part?" she teased, feeling bold. "Finding my long-lost father or kissing you in the middle of Pike Place?"

His laugh warmed her. "Both were pretty memorable, though I admit I've been thinking about one a bit more than the other."

Chance crossed the room toward her, and without hesitation, she reached for his hand, lacing their fingers together.

"I've wanted to do that for a while," she admitted. "I just needed to—"

"Find your father first," he finished. "I know. It's why I waited." His thumb traced slow circles on her palm. "Some things are worth being patient for."

Chance leaned forward, then caught himself with a self-conscious grin. "I should probably brush my teeth first."

"I was thinking the same thing," Abbeline laughed, letting go of his hand. "Not exactly romantic, is it?"

They both moved at once—Chance toward the living room bathroom, Abbeline to her en suite. She could hear his chuckle as they separated, their mutual eagerness more funny than awkward.

Abbeline quickly rinsed with mouthwash, ran her fingers through her curls, and returned just as Chance appeared in the doorway, nearly colliding with her.

"Sorry," they said in unison, then laughed.

"I was just—" he began.

"Me too," she finished, sliding her hands up his chest.

Their lips met in a kiss that deepened quickly, months of restraint giving way to newfound freedom. His arms wrapped around her waist as she melted against him.

When they finally pulled apart, Abbeline rested her forehead against his.

"We should probably get ready," Chance murmured, though he didn't move.

"Five more minutes," she whispered, pulling him back to her.

It was closer to thirty before they finally began preparing for the day, exchanging smiles and casual touches as they moved around the room. The tension that had lingered so long had melted into something warm and easy, yet full of promise.

As they packed for their overnight stay at Edward's cabin, Abbeline paused, struck by the surreal weight of it all.

"What is it?" Chance asked.

"I'm just... processing. Yesterday I found my father after twenty-one years, and I kissed you after eight months of searching together." She shook her head with a faint smile. "A lot of life-changing events for one day."

"Too much?"

"No," she said firmly. "Just right. Overwhelming in the best possible way."

"We'll take it at whatever pace feels right," he said. "The search is over. We've got time for everything else."

She nodded, grateful. As they headed to the car, his hand found hers naturally, their fingers intertwining with quiet certainty.

Morning mist clung to the evergreens as Chance drove north, the city falling away into dense forest. Abbeline watched the shifting landscape, the wooden hummingbird warm in her palm.

Two powerful emotions competed in her chest—joy at finding her father, and something deeper, quieter, growing for Chance. Each tugged at her thoughts, each filling her in different ways.

"Should be just ahead," Chance said, checking the directions Edward had scribbled on a napkin. "Red mailbox, gravel driveway."

"There!" Abbeline pointed as the mailbox came into view, mounted on a post carved like a tree trunk.

The driveway wound through tall firs before revealing a cedar cabin, silvered with age, a stone chimney puffing smoke. The porch wrapped two sides, lined with rocking chairs and potted herbs.

"It's exactly how I pictured it," she whispered. Then, more hesitantly, "Is it weird that I'm bringing you to meet my dad the day after we first kissed?"

Chance brushed his lips over her knuckles. "Nothing about us has followed a script. Why start now?"

Before they could exit the car, the cabin door opened. Edward stepped out with a mug in hand, dressed in jeans and flannel, his posture more relaxed than the day before.

"You found it," he called. "Not many do without detailed directions."

"The mailbox helped," Chance said, offering a handshake.

Edward shook it briefly, then turned to Abbeline. Up close, the years showed more clearly—gray hair, weathered skin, a faint scar on his jaw—but his smile was warm.

"Welcome home," he said.

Something in her chest tightened. The words caught her off guard—so ordinary, yet profound. She hadn't realized how much she needed to hear them until now.

They landed hard. Not just 'my home'—*our* home. As if this place belonged to her too.

"It's beautiful, feels like a sanctuary," she said, taking in the clearing and distant mountain view.

"That was the idea. After years in cities, I needed space. Distance." He met her gaze. "Perspective."

Inside, the cabin was small but meticulously crafted—every piece of furniture handmade, walls adorned with carvings, books on nature, history, and art lining the shelves.

"You built all this?" Chance asked, admiring an inlaid dining table.

"Most of it. The cabin existed, but rebuilding it gave me purpose."

Abbeline moved to a small side table filled with framed photographs—herself as a child, a teenager, a graduate. She recognized Beatrice's hand in the careful curation.

"You had these all along."

"They helped me track the years," Edward said from behind her. "Reminded me what I was working toward."

Chance shifted slightly beside her, his expression unreadable for a moment—as if he, too, was measuring the distance they'd all traveled.

Her thoughts turned to Chance—how he'd waited, supported, believed. A different path, the same quiet strength.

Edward motioned them to the table, where coffee and muffins waited. From beneath it, he produced a wooden box.

"I've been up since dawn," he said. "Gathering things I thought you'd want to see."

Inside: Ranger insignia, discharge papers, photos with his unit. Deeper still—a wildflower, concert ticket stubs, a sketchbook.

"Mom's artwork," Abbeline breathed, opening it. "I've never seen these."

"She gave me that the day we decided to marry," Edward said gently. "Said it captured the moments when she first realized she loved me."

Page after page revealed Abbie's eye—Edward reading, standing post, sleeping in sunlight. Then: a sketch of Big Joe's BBQ.

"That was our place," Edward said, voice thick. "Where I proposed."

"She captured you perfectly," Abbeline whispered. "You look so happy."

"I was. With her, I always was."

Chance leaned closer to see, his shoulder brushing hers. The warmth of it pulled her attention for a heartbeat—two powerful threads weaving together.

"You have her gift," Edward said. "Beatrice sent photos of your art—the portraits. Same way of seeing beneath the surface."

Abbeline looked up. She saw it too now—the thread connecting them. Not just in name, but in how they saw the world.

Edward's gaze lingered, his voice quiet. "I've spent so long preparing for this moment... and now that it's here, I worry I won't know how to be what you need."

Abbeline reached across the table, her fingers brushing his. "You don't have to be anything but yourself. This"—she glanced at the sketchbook—"this is what I need. You. The real you."

She paused, then added softly, "Tell me about her. Not the recordings. The little things. What made her laugh? What annoyed her?"

Edward's face softened. "She had this laugh... started as a giggle, ended as a full-body thing. She hated cold feet in bed but always forgot socks. Used me as her heating pad."

For the next hour, stories flowed—untaped, unfiltered memories. Chance quietly stepped onto the porch, giving them space.

Abbeline was grateful for the gesture—his intuition another thread weaving this new life. And yet, she already missed the weight of his presence beside her.

The day continued in a blur of meaningful moments— Edward showing his workshop, teaching woodcarving, making a recording together. When evening fell, Abbeline found Chance on the porch, staring at the stars.

"Hey," she said. "Sorry for all the family drama."

"Don't be," he said. "Watching you with your dad—it's been an honor."

"It still doesn't feel real."

"It is," he said. "And it's just the beginning."

They stood in silence, the night wrapping around them. From inside came the sounds of dishes—ordinary, comforting.

"What happens when we go back to Atlanta?" Chance asked. "With your life... your art... us?"

She turned to face him. "I keep painting. I stay connected to my father. I keep becoming Abbeline Stuart."

She reached up, fingers tracing his jaw. "And we explore what started here. I've spent so long looking back. I'm ready to look forward now."

"You're sure? This isn't just the emotion of today?"

"Finding him helped me find me. And that me wants you."

He pulled her closer. "Then I'd like to be part of that journey. Every step."

"Good," she whispered. "Because I'm not letting you go."

Their kiss was slower this time—no urgency, just certainty. A promise, not a question.

When they finally broke apart, he rested his forehead to hers. "I've been waiting for this since that night in your studio."

"You saw me before I did," she said. "Thank you for waiting."

Inside, Edward called about hot chocolate. Abbeline smiled, reluctant to move.

"We should go in," she murmured.

"One more minute," Chance whispered, holding her tighter.

She leaned into him, eyes on the sky. Twenty-one years ago, a father chose silence to protect his daughter. Today, that silence was broken—by persistence, by faith, by love.

The search had ended—but something new was just beginning.

Chapter 8

Becoming Whole

Three months after the reunion

Abbeline's brush moved in confident strokes, layering color in rhythm with the filtered summer light through her studio windows. Atlanta's heat clung to the glass, but the ceiling fan stirred her curls with a welcome breeze. When her phone chimed, she didn't look up.

"Just a sec, Dad," she called, finishing a final stroke before setting down the brush. Blue smudges marked her fingers as she accepted the video call, and Edward's face appeared onscreen.

"Am I interrupting?" he asked, noting the paint on her skin with a fond smile.

"Perfect timing. I needed a break." She turned the phone toward the canvas. "Thoughts?"

Bold colors and organic shapes formed a stylized landscape of the Pacific Northwest—a visual homage to the place where she'd found her father.

Edward studied it. "It has movement. Like the forest is breathing." His voice softened. "Your mother would've loved it."

"I think about her a lot when I paint now," Abbeline said, settling on her stool. "Like I finally understand what it meant for her—being pulled into something she had to get out of her head and onto the canvas."

"Exactly like that. She'd disappear for hours. You've got that same look."

The easy comparison still felt like a gift, especially after years in Randolph's house where her mother's name had been erased by silence. These calls were part of her new routine— Edward in his Seattle workshop, she in her Atlanta studio. Together, they were bridging twenty-one years, one conversation at a time.

"How's the commission going?" she asked, eyeing the carved panels behind him.

"On track. The client's into the forest motif." He turned the camera to show a panel of intertwined trees and hidden wildlife. "But enough about work. What's the latest on the gallery showing?"

"Aunt Bea dropped off the contract yesterday. I need to finish fifteen pieces by September." Her voice lifted. "My first solo exhibition."

"I'm not surprised," Edward said, pride unmistakable. "Your mother's talent, your vision. The world deserves to see it."

A knock interrupted them. Chance poked his head in. "Sorry to crash," he said, then spotted the phone. "Hey, Mr. Stuart!"

Their informal title had emerged naturally—after "sir" had made Edward wince and "Edward" felt too bold. "Mr. Stuart" was the truce that worked.

"Chance," Edward greeted, his expression warming.

"I brought lunch." Chance held up a takeout bag, the smell of garlic and spice filling the studio instantly. "Marco made lasagna—our nonna's recipe."

"I'll let you two eat," Edward said. "Call tomorrow?"

"Wouldn't miss it. Love you, Dad."

The words still felt fresh, but less foreign. Edward smiled gently. "Love you too, Bella."

Abbeline ended the call and stretched, easing out the stiffness in her shoulders. At the sink, she scrubbed away the paint while Chance crossed to wrap his arms around her, careful of the drying canvas.

"How's your dad?"

"Good. Busy." She leaned into him. "He's thinking of visiting before the exhibition."

"Perfect timing. He could help pick the final pieces." He kissed her temple before letting go. "But first, mangia. Marco outdid himself."

Their rhythm was easy now—weeknights after his finance classes, weekends shared between her studio and social outings, comfortable silences that didn't need filling. That kind of ease still surprised her after years of curated interactions and social performance.

She took a bite and groaned. The flavor overwhelmed her.

"That good, huh?" Chance grinned.

"Unreal." She licked sauce off her lip, then glanced at her reflection in the mirror above the sink. Her curls were longer now, sunlit highlights glinting gold. She no longer hid her freckles. She barely recognized the polished young woman she used to be. This version felt real, messy, and completely her own.

"You're doing that thing again," Chance said, grinning as he unpacked the rest of the food.

"What thing?"

"The 'catalogue-the-moment' look." He handed her a napkin. "Should I worry you're immortalizing me with tomato sauce on my shirt?"

"Maybe." She smiled, then softened. "How was your career counseling meeting?"

He hesitated. The shift was subtle but unmistakable—his hand rubbed the back of his neck, his eyes dropping briefly.

"Actually… I need to talk to you about something."

She tilted her head. "That sounds ominous."

He sighed. "It's complicated."

"That sounds worse."

"Remember when I told you my father and I had an agreement about my career path?"

She nodded, already sensing the turn.

"The plan was always that I'd work somewhere else for three years before joining the family business. Get experience, prove myself on my own merits." His words came faster now, as if he needed to get them all out before losing his nerve. "The thing is, before we... before Seattle. Before things got serious between us, I accepted a position in New York. Starting after graduation in May."

The silence that followed wasn't cold, only stunned.

"New York," she repeated, the words clicking into place. "That's... far."

"It is. It's with Karrington Financial. Great firm."

"When were you going to tell me?"

"I should've said something sooner. At first, it didn't feel relevant—we were focused on finding your dad. Then everything happened so fast... I didn't want to add a time limit to what was still forming." He raked a hand through his hair. "But not telling you felt worse."

She set down her fork. Her chest tightened—not from betrayal, but from the weight of uncertainty. This wasn't like Randolph's secrets or her old life's manipulations. Still, it hurt.

"So you're leaving in May."

"That was the plan," he said. "Before you. Now... I don't know. I just knew you deserved honesty."

She studied his face and found no deceit—only worry, hope, and something like regret.

"I get it. You made a smart move. And it predates us."

"Abbeline," he said gently, taking her hand, "this doesn't have to be an ending. We can figure it out. New York isn't the moon. It's just... three years," he said, like the number itself might soften the impact.

"Just." Her tone sharpened. "Longer than we've known each other."

"I don't have the perfect answer. But I know this matters. You matter. And I'm not walking away."

His sincerity muted the sting. This wasn't abandonment. It was life colliding with love.

"I need time," she said. "To think."

"Of course. Take whatever you need."

Her phone buzzed with a text. She glanced down, her brow furrowing.

"Speaking of complications—Aunt Bea wants dinner Saturday. Says it's important."

"Wedding plans?" Chance guessed, latching onto the shift in tone.

"Maybe." But Beatrice's text hinted at something weightier than floral arrangements. Abbeline had learned to read the subtext in her aunt's messages. This felt strategic.

"Penny for your thoughts?" he asked.

"Just wondering what she's not saying. But we've got four days to speculate."

He reached for her hand again. "Whatever it is, we'll handle it. Together."

The word held firm. Through studio paint and cross-country job offers, found father and uncertain futures—this was their rhythm now.

"Right," she said, fingers tightening around his. "Together."

For now, that was enough.

***

The gallery's white walls gleamed under track lighting, blank spaces waiting for Abbeline's vision. She walked the perimeter slowly, measuring dimensions with her eyes, mentally placing each painting in the sequence she'd been visualizing for weeks.

"The lighting is excellent," said Miranda Wu, the gallery owner who'd taken a chance on an unknown artist with an unusual story. Her sleek bob swung as she gestured toward the ceiling. "We can adjust the spots to highlight specific textures in your work. Those impasto sections will cast beautiful shadows."

Abbeline nodded, grateful for Miranda's enthusiasm. At thirty-five, Miranda had already built a reputation for spotting breakout talent. Two months ago, after visiting Abbeline's studio, she'd offered the exhibition without hesitation, drawn by the emotional intensity and technical depth of the collection.

"I'm thinking we open with the forest series," Abbeline said, pointing to the largest wall. "The journey starts there, in the Pacific Northwest, where I found my father."

"Perfect," Miranda agreed. "And we'll place Fragments and Reclamation on either side of the entrance, bookends for the narrative arc." She made notes on her tablet. "The shift in your palette, from cooler greens and blues to warm earth tones, will guide viewers through the emotional arc beautifully."

Chance appeared from the back office, where he'd been handling insurance paperwork. "All set. Coverage kicks in the moment your work arrives."

His presence steadied her, even as it complicated her thoughts. Four days had passed since the New York revelation, and while they hadn't argued, a subtle distance lingered. The conversation they needed to have still waited—quiet, un-resolved.

"I need to check on a delivery," Miranda said, glancing at her watch. "Take your time. Lock up when you're done—the code's by the door."

After she left, the gallery fell into a companionable quiet. Abbeline and Chance resumed their circuit of the space. He kept a slight distance, respectful of the space she'd asked for, but he was still unmistakably present.

"It's really happening," she said softly, stopping in front of the main wall. "Eight months ago I was just starting to paint again. Now…"

"Now your first solo exhibition is around the corner." His pride was evident despite the tension between them. "It's extraordinary, Abbeline."

"It's terrifying," she admitted, voice low. "What if no one connects with the work? What if Miranda only offered me this show because of the Hartwell name—even if I don't use it anymore?"

Chance shook his head. "Miranda doesn't waste wall space on anyone she doesn't believe in, and you know that. She saw what I saw that first day in your studio. Not just talent, but perspective. Truth. People will connect."

His certainty anchored her, just as it had so many times before. She drew a breath, tension easing.

"Dad's flying in next Friday," she said, shifting the subject. "He wants to help finalize the selection. He's booked a place near Aunt Bea's."

"Perfect timing. Ten days will give you two plenty of space to work together." Chance hesitated. "I told my parents about the exhibition. They want to come opening night."

Abbeline looked up, surprised. She'd known them socially for years, but the idea of seeing them now—as herself, not as Randolph's granddaughter—brought a flicker of unease.

"Do they know about… everything?"

"They know the essentials. That you found your father, that you're reconnecting. That we're together." He paused. "My mother had questions about Randolph, but I didn't go into details."

The mention of her grandfather stirred something old and unresolved. Though she'd stayed silent since their confrontation, he hadn't. Messages, letters, even flowers delivered to Beatrice's home—always respectful, always laced with quiet manipulation.

"I'll need to address his absence," she murmured. "Atlanta's art world is small. People will notice."

"You don't owe anyone that explanation."

"No," she agreed. "But the silence might speak louder than any painting. I should at least tell him about the show."

They moved to the window, watching pedestrians drift past below. He stood beside her, not touching, but close.

"Whatever you decide, I'm with you," he said. Then, after a beat, "Even if I'm supporting from New York."

The words shifted the air between them—a soft echo of what still needed saying.

Abbeline turned. "I've been thinking about that," she said. "About us. About what happens next."

"And?"

"I don't have an answer yet." She met his eyes. "This isn't just about distance, Chance. It's about finally feeling grounded—finding my father, reclaiming my name—and now…" She trailed off.

"Now I've introduced more uncertainty," he said gently. "If I could change the timing, I would."

"I know." She folded her arms. "Three months ago, I would've told you to go. No hesitation. Take the opportunity. But now…"

"Now there's us."

"Yes." One word, filled with weight—with everything they'd built: late-night studio conversations, the Seattle trip, the silence that had never felt empty.

Chance stepped closer. When she didn't pull away, he reached to uncross her arms, taking her hands in his.

"When I took that job, I was following a checklist—degree, job, promotion." He smiled slightly. "But then I watched you build something meaningful out of grief. I realized I wanted that kind of life, not just a résumé."

"I don't want to be the reason you give up your plans."

"Abbeline. You're a priority, not a compromise." He squeezed her hands. "We'll find a way that doesn't force either of us to choose."

Her breath caught—his sincerity touched something deep and steady within her.

"What are you saying?"

"I'm saying I'll explore other options. Atlanta jobs. Or we try long-distance temporarily. I don't have all the answers. But I'm not asking you to wait or pause your life. You've come too far."

The honesty steadied her more than any declaration could—not a perfect plan, but a real one, grounded in care and commitment.

"We'll talk more after Beatrice's dinner," she said. "One life-altering conversation at a time."

He smiled, some of the tension in his shoulders releasing. "Fair. Though knowing your aunt, it could be anything from wedding plans to guest room renovations."

The line worked—she laughed, remembering. "Last time she called a 'family meeting,' it was to announce her return to jiu-jitsu."

Each step between canvases felt easier than the last—the weight of uncertainty still there, but shared now. As they locked up, Chance's hand found hers, their fingers lacing as naturally as breathing.

The gallery stood in Atlanta's arts district, surrounded by converted warehouses and indie cafés, a far cry from Buckhead's formality. Here, the city felt alive, imperfect, evolving. Like her.

"Coffee?" Chance gestured across the street. "We can keep working on your artist statement."

The suggestion grounded her. Amid the uncertainty—New York, Randolph, Beatrice—this remained: ritual, partnership, connection.

"Yes," she said, squeezing his hand. "But I'm buying. You've endured too many bad drafts to go unpaid."

His laugh followed them into the sunlight, the afternoon stretching ahead—uncertain, full of promise, just like the empty walls waiting to tell her story.

***

Familiar streets took on new meaning as Edward guided the rental car through neighborhoods he hadn't driven in for over twenty years. From the passenger seat, Abbeline watched his gaze linger on certain buildings and intersections—landmarks from a life left behind.

"It's changed," he said, weaving around construction cones and detours. "More built up. Busier."

"Atlanta's always under construction," she replied, knowing small talk couldn't quite contain the weight of the moment. How could they talk traffic when he was returning to the city where he'd lost everything?

He'd arrived just an hour ago, and the surreal quality of their reunion hadn't yet faded. Every time she saw him, Abbeline felt the dissonance between the stranger she recognized from old photos and the man she was beginning to know—steadily, intimately, over months of conversations and growing trust.

"The exhibition space is just ahead," she said, pointing toward the gallery district. "I thought we'd start there, before heading to Aunt Bea's."

Edward nodded, his focus sharpening as they entered the arts district. Though he hadn't said it outright, Abbeline understood this visit wasn't just about her show. It was a kind of return—an attempt to reclaim space in a city where joy and grief had once collided.

They parked on a quiet side street. Abbeline unlocked Miranda's gallery, having been granted access during installation week. Her pulse quickened. Edward had seen her work in photos and over video calls, but this would be the first time he stood before her canvases in person. His opinion mattered more than she was willing to admit.

"Here we are," she said, holding open the door. "My first solo exhibition space."

Edward stepped inside, scanning the room with a practiced eye—part soldier, part father. But when his gaze landed on the forest series arranged along one wall, that professionalism softened.

"Bella," he said softly, stepping forward. "These are extra-ordinary."

Relief and warmth rushed through her. She'd feared the paintings might seem naïve to someone who had lived those landscapes firsthand, but his expression held nothing but admiration.

"You've captured it," he said, standing before a misty evergreen scene. "Not just how it looks, but how it feels to be there."

"That's what I was aiming for," she said, joining him. "The emotional resonance, not realism."

They moved through the space together. Abbeline explained her layout and vision while Edward listened with quiet intensity, occasionally asking thoughtful questions or offering gentle suggestions, but mostly just observing—his pride unmistakable.

"Your mother would be stunned," he said, stopping before Fragments, an abstract work representing Abbeline's fractured identity before discovering the truth. "She was gifted, but you've made it your own."

The compliment hit deeper than expected, bringing a sudden sting of tears. Comparisons to Abbie weren't new—but this was different. This acknowledged her voice, side by side with her mother's, not beneath it.

"There's one more piece I haven't brought over yet," she said, blinking quickly. "Still in my studio. I was hoping for your opinion before finalizing it."

"I'd be honored."

Outside, her phone buzzed. A text from Chance:

Meeting running late. Will meet you at Beatrice's. Everything okay with your dad?

She typed back: *Perfect. Taking him to the studio now. See you later.*

The brief exchange tugged at her thoughts, pulling her momentarily toward the tension still lingering with Chance. Since their talk at the gallery, they'd deferred deeper discussions until after Edward's visit. Beatrice's dinner—postponed last weekend—was another question mark waiting.

Edward, noticing her slight frown, spoke gently. "Your young man seems invested in your work."

"He's been supportive from the start," she said, her voice shading with uncertainty.

"But?"

"It's nothing." Then, pausing: "Actually—it is. He accepted a job in New York before we were serious. Starts in May."

"Ah." Edward took this in with the calm deliberation she'd come to expect from him. "And now you're at a crossroads."

"I've worked hard to build something here—my art, my relationships. And now…"

"And now your heart is involved," he said, finishing the thought. "Distance complicates things."

She nodded, guiding him back toward the car. "I've spent so much energy finding solid ground. The idea of risking that again feels… heavy."

Edward was quiet as he drove. Then he said, "Your mother and I faced something similar. When we married, I had only one job offer—Columbia. She had gallery contacts here in Atlanta. But we had to leave. Thank goodness Columbia was still close to Beatrice, but far enough to start fresh.

Abbeline hadn't known that. "How did you know it was right?"

"We didn't," he said. "We just knew we wanted to face it together. That mattered more than location."

His words settled in her chest as they pulled up to the converted warehouse that now housed her studio. A few weeks after Seattle, she'd moved her work here—needing not just space, but something fully her own.

She unlocked the door. The scent of linseed oil and gesso greeted them. Sunlight streamed through the tall windows, casting warmth on paint-streaked drop cloths and canvases propped along every wall.

"This suits you," Edward said, looking around. "Built with your own hands, on your own terms."

"Exactly." She led him to a cloth-covered canvas in the corner. "This is the one I wanted your opinion on. It's more personal than the others."

With a careful pull, she uncovered the painting.

It was Edward, standing at his Pike Place stall, surrounded by wood carvings. A translucent image of baby Abbeline hovered in the background—memory and presence overlapping in luminous layers of paint. The technique bridged realism with dream, past with present.

Edward stared, silent. His hand twitched slightly, as if to reach out.

"It's called Reclaimed," she said. "If it's too much, I can leave it out."

"Include it," he said quietly, voice thick. "It's truth, Bella. Uncomfortable, beautiful truth."

He turned to her. His eyes—so familiar now—were wet.

"Your courage in facing our history... it's more than I ever deserved. But I am grateful beyond words."

The rawness in his voice cracked something open between them. No longer careful or cautious, Abbeline stepped into his arms.

His flannel shirt smelled faintly of cedar and oil, grounding her in the reality of him—not a story, not a photograph, but her father, present and real.

His arms tightened, steady and sure.

This wasn't just reunion. It was recognition.

When they finally pulled apart, Edward cleared his throat, his composure returning.

"Your mother would be proud. Not just of your talent, but your strength."

"I get that from both of you," she said, steady now. "Learning our story helped me understand myself in ways I didn't know I needed."

They spent another hour together in the studio, discussing her final selections and sharing stories sparked by colors or symbols in her work. Their rhythm had shifted—less like strangers learning each other, more like family rediscovering what had always been there.

As they prepared to leave, Edward paused before a small painting of a wooden horse—one of Abbeline's earliest post-discovery works.

"You kept it," he said, recognizing the carving from memory.

"It was my most treasured thing," she said. "Even when I didn't know why."

He smiled, his weathered face softening. "Some connections transcend understanding. Like the way I used to dream about you on your birthday without knowing what day it was."

"Or how I always loved carved wood," she said, smiling back. "Even when I didn't know where that love came from."

Something quiet and whole settled between them.

As they drove toward Beatrice's house, late-afternoon light cast long shadows across familiar streets that now bore new significance.

"I have something for you," Edward said. "It's in my suitcase. I'll bring it tonight."

"What is it?"

"A piece I've been working on since Seattle. Something to mark our new beginning."

Abbeline spotted Chance's car in the driveway. A familiar pang of uncertainty stirred—but this time, something steadier rose to meet it.

Edward seemed to sense it.

"Whatever you decide about New York," he said, "just remember—real connections stretch. They don't break. Not when they're rooted in truth."

She nodded, letting the words settle.

Today had clarified things—not in simple solutions, but in the strength she now carried. Through art, through truth, through rediscovery, she had reclaimed not just a father—but herself.

As they walked to Beatrice's front door, Edward beside her, she felt the closing of one circle and the opening of another. Not an ending. A beginning.

Candlelight glowed in Beatrice's dining room, casting warm shadows over the faces that now defined family for Abbeline. Edward sat at one end of the table, more at ease than she'd ever seen him in Atlanta. Roderick occupied the other, his usual courtroom gravitas softened by obvious joy. Chance sat beside Abbeline, his knee brushing hers beneath the table in silent rhythm.

"I think we've kept them in suspense long enough," Roderick said, sharing a glance with Beatrice.

"Indeed," Beatrice agreed, setting down her wine glass. "We invited you all here tonight because we have news."

Abbeline exchanged a look with Chance, who raised his brows. After the postponed dinner, they'd speculated endlessly.

"First," Beatrice said, "Roderick and I have finally set a wedding date—October."

"Congratulations," Edward said, lifting his glass. "A long time coming."

"Over twenty years of on-again, off-again," Roderick admitted with a chuckle. "But that's not all."

Beatrice reached for his hand. "We've been approved to adopt siblings—Abigail, ten, and Bau, seven. If all goes smoothly, they'll move in next month."

Stunned silence followed. Abbeline blinked, then gasped. "You're adopting? I had no idea you were considering it."

"We've been navigating the process quietly for nearly a year," Beatrice explained. "We wanted to be certain."

"We met them through one of my cases," Roderick added. "We felt a connection immediately."

"Abigail?" Abbeline repeated, hearing the significance.

Beatrice nodded, eyes shimmering. "Same as your mom's. When we heard her name, it felt like a sign."

Emotion swept the room. Edward stared at his plate, steadying himself. Abbeline felt tears prick her eyes at this quiet extension of her mother's legacy.

"That's... beautiful," she said finally, voice thick. "You'll be amazing parents."

"There's more," Beatrice added. "Abigail's already showing talent—she draws constantly. And Bau's fascinated by architect-ture. He builds elaborate structures from anything."

Chance squeezed Abbeline's hand, knowing the emotional weight those details carried.

"When do we meet them?" she asked.

"Next weekend," Roderick said. "They'll visit for the day. If all goes well, they'll move in permanently after the court date."

"We're converting the guest room for Abigail," Beatrice said, "and turning the office into Bau's space. We'd love your help designing their rooms—maybe murals?"

"I'd love that," Abbeline said, deeply touched. "Something inspired by their interests?"

"Exactly," Beatrice said, her smile beaming.

The conversation shifted into plans—decorations, school options, building routine. Edward's initial silence gave way to quiet contribution, offering insights from his work with youth in his wilderness program.

"The most important thing," he said, "is consistency. After all they've been through, your presence needs to be the one constant."

"Exactly our focus," Roderick said, grateful.

Later, as Beatrice served crème brûlée cheesecake, Abbeline looked around the table with new perspective. Each person here had endured loss, wrestled with change, and chosen love anyway. And now they were extending that love—two children joining a family already formed by survival and devotion.

"A toast," Chance said, lifting his glass. "To Beatrice and Roderick—and to Abigail and Bau. May your new family bring you joy and the belonging we all deserve."

"To family," Edward echoed, his eyes meeting Abbeline's.

After dessert, Beatrice pulled Abbeline aside. "Thank you for inviting your grandfather to the exhibition," she said quietly. "That couldn't have been easy."

"It wasn't," Abbeline admitted. "But after what Dad said about letting go, it felt right." She touched her mother's necklace absently. "We're not warm yet. But we're texting—briefly."

"He values that more than he shows," Beatrice said. She hesitated. "His heart's getting worse. The doctors are concerned."

The news dimmed the moment. Complicated as he was, Randolph had shaped her world once.

"I'll talk to him at the show," she promised. "A real conversation, not just gallery small talk."

"That's all anyone can ask," Beatrice said gently. "You've come so far, Bella. Reclaiming your name, building something new—and still finding room to forgive. I'm proud of you."

They rejoined the others in the living room. Edward stood, a small wooden box in hand.

"This is what I mentioned earlier," he said, offering it to Abbeline.

The box itself was art—carved cedar, its patterns reminiscent of Pacific Northwest Indigenous designs. Inside, nestled in velvet, was a complete set of miniature animals. Each represented a carving he'd sent during her childhood, now joined by new pieces made since Seattle.

"Dad," she whispered, lifting a tiny fox. "They're exquisite."

"The set is whole now," Edward said. "The ones I made when we were apart—and the ones I've made since finding you. Our story, in wood."

Abbeline gently examined each. There was the horse from her eighth birthday, the bear from her twelfth, the owl from her sixteenth. Pieces she'd discovered in the attic now connected to the man who'd made them.

"Look inside the lid," Edward said.

Engraved in delicate script: *For Abbeline—Separated by circumstance, connected by love, reunited by courage. Your father, always.*

Tears spilled freely as she wrapped one arm around him, the box held carefully between them. "Thank you," she whispered—words too small for the feeling rising inside her.

As she shared the gift with Beatrice and the others, something shifted inside—a settling. Despite everything with Randolph, despite the questions still ahead, she knew who she was: not a fractured inheritance, but a whole identity, chosen and reclaimed.

As the evening wound down, Roderick pulled Chance aside while Beatrice and Edward discussed artwork for the children's rooms.

When Chance returned, his smile was there, but something in his eyes lingered.

"Everything okay?" Abbeline asked.

"Fine," he said quickly. "Just legal advice about a property thing."

She let it be. He'd share when he was ready. For now, she focused on saying goodnight to her father, arranging to meet him the next morning at the gallery.

Outside, the night wrapped warm and humid around them. Chance opened her car door, then paused.

"Would you mind a small detour?" he asked, a quiet tension in his voice.

"Of course not," she said. "Where?"

"You'll see."

Twenty minutes later, they parked in front of the university's darkened arts building. Campus was quiet under summer break.

"What are we doing here?" Abbeline asked.

"Do you remember our first real conversation?" Chance asked. "Not small talk. Real?"

Understanding dawned. "The fundraiser. Two years ago. I was sketching outside."

"You were hiding from donors," he corrected, smiling. "I remember thinking—you were different."

"I didn't know it stuck with you."

"I never forgot," he said, leading her to the same courtyard. Moonlight silvered the benches and water of the fountain. "I volunteered to help with your search partly because I wanted to spend time with you. And these last three months..." He paused, took her hands. "Abbeline, I love you. And I want to make this work, even with New York."

Her breath caught.

She thought of Edward's words earlier: real connections stretch, but don't break.

"You don't need to worry about New York," she said, her decision clear at last. "Take the position. We'll make it work."

His eyes searched hers. "Are you sure?"

"I'm sure," she said. "You're not choosing New York over me. You're choosing a future—and I want to be part of it. Visits, calls, trips. Maybe even gallery scouting in the city. We'll figure it out."

Relief softened his features. "I love you so much, Bella."

The name caught her breath—it was the first time he'd used it. She saw him searching her eyes, checking to see if she was comfortable with it, but she gave him a wide smile, entirely at ease.

"I love you too," she whispered. "And I believe in us. Not because it's easy, but because it's real."

As his lips met hers in the quiet courtyard, Abbeline leaned in—into the kiss, into the future they were daring to build. The wind moved gently through the trees above them, rustling like applause.

✳✳✳

The gallery hummed with pre-exhibition energy as Abbeline and Edward worked side by side, installing the final pieces for tomorrow's opening. Ladders, tools, and measuring tapes lay scattered across the polished concrete floor, while Miranda directed lighting adjustments. Over three days, the collection had taken shape—canvases arranged to guide viewers through Abbeline's emotional and artistic journey.

"A little higher on the left," she directed as Edward adjusted Reclaimed, the portrait that had moved him so deeply in her studio. Though he'd been in Atlanta just five days, they'd fallen into a rhythm—her artistic vision, his quiet precision.

"Perfect," she said when the canvas hung level. "That completes the central wall."

Edward stepped back, surveying the space. "It tells your story beautifully. From fragmentation to wholeness. From loss to reunion."

"Ours," she corrected softly, joining him. "None of this would exist without you."

The gallery had transformed under their hands. Miranda had given Abbeline full control over the installation, and she'd arranged the works chronologically—starting with abstract explorations of pre-discovery identity, moving through the emotional chaos of the search, and ending with the vibrant clarity of her reunion pieces. It was both personal narrative and broader exploration—of identity, belonging, and reclamation.

"Are you nervous about tomorrow?" Edward asked as they began gathering tools.

"Terrified," she admitted with a smile. "Not just about the critics. About seeing Grandfather again. I haven't spoken to him face-to-face since I left his study."

Edward nodded. "First reunions are never easy. But you were right to invite him. Whatever happens, you'll know you extended a hand."

Since sending the invitation, she'd oscillated between doubt and certainty. Her text exchanges with Randolph were sparse—her replies brief—but they were contact nonetheless. Her dad's ability to speak of Randolph without anger had helped shift her own lens, allowing space for complexity without justification.

"Mom would want me to try, wouldn't she?" she asked, placing price lists on the front desk.

Edward paused before answering. "Your mother had a gift for forgiveness. But she also believed in boundaries. She'd never ask you to forget—just to choose peace when you're ready."

Abbeline nodded. "That's what I want too. Not to pretend everything's fine, just to stop letting anger define the relationship."

"A wise approach," Edward said gently. "I've learned that bitterness keeps you tied to the past. Letting go is how you move forward."

Miranda approached, tablet in hand. "Final approval needed," she said, passing it to Abbeline. "Once you sign, it goes live tonight."

Abbeline reviewed the digital catalog—images of her work, her bio, and the artist statement she and Chance had labored over. The words leapt from the screen: *'Reclaimed' explores the journey from inherited identity to authentic self... through color, texture, and form.*

"It's perfect," she said, signing. "Thank you, Miranda. For trusting me."

"Don't thank me yet," Miranda said with a grin. "Wait for the reviews. But between the buzz and your story, I'm predicting a full house."

The "story" had become unavoidable. Though Abbeline valued privacy, the art world thrived on narrative—and hers was potent. The heiress who discovered her true heritage, found her lost father, and reclaimed her identity through art. The Atlanta

Journal-Constitution had already reached out, and several TV crews had shown interest.

"Just breathe tomorrow," Edward advised once Miranda stepped away. "Let the art do the talking."

She smiled at him, grateful for his steadiness. "Will Desiree be joining us?"

Edward's relationship with Desiree, a Seattle landscape architect, had come up slowly over their conversations. Though not serious, the connection had meant something.

"She couldn't get away," he said. "But she sends her best and expects photos."

"Next time, then," Abbeline said—the phrase a quiet acknowledgment of future visits, of continuity.

Moments later, the door swung open as Chance arrived, arms full of takeout. He greeted Edward, kissed Abbeline lightly, and took in the space with a grin.

"It looks incredible," he said. "You're going to blow people away."

Even after deciding on New York, his enthusiasm hadn't dimmed. They'd spent hours planning—rotating visits, video calls, gallery scouting. A challenge, yes, but not a barrier.

"I brought enough for everyone," he added. "Let's eat."

They carried dinner into the gallery's modest break room and gathered around a cramped table, the closeness lending intimacy to their meal.

"Beatrice texted," Chance said between bites. "Abigail and Bau are excited. She called it their first official family outing."

"They seemed to enjoy last weekend," Abbeline said. The children had warmed to her quickly—Bau building towers from kitchen objects, Abigail sketching flowers with startling detail.

"They're good kids," Edward agreed. "Resilient."

After Miranda stopped by with final logistics, they drifted into conversation—about the exhibition, the adoption, Chance's final semester. Edward and Chance had grown surprisingly comfortable with each other, their mutual respect grounding the moment.

When they finished eating, Chance checked his watch. "Early class tomorrow. Need a ride?"

"Actually," Abbeline said, "I'm going to stay a bit. A few last-minute tweaks. Dad can drop me off."

Chance kissed her goodbye and promised to pick her up an hour before the opening. When the door closed behind him, Abbeline and Edward returned to the main gallery in thoughtful quiet.

"You're lucky," Edward said. "Not many young men would be so steady with a long-distance future ahead."

"I know," she said. "He reminds me of you, actually— putting love first."

Edward blinked at the comparison, then smiled. "Thank you."

He patted the bench beside him. "There's something I've been thinking about. Since Seattle."

She looked at him, curious. "What is it?"

"I'm considering moving back to Atlanta."

The words landed like a stone in still water.

"Atlanta? But your life is in Seattle—your shop, your clients, Desiree…"

"My clients mostly order remotely now. The workshop can move. And as for Desiree…" He exhaled. "We care about each other, but we've always kept it casual. Part of me was still here—with you, with her memory."

Abbeline hesitated. "But you've built a life there."

"I built a hiding place," he said softly. "A good one. But still a place I went to survive, not to live fully. Reuniting with you, reconnecting with Beatrice, even walking these streets again… I realized I don't want to live halfway anymore."

She searched his face, her chest tight. "What if it complicates things with grandfather?"

"Atlanta's a big city. And I have no interest in reigniting the past. I've made my peace. What happens between you and your grandfather is yours to navigate. I won't interfere."

"You've really forgiven him?" she asked quietly.

"Forgiveness doesn't excuse what he did. It just stops him from owning any more of my life."

She sat with that truth for a moment, feeling it settle beside her own. "When would you come?"

"Not immediately. I need to wrap up some commissions, find a workshop space. But maybe by the end of the year."

She nodded, her heart opening to the idea. "I'd like that. Having you here."

"Then I'll make it happen," he said, his voice full of gentle resolve.

As they tidied the space one last time, Abbeline felt the shape of her life adjusting again—new contours forming around connection and choice, not legacy or expectation.

Later, as Edward drove her back to Beatrice's, the Atlanta skyline shimmered. The city felt different now—less a map of constraint, more a field of possibilities. Where once there had been silence, now there was support. Where once there had been distance, now intention.

"You know what I just realized?" she said as they neared Beatrice's house. "This show—it's happening exactly one year after I found those photographs in the attic."

Edward glanced at her. "A year already?"

"A year," she said. "From hidden past to opening night. From Hartwell to Stuart."

He smiled, pride lighting his face. "Quite a journey. And just the beginning."

As they pulled into the driveway, a quiet certainty settled in her chest. Tomorrow would bring critics, questions, and Randolph. But she would meet all of it grounded in truth, surrounded by love.

One year ago, she had uncovered fragments of her past. Now, those fragments had become something whole—not perfect, but hers. A life shaped by choice, by courage, and by connections that had survived distance and time.

She said goodnight to her father, promising to see him early tomorrow, then stepped inside the house that had once been a refuge and was now a launchpad.

The gallery was ready—and so was she.

Chapter 9

Connection Points

THE GALLERY LIGHTS were adjusted to perfection, each beam illuminating the textures and tones of Abbeline's canvases. An hour before the opening, she stood alone, absorbing what she had created. Her journey was mapped on these walls—from fragmented identity to reclamation, from loss to discovery, from Hartwell to Stuart.

"Ready?" Edward's voice was soft behind her.

She turned to find her father in the doorway, his charcoal suit complementing the silver in his hair. Even after months of calls and visits, seeing him here still carried a quiet wonder. He looked slightly out of place, yet entirely at home, a man who shaped beauty from raw materials now standing among his daughter's art.

"I think so," she said, smoothing the skirt of her midnight-blue dress. It had taken days to choose—elegant yet understated, honoring her evolving identity. She wore her mother's silver necklace and let her natural curls fall freely, catching the gallery lights.

"Nervous?" Edward asked, stepping beside her.

"Terrified," she admitted with a soft laugh. "Not just about critics, but…" Her eyes drifted to the guest list on Miranda's desk. Randolph Hartwell's name bore a small star—Miranda's code for VIPs.

Edward followed her gaze. "You okay?"

She didn't answer right away. "I'm trying to be."

He nodded, offering no judgment, only quiet reassurance. "Whatever happens tonight, these," he gestured to the paintings, "are yours. Your vision. Your truth. No one can take that from you."

Abbeline squeezed his hand, grateful for his steady presence. One of the gifts of their reunion had been discovering his quiet, expectation-free wisdom.

"Mr. Stuart? Ms. Stuart?" Miranda's voice called from the entrance. "The caterers need final approval."

"We'll be right there," Abbeline said, giving his hand a final squeeze as she let go.

As they moved forward, the practical details provided a welcome distraction. Beatrice arrived early, her innate precision smoothing last-minute chaos. Roderick followed, carrying a bouquet of wildflowers—the same variety Edward had once pressed into a letter she received on her twelfth birthday, a detail she'd shared during dinner months ago.

"These are from both of us," Roderick said, handing her the flowers. "For new beginnings."

Chance had arrived with her and Edward but had stepped aside to help Miranda with early setup. Now he moved beside her, his navy suit making his eyes startlingly blue, his hand grounding at the small of her back.

"The gallery looks incredible," he murmured, leaning close. "And so do you."

She glanced at him, her nerves steadying under his touch. "You've said that twice already," she said, smiling. "Still nice to hear."

"I had motivation." His gaze held hers, and that flutter in her chest—both thrilling and bittersweet—rose again. His departure for New York was just days away.

By seven o'clock, Miranda had gathered them for final instructions and a quiet toast in the gallery office.

"Remember to breathe," she advised, handing Abbeline a glass of champagne. "Let the work speak. Share what feels right. This is your story, your night."

They clinked glasses, the cheerful sound mingling with the tension beneath. This wasn't just an exhibition; it was a declaration, a reclaiming.

"To Abbeline Stuart," Edward said, pride clear in his voice, "and to truth that transforms rather than destroys."

"To truth," they echoed, just as the front door chimed with the arrival of the first guests.

What followed was a blur—greetings, introductions, polite questions. Miranda had curated a blend of critics, collectors, and select members of Atlanta society. Abbeline explained her process repeatedly, thankful for the rehearsal during installation.

Most guests focused on the art, but she sensed the undercurrent of curiosity: the whispered recognition of her transformation from Hartwell heiress to self-made artist.

An hour in, the gallery was comfortably full. Edward stood near "Reclaimed," their father-daughter portrait, answering quiet questions about his woodwork. Chance moved fluidly through the space, offering water or gently intercepting overzealous guests.

Beatrice touched Abbeline's arm gently, drawing her gaze to the entrance.

Randolph Hartwell stood just inside, surveying the room. His tailored suit and composed expression marked him as a man of influence, but the sharpness had dulled. His shoulders sloped slightly, his complexion grayer than she remembered.

Their eyes met across the room—years of expectations, betrayals, and unspoken truths suspended in that gaze. Abbeline excused herself and walked toward him, heart pounding.

"Grandfather," she said, voice steady. "Thank you for coming."

Randolph's gaze moved over her—her curls, her posture, the quiet elegance that was wholly her own.

"Abbeline," he said, voice thick. "The exhibition is impressive."

The words were small, but the effort behind them was not. She inclined her head, accepting both the compliment and what it represented.

"Would you like me to show you around?" she offered, surprised by her own willingness.

Something flickered—relief, perhaps. "Yes. I would like that."

As they moved through the exhibition, she felt the watchful eyes of Beatrice, Edward, Chance. But this moment belonged to them.

The first paintings were restrained, compositions from before the attic, before the truth. Randolph studied them silently, absorbing them with a businessman's intensity.

"These are from before," she said softly. "Before the attic."

He nodded, adjusting his signet ring—a familiar gesture that tugged unexpectedly at her.

At "Seventy-Two Hours"—a raw depiction of Edward's final moments with baby Abbeline—Randolph's breath caught.

"You know everything, then," he said, barely audible.

"Yes." Her eyes didn't waver. "Everything."

The acknowledgment passed between them like current—not absolution, just truth.

At "Reclaimed," he paused long, taking in the ghostly overlay of baby Abbeline behind Edward's portrait. The craftsmanship was undeniable, but it was the emotion that stilled him.

"He's here tonight," Randolph said.

"He is." She gestured toward Edward, who was deep in conversation with a collector.

Randolph's gaze followed. Something in his expression shifted—not soft, but complex.

"Beatrice tells me Edward is considering moving back permanently."

"He is." she said looking at him, "He's rented a workshop near my studio. The lease starts next month."

He nodded, gaze drifting back to the canvas. "Your mother had this same gift," he said quietly. "Capturing what's beneath the surface."

The unexpected comparison to Abbie felt like a hand extended across distance.

"I didn't know that," she said. "Thank you."

They continued in silence until they reached "Seeds of Change"—tiny seedlings pushing through rich, dark soil.

"This is your most recent work?" he asked.

"Finished it two days ago."

He nodded, studying it closely. "I see." He adjusted his ring again, his hand trembling faintly. "And this arrangement, does it work for you?"

"It does," she said. "Having him here—it's good."

Another nod. Then, softer than before: "When you came to my study that day, paint on your clothes, hair wild... I didn't recognize you. But now, looking at these paintings—I see you. For the first time."

The words hung in the air. Before she could respond, Miranda appeared beside her.

"Sorry to interrupt, but the *Atlanta Arts Journal* critic would like a word, and there's a collector very interested in 'Forest Whispers.'"

Abbeline glanced at Randolph, reluctant to step away. He straightened, slipping back into poise.

"You should attend to your guests. This is your night."

She hesitated, then nodded. "Thank you for coming. It meant a lot."

Something softened in his expression—not quite a smile, but close. "The work is exceptional, Abbeline. Your mother would've been proud."

He turned and walked toward the exit, posture still impeccable, steps slightly slower.

Abbeline watched him go, emotions churning. No resolution, not yet, but something had shifted.

Across the room, Edward caught her eye. She offered a nod. Later, they would talk.

The gallery hummed around her—conversations, red dots appearing beside sold pieces. Chance slipped to her side, hand finding hers.

"You okay?" he asked softly.

"Yes," she said, surprised by her own certainty. "I think I am."

Chance's fingers curled gently around hers.

Together, they moved through the gallery she had once only dreamed of. A year ago, the truth had shattered her. Tonight, it had shaped her. Not closure—just a doorway.

***

The morning after the exhibition opening, Abbeline woke to the persistent chime of her phone. Sunlight spilled through the curtains as she reached for it, still heavy with the exhaustion of the night before. Her screen lit up with missed calls, texts, and notifications, all tied to her debut.

"Is your phone having a seizure too?" Beatrice asked from the doorway, already dressed and holding out a mug of coffee like an olive branch. "I've had alerts going off since before sunrise."

"What's happening?" Abbeline sat up, taking the mug gratefully.

Beatrice perched on the edge of the bed, phone in hand. "You've gone viral, at least in Atlanta art circles. The *Journal* posted their review at midnight. Glowing. Then the *Chronicle* followed early this morning. Social media picked it up like wildfire."

Abbeline took a sip of coffee and opened the *Journal*'s review:

"Stuart's debut exhibition 'Reclaimed' announces the arrival of a formidable new talent on Atlanta's arts scene. Her technical skill is matched only by the emotional authenticity that infuses each canvas. Particularly notable is her masterful use of color to convey psychological states—from the muted, controlled palette of her earlier works to the vibrant expressionism of her recent paintings…"

The review continued with thoughtful analysis and closed by praising her "courageous exploration of identity and emotional truth." The *Chronicle*'s piece took a more narrative angle, spotlighting her artistic journey while tactfully acknowledging her connection to "one of Atlanta's most established families," carefully skirting the Hartwell name.

"This is… overwhelming," Abbeline murmured, setting the phone down as another buzz rattled her nightstand.

"And that's just the beginning," Beatrice said, her smile proud but edged with caution. "Three collectors already called Miranda this morning asking about commissions. But," her tone shifted, "there's some society chatter too."

Before Abbeline could ask, her phone rang. Madison.

Abbeline blinked. Her former society friend had breezed through the exhibition with a glossy compliment before vanishing. They hadn't spoken meaningfully in months.

"I should take this," she said, uncertain.

Beatrice gave her shoulder a gentle squeeze. "I'll be downstairs. Just remember—you don't owe explanations."

Once alone, Abbeline answered with careful neutrality. "Hello, Madison."

"Abbeline!" Madison's voice spilled out, sugary and rehearsed. "Darling, I've been trying to reach you since I saw the *Chronicle* piece. Why didn't you tell me your exhibition would be such a sensation?"

"I didn't know myself," Abbeline said honestly, already bracing for what was coming.

"Well, it's everywhere," Madison continued. "Rebecca Thompson's hosting brunch today and specifically asked me to invite you. Everyone's talking about your reinvention, especially the name change. It's caused quite the buzz."

Abbeline closed her eyes for a moment. The same social sphere that had exiled her was now knocking—not out of care, but because success had made her relevant again.

"That's kind of Rebecca," she replied evenly, "but I already have plans today."

"Oh." Madison's disappointment was unmistakable. "With your... father?"

The pause before *father* said more than the word itself. Abbeline felt her shoulders tense.

"With my family, yes," she said, her tone polite but distant. "And I need to be available for collectors reaching out about commissions."

"Of course, of course," Madison backpedaled. "Perhaps dinner later this week? Just the two of us. I've missed you terribly."

Abbeline almost laughed. Madison had vanished the moment it became clear she wasn't going to fall back in line. Now, here she was, eager to reclaim proximity.

"I appreciate the thought," Abbeline said, still cordial. "But I'm quite busy preparing for Chance's departure and following up from the show. Perhaps another time."

She ended the call with minimal promises, then sat for a moment, coffee cooling in her hands. Fame, however niche, had shifted the dynamic. She was being reclaimed by the very circles that had once cast her out.

A text from Chance lit her screen:

Have you seen the reviews? You're officially Atlanta's artistic revelation. Told you so. See you at 11 for celebration brunch?

The simple, unadorned message brought a smile. She replied quickly, then headed for the shower—determined to focus on the people who had stayed.

Miranda's gallery buzzed with activity when Abbeline arrived. This crowd was different from opening night: fewer society regulars, more art lovers lingering over each canvas. Miranda greeted her with an enthusiastic hug and led her to the office.

"Three pieces sold during the opening, two more overnight, and inquiries on nearly everything else," she said, barely containing her excitement. "Plus, a commission request from the Westside Development Committee for their new cultural center."

"That's incredible," Abbeline said, her pulse quickening. "I never imagined—"

"I did," Miranda interrupted, beaming. "Authentic work that speaks to people and demonstrates skill? That's the formula."

They mapped out next steps—commission logistics, pricing tiers, potential follow-up exhibitions. With each detail, Abbeline's confidence solidified. This wasn't luck or legacy, this was earned.

After wrapping up, she stepped into the sunlight where Chance was waiting.

"I'd say this calls for a proper celebration," he said, offering his arm. "How does it feel to be Atlanta's newest artistic sensation?"

"Surreal," she admitted, linking arms with him. "Especially watching certain people change their tune."

"Let me guess—Madison called?"

"Madison and a brunch invite from Rebecca Thompson."

Chance let out a low whistle. "Ah, the society pivot. Success forgives all, even renouncing the Hartwell name."

Abbeline's smile faded. "I also saw some online comments. Speculation about my 'family situation.' Someone spotted Randolph and Edward at the show."

Chance squeezed her hand. "Let them guess. You don't owe anyone the real story."

"I know," she said. "But it feels like I've traded one kind of scrutiny for another. I used to be the Hartwell heir expected to perform. Now I'm the artist with the 'fascinating backstory.'"

They reached the quiet restaurant, far from their former society haunts. Seated in a cozy corner booth, Chance looked at her carefully.

"The difference is—now you decide what to share. Your worth isn't tied to appearances."

His words settled deep. This visibility was different. She was navigating it by choice.

As they ate, their conversation turned to logistics—Chance's departure in three days, plans for his first visit back. Their time felt threaded with a quiet urgency, each moment more precious for being finite.

"Have you talked to your dad about the workshop?" Chance asked.

"Briefly. He's signing the lease Thursday." She smiled. "He said watching me find my voice helped him stop hiding in Seattle."

"Like father, like daughter," Chance said. "Both reclaiming your lives."

It was a parallel she hadn't seen, but it felt true. Both of them had defined themselves by absence—until now.

Her phone buzzed again. "Forest Whispers" had just sold—six pieces in total now.

"I didn't expect this," she murmured, showing him the message.

"It's because you stopped performing and started telling the truth," he said simply. "That's what people respond to."

As they left the restaurant, a photographer appeared, snapping shots before they could react.

"Ms. Stuart! Can you comment on your relationship with Randolph Hartwell? Is it true you changed your name to distance yourself from the family?"

Chance stepped in front of her. "No comment. Please respect her privacy."

The photographer tried again. "There's strong public interest—especially after last night."

Abbeline's heart raced. For a split second, old fears stirred. But she remembered Edward's words from the night before, and her voice steadied.

"My art speaks for itself," she said clearly. "That's all the public needs to know. Good day."

Taking Chance's arm, she walked away. Her hands trembled, but inside, something had solidified.

"That was perfectly handled," Chance said once they were in the car. "Firm, professional. Very artist-in-command."

She laughed. "I channeled Miranda."

At Beatrice's, Edward's truck was already in the driveway. Inside, he and Beatrice were mid-conversation about Abigail and Bau's upcoming visit.

"There you are," Beatrice said with a smile. "The *Chronicle* piece has been shared over a thousand times."

"Which means more attention—good and bad," Edward added. "Your mother dealt with that too, before we left Atlanta."

The unexpected link to Abbie—more than genetics, something shared—landed deep. Beatrice must have seen it, because she smoothly changed the subject.

"The kids are excited for the visit," she said. "Especially Abigail. She wants you to teach her to paint."

Plans for decorations and activities followed. For the first time, the idea of "family" didn't feel inherited or aspirational—it felt real.

Later, while Edward and Chance loaded tools into the truck, Beatrice and Abbeline lingered in the kitchen.

"How are you really doing with all this?" Beatrice asked.

"It's a lot," Abbeline admitted. "But it's validating, too. They're responding to my work, not my name."

Beatrice nodded. "That's what resonates—what's real. And it lasts longer than appearances ever will."

"I just hope the focus stays on the art," Abbeline said. "The speculation about grandfather, dad—it's already started."

"You can't control what people find fascinating," Beatrice said. "But you can control what you give them access to."

Abbeline let that sink in. It echoed what Chance had said— what Edward had reminded her of. Maybe that was the real transformation: not just finding her voice, but learning how to protect it.

As Edward and Chance returned, talking easily, Abbeline looked at this new configuration of family—chosen, reclaimed. Whatever scrutiny came, this was the truth she'd fought for.

The exhibition had made her visible. But unlike the old spotlight, this one illuminated what she created. That made all the difference.

***

Four days after the exhibition opening, Abbeline stood in her studio, surrounded by the artifacts of recent success—newspaper clippings, handwritten notes from visitors, a spread-sheet of commission requests growing by the hour. Yet her gaze stayed fixed on the clock above her worktable, its hands moving steadily toward 7:15 PM.

In nine hours, Chance would board a flight to New York, beginning the next chapter of his career—and the longest they'd been apart since they started dating. They had made plans:

weekly calls, monthly visits. But the nearness of his departure pressed against her chest with real, familiar weight.

She picked up her phone, considered calling—and set it down again. They'd agreed to spend the morning separately: he finishing his packing, she working on a time-sensitive commission. Their goodbye would begin with lunch at one, followed by the airport drive. Practical, organized, just as Chance had suggested.

Footsteps on the studio stairs pulled her from her thoughts. Edward appeared in the doorway, a small wooden box in his hands.

"I hope I'm not interrupting," he said, reading her silence with ease.

"Not at all." She set down her palette, grateful for the pause. "I was just... thinking."

"About Chance leaving," Edward said gently, stepping into the studio and placing the box on her table. "Thought you might need something to keep your hands busy today."

Inside the box was a set of woodcarving tools, their polished handles warm to the touch.

"They're beautiful," she murmured, fingers grazing the smooth wood.

"I noticed more texture in your recent work," he said. "These might help with impasto layering."

His attention to her evolving technique, his thoughtfulness in supporting it, brought unexpected emotion to the surface. She blinked fast, the tears about more than the tools.

Edward noticed. "The first separation is always the hardest," he said. "Even when you know it's temporary."

"I keep telling myself it's just distance. Three hours by plane. But it feels... bigger."

"Because the future always holds some unknown," he said. "Plans are comforting. But eventually, they meet real life."

She looked at him, struck by the depth of understanding in his voice—not just because of her and Chance, but because of his own long history with distance.

"How did you do it?" she asked quietly. "Say goodbye to Mom, knowing you'd never see her again?"

Pain flickered in his expression before he carefully composed himself. "That was different," he said. "Final in a way your goodbye with Chance isn't."

"I'm so sorry," she said quickly. "That was thoughtless—"

"No. It's fair." He paused. "What made it bearable was knowing she'd live on in you. That something of us would remain, even if I couldn't be there to see it."

He glanced at her canvas. "It's why I pushed through those first years apart from you. I knew you were out there, even if I couldn't be with you. That gave me purpose."

The perspective settled something in her. Chance's move to New York was a challenge, yes—but not an ending. Not a loss like Edward had faced. Not the twenty-one years they had spent apart.

"Distance is just geography," Edward said. "It can test a bond, but it can't break one built on truth."

She nodded, the words anchoring her again. "Thank you." The gratitude was for more than the tools.

Edward smiled, sensing what remained unspoken. "I should let you get back to work. That commission won't finish itself."

After he left, she returned to the canvas with renewed focus. By the time she needed to clean up for lunch, she'd finished the most difficult section, feeling more grounded than she had all morning.

Chance was waiting at their favorite café, tucked into their usual corner booth with her lavender latte already on the table. He stood as she approached, smiling despite the shadow of goodbye.

"I ordered your usual," he said. "Hope that's okay."

"Perfect," she replied, accepting the light kiss he offered before they sat. "How's the packing?"

"Done. Marco helped, though his version of packing is... creative."

She laughed, picturing the cousin who had become part of their makeshift family during the search for her dad.

"I have something for you," Chance said, pulling a small brown-paper-wrapped package from his bag.

Inside was a framed photograph—not of them, but of her studio. Morning light streamed through the windows, her easel silhouetted against the glow.

"It's where I picture you when we're apart," he said. "Not at parties or Beatrice's. Here. Doing what you love."

It caught her breath—the intimacy of being seen so clearly.

"It's perfect," she said softly.

"I've got a matching one for my desk," he added. "Madison called me sentimental."

"Madison's at your place?"

"Dropped off some documents from my father. She's interning at the firm this summer."

The mention gave her pause, but she didn't linger on it. They both knew Madison's sudden reappearance had more to do with appearances than friendship.

"She asked if you'd be at the airport," he added, amused. "I said our goodbye would be private."

"Thank you," she said, relieved to avoid the pretense.

They moved on to planning—his orientation schedule, temporary housing, which weekend she'd visit. The logistics gave structure to their impending distance, a buffer against rising emotion.

"Dad stopped by this morning," she said. "Brought woodcarving tools. Said he noticed more texture in my pieces."

"Thoughtful," Chance said. "How's the workshop setup going?"

"Faster than expected. He's already started moving things in."

"Good timing," he said. "You'll have your dad close just as I'm getting farther away."

There was no envy in the comment. Just steady support—the kind she'd come to count on.

As lunch ended, the weight of the clock returned.

"We should probably head to the airport," Chance said, glancing at his watch. "Traffic's going to be brutal."

They drove in comfortable silence, hands linked over the console. Each familiar landmark felt like a touchstone. The city faded into airport signage, and the minutes felt both fast and slow.

At the terminal, they parked instead of using the drop-off lane, stretching their final moments. The security line was already long.

"This is it," Chance said, setting down his bag.

"For now," she replied, firm but gentle. "Twenty-three days."

"Approximately five hundred fifty-two hours, but who's counting?"

She smiled through the ache. "Certainly not Mr. Finance."

"I made a spreadsheet," he confessed. "Color-coded. Our visits, calls, flights."

That, more than anything, undid her composure.

"Of course you did," she said, tears brimming.

"Hey," he said, brushing her cheek. "This isn't an ending. It's a new chapter. With... annoying travel logistics."

"I know," she said. "It's just harder in the moment than I expected."

"For me too," he admitted, voice low. "It's the right move—but leaving you feels like stepping away from everything that matters most."

She took his hand. "We'll make it work. One day at a time."

"One visit at a time," he echoed. "One call at a time."

When the moment came, their kiss was long, lingering, full of all the things they couldn't say fast enough. Then, forehead to forehead, they held still in the midst of the airport's motion.

"I love you, Bella," he whispered.

"I love you too," she said, the words steady despite the tears. "Text updates. Every stage."

"Every step," he promised.

With one last squeeze, he turned and disappeared into the crowd. She watched until he was gone.

On the drive back, she cataloged the changes of the past year: from Hartwell heiress to Stuart artist, from fatherless to reconnected, from socially curated relationships to something real. This separation was hard—but it wasn't loss.

At her studio, she set up her laptop for their video call. Beside it, she placed the photograph—her studio in morning light, as Chance saw it. As he saw her.

She returned to her painting, her phone nearby. One by one, texts arrived: boarding, takeoff, in-flight movie choice. Each, a thread between them.

Eventually, when the brushstrokes began to blur and the studio lights felt too bright, she packed up for the night and headed home.

When her phone rang just after 11, she answered immediately.

"Hey," Chance said, the sounds of JFK chaos in the background. "Landed. Fighting for my suitcase."

"How was the flight?"

"Uneventful. Except the guy next to me really wanted to talk about his golf game."

They chatted as he found his ride and headed to his temporary place. Familiar rhythm returned. Steady, easy, them.

"I should unpack and crash," he said eventually. "Video call tomorrow. Earlier this time."

"I'll be waiting."

After they disconnected, Abbeline lay back on her bed, staring at the ceiling. The house felt quieter, but not empty. Her eyes fell on the calendar—her visit, circled in blue.

This separation was a test. But not one they feared. They had chosen this. Believed in this.

Distance was just geography. It could stretch a bond, but not sever it—especially one built on truth.

And if the last year had taught her anything, it was this: truth, once claimed, becomes a foundation that holds.

***

The weekend following Chance's departure brought a welcome distraction as Abbeline helped prepare for Abigail and Bau's visit to Beatrice's home. This would be their second visit, and their first full weekend stay—an important step before their upcoming permanent placement.

Abbeline had poured herself into helping convert the guest room and office into proper children's bedrooms. The walls now featured murals she'd painted throughout the week—a magical forest with hidden animals for ten-year-old Abigail, and a cityscape for seven-year-old Bau, blending his homeland's architecture with Atlanta landmarks.

Saturday morning found her in Abigail's room, perched on a ladder, placing glow-in-the-dark stars in constellation patterns mapped out with Edward.

"Ms. Beatrice says you're an artist," a small voice said from the doorway. "A real one. With galleries and everything."

Abbeline turned to find Abigail standing just inside, wide-eyed, taking in the mural. Though they'd met during the children's first visit, this was their first real moment alone.

"I am," Abbeline said, climbing down. "And you must be Abigail. I'm Abbeline—Beatrice's niece."

The girl nodded, her long braids dotted with colorful beads. "You made this?"

"I did. Do you like it?"

Abigail stepped closer, fingers hovering above the wall. "There are animals hidden in it," she said, spotting a fox among the tree roots. "It's like a secret world."

"Exactly that," Abbeline smiled. "I thought you might like discovering new ones over time."

Abigail looked at her then, a hint of a smile softening her face. "I draw too," she said, a mix of pride and caution. "Ms. Beatrice said you might teach me how to paint properly."

The way she said "Ms. Beatrice"—formal, tentative—reminded Abbeline how carefully these children were navigating connection. After two years in foster care, they were still testing the edges of safety.

"I'd love to teach you," Abbeline said. "I brought supplies if you'd like to try."

Abigail considered the offer. Finally, she nodded. "That would be acceptable."

The formality made Abbeline smile. "Wonderful. Let's go downstairs. Your brother might want to join us."

"Bau doesn't draw," Abigail said as they walked. "He builds. He takes things apart. Sometimes clocks. Then people get mad."

"Maybe we can find him something meant to be taken apart," Abbeline said.

Downstairs, the living room had become an impromptu gathering place. Beatrice and Roderick sat on the couch; Edward in an armchair nearby. To Abbeline's surprise, Randolph was also present, seated by the fireplace—his first social outing since his hospital release.

The conversation paused as Abbeline and Abigail entered. She felt a flicker of tension—Edward and Randolph in the same room—but both men seemed relaxed, or at least civil.

"There you are," Beatrice said warmly. "Did Abbeline show you your mural?"

"Yes," Abigail nodded. "It has secret animals. And stars on the ceiling."

"Constellations," Edward added, smiling. "The real ones you'd see in the night sky."

Abigail studied him. "Are you an artist too?"

"A woodcarver," he said, matching her tone. "I make animals and objects from wood."

"Like the fox?" she asked, surprising both Edward and Abbeline. She'd noticed his carving on Beatrice's mantel.

"Exactly like that," Edward nodded. "You have a good eye."

Just then, Bau burst in, a half-dismantled remote-control car in hand.

"I didn't break it," he announced. "I'm fixing it. Mr. Roderick said I could."

"I did," Roderick confirmed, his expression amused. "It wasn't working. Bau's investigating."

Bau's gaze shifted to Edward's gloves. "Are you a builder?"

"Among other things," Edward said. "I build furniture, repair houses, carve animals."

"Can you teach me to build real stuff?"

"If your guardians approve," Edward replied, glancing to Beatrice and Roderick.

"We'll discuss it," Beatrice said carefully. "For now, Abbeline brought art supplies for everyone."

Abbeline unpacked her tote: paints, brushes, pencils. "Enough for anyone who wants to join."

Bau looked skeptical until she revealed modeling clay. "For sculptors," she said. "You can build in 3D."

For the next hour, the living room became a creative workshop. Abigail sat beside Abbeline, focused and serious as she practiced watercolor techniques. Bau sprawled on the floor nearby, molding the clay into towers and bridges, asking Edward questions about materials and support beams.

Beatrice and Roderick had settled in behind them, sketching the garden. Their interactions—Roderick adjusting the angle of Beatrice's hand, Beatrice gently redirecting Bau when his clay threatened the coffee table—showed a quiet teamwork. They moved fluidly, offering reassurance without smothering, guidance without control. The rhythm of parenting was already forming between them.

Randolph remained apart, watching from his chair. He'd declined to participate, citing his recovery, but his gaze often drifted to Abigail. When she completed her first painting—a bird, rendered with startling precision—he spoke.

"You have quite a talent," he said. "Much like your namesake."

Abigail looked up. "My namesake?"

"You have the same name as my daughter," Randolph said. "Abbeline's mother. We called her Abbie. She had a gift for seeing what others missed."

The room quieted. Randolph rarely mentioned Abbie. His voice had softened.

"Was she good at painting?" Abigail asked.

A.T. Rhode

"Very good. She captured people with just a few strokes." He glanced at Edward. "She would've appreciated your eye for detail."

Abigail digested this, then asked, "Did Ms. Beatrice and Mr. Roderick choose me because I have the same name as her?"

Beatrice stepped in gently. "Oh no, sweetheart, but it felt like a sign—a connection already in place."

Bau looked up. "Like destiny?"

"Like synchronicity," Roderick offered. "Meaningful coincidences."

"Like puzzle pieces fitting together," Abbeline added.

Abigail turned to her. "You're named after her, too."

"Yes," Abbeline nodded. "Though my name is Abbeline, not Abigail."

"And you paint like her. And I paint like both of you. Even though we're not related."

The clarity in her words startled Abbeline.

"Family isn't always about blood," Edward said gently. "Sometimes it's about who sees you—and loves you—as you are."

Bau, uninterested in philosophy, had a practical question. "If we live here forever, does that make you our cousin?"

"I suppose it does," Abbeline said. "Through Beatrice and Roderick."

"And Mr. Edward?"

"I'd be your cousin's father," Edward said. "No exact name for that. But it means we're connected."

Bau just nodded and went back to his clay. Abigail remained still, looking at Randolph.

"Are you part of the family too?" she asked him.

254

The question landed heavy in the room. Randolph's expression shifted, then steadied.

"I am Beatrice's father. Abbeline's grandfather. Which would make me... your grandfather, too, once the adoption is complete."

His voice was measured, but there was something raw in the way he included himself.

Abigail accepted the answer. "Our mom and dad died in a car accident. Ms. Lopez said they didn't want to leave us—they just couldn't stay."

Her words—plain, grief-laced—reverberated. Beatrice touched her shoulder gently. Roderick shifted closer to Bau, who leaned into his side.

"They loved you," Beatrice said. "They would've stayed if they could."

"Like my mom," Abbeline added. "She died when I was born. But she didn't choose to leave either."

Abigail blinked. "You didn't have a mom either?"

"No. But I had Aunt Bea. Like she and Roderick want to be for you and Bau."

"And my dad came back," Abbeline said, gesturing to Edward. "Sometimes family finds its way back."

Bau chose that moment to announce his clay structure was finished. Everyone gathered to see it: a model of Beatrice's house, complete with garden and tiny figures.

Edward studied it. "Great proportions. Strong structure."

Bau beamed. "I want to build buildings that don't fall down."

"We'll look into programs at Georgia Tech," Roderick said. "I know someone there."

The conversation shifted to dinner plans, a possible movie, and Bau's request to visit Edward's workshop.

As the others moved to the kitchen, Abbeline stayed behind with Randolph.

"How are you feeling, Grandfather?"

"Better than predicted. Not as fast as I'd like."

"Recovery takes time," she said.

He studied her face. "Beatrice said your exhibition was extended."

"Three more weeks," she said. "The response surprised me."

"It shouldn't have," he said. "The work speaks for itself."

The simplicity of the compliment caught her.

"Thank you. That means a lot."

They both looked toward Abigail, now cleaning her brushes.

"She reminds me of you," he said. "Serious. Observant."

"She's been through a lot."

"And yet resilient," Randolph said. "As you were. As you've had to be."

There was a pause before he added, "I imagine I haven't made that easier."

Abbeline didn't look away. "Did you mean what you said? At the hospital?"

"Yes," Randolph said. "Facing death didn't teach me anything new—it forced me to admit what I'd long avoided. I was wrong. About your father. About controlling your life. About erasing parts of you."

He met her eyes. "I don't expect forgiveness. Some things can't be undone. But I want you to know—I see it now. I live with it."

She absorbed his words. Not forgiveness—but perhaps the space where it could begin.

"I appreciate the honesty," she said. "It means a lot."

Beatrice called everyone to dinner. Edward and Randolph moved through the same space without friction—not avoiding, but not forced. Coexistence.

At the table, Bau dominated the conversation, bouncing from ideas to inventions. Abigail listened more than she spoke, but her eyes followed every shift. Beatrice and Roderick managed the chaos with calm precision—Beatrice gently steering Bau's enthusiasm, Roderick answering every question like it was the most important one asked.

Later, in the living room, the children chose a movie. Bau campaigned for action; Abigail wanted animals. They settled on both.

Abbeline ended up seated between Edward and Randolph. Unplanned—but somehow fitting.

"They're adjusting well," Edward murmured.

"Beatrice always had a way of creating safety," Randolph said. "Even as a child."

Edward nodded. "Abbeline had that. And now these two will too."

The simple, civil exchange felt monumental. Not friendship. But peace.

As the movie played, Abigail got on the couch and leaned gently against Abbeline's arm.

"Will you show me how to mix colors like in the forest mural?"

"Anytime you want."

"And maybe we can see your gallery?"

"Yes," Abbeline smiled. "Next weekend, if it's okay with Aunt Bea."

As Abigail nodded, eyes on the screen, Abbeline looked around the room—at Edward, at Randolph, at Bau by Edward's feet. Not perfect. Not planned. But family.

Not born of blood or bound by obligation, but shaped by effort. By choice.

As Edward had said: family was who sees you—and loves you—as you are.

And this, for all its imperfections, was theirs.

***

Six weeks after the exhibition opening, Abbeline stood in the bustling terminal of JFK Airport, her heart pounding with anticipation. After weeks of video calls and messages, she was finally here—for her first visit to see Chance in New York. The four weeks since his departure had felt both endless and surprisingly manageable. Daily contact had kept their connection strong, but the physical absence still hummed beneath her routine.

As she moved through the crowded arrival area, her eyes scanned until they found him—standing slightly apart from the crowd, his face lighting up the moment their eyes met. Without hesitation, she broke into a half-run, weaving between travelers until she reached him.

Chance caught her in an embrace that lifted her briefly off the ground, arms wrapped tight around her, dissolving the last remnants of separation. When they kissed, it felt like a conversation resuming mid-sentence—the gap between them vanishing in the certainty of touch.

"You're really here," he murmured into her hair.

"I'm really here," she replied, breathing in the scent of him—coffee, cologne, and something uniquely Chance that no screen could convey.

The ride into Manhattan passed in a blur—catching up, laughing, their hands intertwined in the backseat. Every glance, every casual brush of fingers carried the weight of absence now relieved.

"How's my favorite artist adjusting to her growing fame?" Chance asked, his thumb drawing idle circles on her palm.

"Still surreal," she said. "Miranda called yesterday—there's interest from galleries in Chicago and San Francisco."

"I'm not surprised," he said, pride shining in his eyes. "You're capturing something real—people feel it."

His easy validation had always grounded her. Even more now, spoken from a separate path still firmly tethered to hers.

She studied his profile as the taxi moved through the city— a slightly sharper jawline, a more focused intensity in his eyes. Change, but not distance.

"You look good," she said softly. "New York agrees with you."

"Parts of it do," he said. "The work's demanding in all the ways I hoped. But it's better with you here."

Simple, honest, and exactly what she needed to hear.

Chance had booked her a room at a boutique hotel, not yet ready to host in his still-sparse apartment. The windows framed the skyline in a way that sparked her artist's eye.

"I thought you might want to sketch from here," he said. "The light changes all day."

The thoughtfulness made her heart swell. He still saw her— truly and instinctively—in the way that had made their bond so natural from the start.

They spent the afternoon walking—Chance's essential "first-time New York" tour, a mix of landmarks and local gems. They visited a tiny Italian deli Marco had recommended, strolled through sunlit parks tucked between towers, and wove through crowds speaking every language imaginable.

By evening, they were seated in a cozy jazz club, close enough to the stage to feel each note. The room buzzed with life, but between them, a calm settled.

"I haven't felt this inspired in weeks," Abbeline said, her eyes bright.

"This city reminds me of your recent work," Chance said. "Structure and chaos in harmony. Intention and spontaneity."

She took his hand across the table, her smile soft. He was right. The city's rhythm mirrored her own evolution—reclaiming truth, honoring complexity, letting art hold contradiction.

"I like seeing where you're building your life," she said. "It helps me picture you when we're apart."

"It's not home yet," he said. "But it's getting closer. Especially now."

Later, back in the hotel, they stood at the window watching Manhattan glow beneath them. Chance wrapped his arms around her from behind, his chin resting lightly on her shoulder.

"Four weeks felt like forever," he whispered. "But this... this was worth the wait."

She turned in his embrace, kissing him with all the emotion that weeks of absence had condensed. It wasn't just about missing—it was about returning.

Lying beside him afterward, they talked in the dark. Abbeline shared Edward's upcoming Portland trip—the photographs he hoped to reclaim, the memories he wanted to share.

"That's perfect," Chance murmured, fingers tracing gentle shapes along her arm. "Another piece falling into place."

"He's showing me so much," she said. "Even the hard parts. It helps me understand how he survived those years apart from me. How he held on."

Chance's voice was quiet. "And it's showing you something about us too. About what we can hold."

The parallel clicked into place—Edward's quiet endurance, his long-distance love—and Abbeline felt something loosen inside.

"Twenty-one years he stayed connected without knowing if we'd reunite. We've got visits, texts, calls... it's not the same."

"Exactly," Chance said. "We have so many tools. And we have each other, fully. No secrecy. No distance of the heart."

Perspective settled her. What they had was real—and manageable.

The next day, Chance brought her to his office. He introduced her proudly to his colleagues, who clearly knew all about "the artist from Atlanta." Despite the contrast between their worlds, Abbeline found herself appreciating this window into his.

"They're lucky to have you," she said afterward. "I could see how much they appreciate your work."

"It's pushing me," he admitted. "Beyond family expectations, beyond school. I'm building something that's mine."

Just like she was. Their journeys mirrored each other—separate but deeply in sync.

The rest of the weekend unfolded in balance: museum visits, architectural walks, late-night conversations that picked up where their daily calls had left off. They moved through the city and through each other's stories with ease.

On Sunday, Chance brought Abbeline to his Aunt Margo's house in Queens—a narrow brick home brimming with voices, music, and the smell of garlic bread. Inside, three generations of family were already in full swing, clustered in the kitchen and spilling out onto the back patio.

"Finally!" Margo bellowed as they stepped through the door, arms already outstretched before Chance could get a word in.

"My goodness, you are gorgeous! My nephew's got good eyes!" she exclaimed, pulling Abbeline into a tight hug. "And so tall, too!"

Chance grinned, leaning down to kiss her cheek. "Well, Aunt Margo, everyone is taller than you."

She swatted his cheek playfully. "See how he abuses me? And after all I've done."

Then, turning to Abbeline with mock seriousness: "You're lucky you brought her today, Chance. If not, next Sunday's family dinner was off the table. Capisce?"

Chance clutched his chest dramatically. "You really think I'd do that to you?"

Margo slapped his arm with a smirk. "In a heartbeat."

Abbeline watched it all, smiling. She'd never seen anything like it—and she loved every second.

"Hi, I'm Abbeline," she managed between laughs as Margo pulled her into a firm, fragrant hug. "It's so nice to finally meet you."

"Nice?" Margo scoffed, drawing back just enough to cup Abbeline's face. "Nice is for strangers. You're already family. Come meet your Nonna before she falls asleep on us."

In the living room, Nonna Russo—stoic and regal in her armchair, a hundred years of life resting in her gaze—held court with silent amusement.

Margo approached Nonna, guiding Abbeline gently by the arm. "Ma, this is Chance's girl—from Atlanta."

Nonna squinted, leaning forward. "Chance's squirrel from Alaska?"

Margo sighed. "No, Ma. His girlfriend. Abbeline. From Atlanta."

Nonna's eyes twinkled. "Ahhh... Chance's *gift from Santa*! Very lovely."

Just then, Chance strolled over and kissed her cheek. "Nonna, this is my girlfriend. From Atlanta."

Nonna smiled slyly. "I heard the first time, bello. Just wanted to hear it from you."

Margo threw up her hands. "You know what? You old—" she muttered, shaking her head as she walked away, laughing.

Nonna winked at Abbeline and tugged her in for a warm hug. "I've been waiting to meet you, bambina."

The gathering that followed was exuberant and unapologetically loud. Chance's cousins told stories over one another, his uncles argued about the best subway lines, and a five-year-old niece demanded to see Abbeline's "paint hands." At one point, Margo demanded a group photo and refused to let them leave until Nonna approved the final shot. ("She blinked. Do it again. This is history.")

Through it all, Chance moved easily—carrying plates, refilling drinks, translating family shorthand into quiet asides for Abbeline. Watching him here, surrounded by love, not in expectation but in acceptance, Abbeline felt a rare kind of peace.

Later, as they slipped on their coats to leave, Margo tugged Abbeline aside.

"You brought something steady into his life," she said, her tone lowering just enough to carve sincerity into the space. "I've never seen him shine like this. Don't let work or miles trick you out of it. Some things are worth the flights."

As they stepped back onto the street, Abbeline carried the warmth of that afternoon with her—wrapped in laughter, sauce-stained napkins, and the sense that she'd been welcomed not just as Chance's girlfriend, but as part of the family."

On her final morning, they wandered through Central Park beneath soft spring light. Seated on a bench overlooking the lake, she pulled a small canvas from her bag.

"I made this for your apartment," she said.

It was a painting of Atlanta's skyline at sunset—the view from their favorite post-search spot.

Chance studied it, quiet. "It's beautiful. And perfect. It'll remind me of you."

She nodded. "Not to make you homesick. Just... connected."

He traced the canvas edge. "It reminds me of us. What we're building."

Their exchanged gifts—his photo of her studio, her painting of home—were anchors. Symbols of presence, even across distance.

"This weekend made the separation both easier and harder," she said. "Easier because I can picture your life now. Harder because... I miss it already."

"I get that," he said. "But I wouldn't trade this. Showing you this part of my world—it's important."

As they stood to leave, Chance kissed her. "Four weeks and three days until I'm in Atlanta," he said. "Already cleared my schedule for Portland."

"And I booked my next visit here," she said. "June seventh. It's in red on my calendar."

Their carefully plotted visits, their mutual understanding—it all made sense now. This wasn't an obstacle. It was just another pattern to manage, another part of their shared mosaic.

The ride to the airport carried its inevitable hush, but not dread. At security, their goodbye held none of the fear from their first separation.

"Call when you land," he said, reluctant to let go.

"Always," she promised. One last touch, one last look, then she turned toward the gate.

As the plane lifted off, Abbeline watched the skyline shrink into miniature. This visit had given them exactly what they needed—bond reaffirmed, distance reshaped.

By the time her cab pulled up to her studio that evening, Atlanta felt both familiar and changed.

Edward was building in his new workshop. Beatrice and Roderick preparing to welcome Abigail and Bau. Randolph choosing honesty, step by step. And she—no longer Hartwell heiress, but Stuart artist, daughter, girlfriend, teacher.

Imperfect. Unpredictable. But hers.

She opened her sketchbook. Filled it with impressions: Manhattan's shifting light, Central Park's curved paths, Chance's smile at the deli counter. Lines and color. Memory and motion. Another bridge between their worlds.

This wasn't an ending.

It was the beginning of a rhythm.

Spring blurred into summer. One visit at a time, one canvas at a time.

Forward. Together.

Chapter 10

What Binds Us Together

GOLDEN LIGHT STREAMED through Beatrice's dining room, catching on crystal and casting honeyed patterns across the white tablecloth. Abbeline adjusted the centerpiece—rust chrysanthemums, amber maple leaves—her artist's eye seeking balance. She smoothed a hand over the necklace that had been her mother's, the silver pendant warm against her skin.

The table told a story of transformation: the formal Hartwell china she'd grown up with now mingled with Beatrice's eclectic pieces and Edward's hand-carved wooden serving spoons. Steam rose from the sage stuffing and cranberry compote, both made using her grandmother's worn recipe card.

"That looks incredible," Chance said, appearing behind her. His fingertips traced slow circles at her lower back—a casual intimacy honed over six months apart.

"Though I'd expect nothing less from your artistic touch."

She leaned into his solid warmth. Since his move to New York, moments like this had become treasures.

"Five days together feels like a gift," she murmured. "I was prepared for a Thanksgiving video call if your meetings ran over."

"Miss this?" Chance's hand found hers, his thumb automatically tracing familiar patterns across her palm. "Not a chance." His eyes crinkled with the familiar wordplay.

"Two o'clock was definitely the right call," Beatrice said, emerging from the kitchen with a basket of warm rolls, the air sweet with yeast. Her chestnut hair was pulled into a loose bun, wisps escaping after hours in the kitchen. "Daddy's meds are at six, and the kids do better with routine."

"And we'll need to head to the Bianchi mansion after dessert," Abbeline added, straightening a napkin.

This year's gathering held weight beyond the usual holiday: Edward was now fully settled in Atlanta, and it was the first Thanksgiving since Beatrice and Roderick had finalized the adoption of Abigail and Bau just last week.

"Aunt Bella, is this correct?" Abigail called from the sideboard, arranging hand-carved wooden napkin rings shaped like forest animals—Edward's gift to his new niece and nephew. At eleven, she carried herself with quiet poise.

Abbeline crossed to her, recognizing the posture of focused attention she herself assumed when creating.

"Perfect," she said. "You've got a remarkable eye for detail."

Abigail gave her a warm smile, the kind that bloomed slowly but reached all the way to her eyes.

The doorbell rang, followed by the thunder of small footsteps.

"I'll get it!" Bau shouted, abandoning his Lincoln Logs in a blur of seven-year-old energy.

"Walk, please!" Roderick's voice carried from the kitchen, calm but firm. A three-tap rhythm on the doorframe preceded his appearance with a gravy boat, his glasses fogged from steam.

Edward's baritone came from the entryway, followed by Bau's excited chattering.

"Uncle Edward! Did you bring your tools? Can we work on the birdhouse after dinner? I drew new plans!"

"Let the man through, buddy," Chance said, tussling his hair with a grin.

Edward entered with wine in one hand and flowers in the other. In his early fifties, he moved with fluid alertness—military precision softened by civilian life. His gaze swept the room: doors, windows, people—before he smiled, creating a map of familiar laugh lines.

"Happy Thanksgiving," he said.

Abbeline stepped into his embrace, breathing in cedar and coffee. After thirteen months rebuilding their relationship, these moments still carried the air of miracle.

"Good to see you, Mr. Stuart," Chance said, posture straightening as he extended a hand. Though Edward had long encouraged him to use his first name, Chance maintained the habit—a respectful nod to his upbringing.

"Chance," Edward replied with a brief smile. "Good to have you home."

He handed the bouquet to Beatrice, who emerged wiping flour from her hands.

"Happy Thanksgiving, sis," he said, hugging her.

"Thanks, bro," she replied, burying her nose in the flowers.

The words hit Abbeline with quiet force. Not just father and daughter reconnecting—family, long fractured, was knitting itself together again.

Roderick followed with appetizers. "The master carver has arrived just in time," he said to Edward. "Turkey's resting."

Edward and Roderick fell into easy conversation: commissions, courtroom wins, knife-sharpening techniques. Their rapport was natural, built from years of shared concern for the women they loved.

Twenty minutes later, the doorbell rang again. Silence fell. Even Bau paused. Beatrice squared her shoulders—a subtle bracing Abbeline recognized from years of managing Randolph—and opened the door.

"Thank you for coming, Daddy," she said, her childhood term of endearment slipping through.

Randolph stepped in—silver-haired, meticulously dress-ed—the bottle of scotch in his hand catching the light off his signet ring. He looked thinner, older; his presence still precise, yet diminished.

"Grandfather," Abbeline said, rising. Their relationship had been cautiously rebuilding in recent months.

"Abbeline," he answered. His voice carried more weight today—a telltale sign of emotional significance. His gaze moved to Edward, who stood in acknowledgment. Something flick-ered—discomfort, confusion, maybe shame—then vanished behind a reflexive ring adjustment.

"Randolph," Edward said, extending a hand. "Good to see you up and about. How's the recovery?"

Randolph hesitated, thrown by the genuine courtesy. Then he accepted the handshake with polished control.

"Making progress," he said stiffly.

Beatrice guided them toward the table. "Everything's ready," she said, quickly tucking away a stack of recipes and notes.

"Before we begin," Roderick said, removing his glasses, "we wanted to thank you all. One week ago today, we officially became Abigail and Bau's parents. Having our family together means everything."

"To family," Edward said, lifting his glass.

"To family," echoed around the table.

Dishes passed. Conversation resumed—Edward's commissions, Abbeline's Seattle exhibition, Chance's transfer to Atlanta. But Abbeline noticed Randolph's attention never strayed far from Edward.

Edward spoke with warmth, recounting Thanksgivings with friends and stories from his wilderness program. He never mentioned the years of absence or resentment—only lessons, connections, and healing.

"It's remarkable work you did with those young men," Roderick said.

"They taught me as much as I taught them," Edward replied. "Helping others gives healing its shape."

A flicker of tension crossed Randolph's face. He lowered his fork and twisted his ring with a tight grip.

Conversation moved on—gallery news, plans for Sunday dinner—but Randolph's responses grew shorter. His scrutiny of Edward intensified, edged with something unspoken.

When Edward praised Abbeline's artwork and linked it to her mother's talent, the tension snapped.

Randolph's knife scraped his plate harshly. Heat crawled up his neck in blotchy patches.

Then—water spilled. A slow stain spread across the white cloth.

"Grandfather?" Abbeline asked. "Are you okay?"

"Fine," he said, voice thin. "Just... a moment of weakness."

Edward observed, then offered gently, "Perhaps some air?"

A pause. Then Randolph nodded.

"I'll just step outside briefly."

Beatrice made to follow, but Edward touched her arm.

"Let me."

———

Outside, the air was crisp, the scent of dry leaves and woodsmoke mingling. Randolph stood at the railing, hands braced.

"It can be overwhelming," Edward said quietly. "Seeing something you thought lost return in a new shape."

"You've waited years to see me like this," Randolph said, voice rough. "Diminished. Dependent."

"No," Edward replied. "That was never what I wanted."

"Then what?" The old force surged in Randolph. "After everything I took from you—your daughter, your family—what could you want but to see me suffer?"

"Peace," Edward said. "For all of us."

Randolph stared. "I don't understand you, Stuart. Never have."

"I was angry," Edward admitted. "Justified. But it only hurt me. I realized moving forward didn't mean forgetting—it meant not letting it define me. Forgiveness wasn't for you. It was for me."

The truth hit Randolph hard. He looked toward the window, where family laughter drifted faintly.

"I tried to destroy all this," he said. "Deliberately. I abandoned Abbie when she needed me most."

Edward didn't contradict him. He simply nodded.

"Yes. You did."

Randolph's voice broke. "What kind of father does that?"

"A human one," Edward said. "Who made a terrible mistake and has been punishing himself ever since."

Randolph swayed slightly, the railing his anchor.

"How can you sit across from me like that?"

"By remembering what I have now. Abbeline. My work. A family healing. The past is unchangeable. The present isn't."

Inside, Abbeline rose, sensing something deeper unfolding. She stepped onto the porch.

Randolph tried to compose himself, but his eyes were red.

"Grandfather?" she asked gently. "Are you all right?"

"No," he said honestly. "I'm not all right. I look at that family and all I see is how close I came to destroying it."

His words were raw, stripped of performance.

"I don't know how to make it right," he added. "But I needed to say it. To both of you. I was wrong."

Abbeline touched the railing, her fingers tracing faint patterns.

"I don't know if forgiveness is possible," she said. "But healing is. It's already happening."

Randolph nodded. After a moment, Edward spoke.

"We should rejoin the others. Dessert's a sacred tradition."

The line broke the heaviness just enough. Randolph nodded again.

As they stepped inside, the atmosphere had shifted—nothing said, but something understood. Beatrice touched her father's shoulder as he sat. Roderick added a pillow behind his back.

"Who wants pie?" Bau announced. "Two kinds!"

"That's right," Chance said. "And we need room for Nonna's tiramisu."

As dessert was served, Randolph grew quiet—but not withdrawn. When Abigail offered extra whipped cream, he accepted with a tired but genuine smile.

By five-thirty, the front hall filled with coats, pie containers, and last hugs. Edward was gathering his things, and Randolph stood with his assistant by the door, coat already on.

Abbeline joined him, sensing the shift in his posture—not quite ease, but something close to it.

"Take care of yourself, Grandfather," she said quietly, meaning far more than the phrase.

"And you as well," he replied, meeting her gaze without the evasiveness of old. "We'll speak again soon."

Moments later, he stepped outside with his assistant, the door closing gently behind them.

Abigail approached with solemn dignity. "When will you teach me how to draw better?"

"Next Saturday," Abbeline promised. "All afternoon, if you like."

Satisfied, Abigail nodded. Bau's goodbye was less restrained—a flying hug.

"Bring the special foam core next time!"

"I won't forget," Chance promised.

Outside, afternoon was slipping quietly into evening. As Chance loaded the car, Abbeline stood a moment longer.

"Ready for round two?" Chance asked, opening her door.

"Absolutely," she said, settling in. "Though I may fall into a food coma before dessert."

They pulled away, heading toward Marco's welcome and Nonna's tiramisu, the day's truths still echoing quietly in their wake.

***

One and a half years after Thanksgiving

The Atlanta Arts District pulsed with summer energy as golden hour cast everything in honeyed light. Crowds drifted between galleries for the seasonal exhibition openings, their conversations creating a gentle murmur that rose and fell like waves. Outside Meridian Gallery, a banner stretched across the entrance: *SECRETS IN SEPIA: NEW WORKS BY ABBELINE STUART.* Spotlights illuminated the elegant lettering, drawing admiring glances from passersby who paused to study the promotional images—landscapes and portraits rendered in Abbeline's signature blend of precision and emotional depth.

Inside, the space buzzed with anticipation. The crisp scent of fresh paint and cut flowers mingled with designer perfume, while soft jazz filled the room with understated elegance. Champagne glasses clinked as servers circulated, their trays catching the light like constellations in motion.

Abbeline stood near the entrance in a midnight blue dress that echoed the sophistication of the evening. Her natural curls fell past her shoulders, her mother's silver necklace catching the light and casting tiny prisms across her collarbone. Her fingers traced faint patterns on her dress, a nervous habit softened into tenderness over time.

"The Seattle series represents a turning point," she explained to an art critic, her voice steady despite the nervous current beneath it. "Finding my father after twenty-one years reshaped my understanding of presence and absence. The landscapes explore that duality—what remains visible even when physically distant."

The critic nodded, clearly intrigued. "Your use of negative space is especially effective. One feels the presence in the void. And this impasto work—texture in the foreground, ethereality in the distance—that's quite compelling."

"Exactly what I was aiming for," Abbeline said, warmed by the insight.

As the critic moved on, she checked her phone discreetly. Still no message from Chance. His text that morning had been apologetic but final: an unavoidable meeting with Karrington's biggest client, no way to reschedule. She returned the phone to her clutch, lifting her chin with a practiced poise.

"He'll be devastated to miss this," she reminded herself. They'd endured two years of distance: video calls, alternating visits, and steadfast emotional presence. One missed opening didn't erase that. Still, her eyes drifted to the door from time to time, holding space for what felt impossible.

"The attendance is impressive," Miranda Wu said, appearing at her side with two flutes of champagne. Her sleek bob swung as she surveyed the room. "We've already sold three pieces. *The Journal's* columnist just arrived." She handed

Abbeline a glass. "You've grown so much since your first show."

"Thank you," Abbeline replied, the cool glass steadying her hands.

"This work feels more cohesive. Intentional."

"More confident," Miranda said knowingly. "Success suits you."

Before she could respond, Edward stepped into the gallery, elegant in a navy suit that framed the silver at his temples. His eyes swept the space in that practiced left-right scan, a residual habit from years in the field. He moved with composed ease, nodding to patrons as he approached.

Over the past year, Edward had firmly settled in Atlanta, his workshop producing commissioned pieces for clients across the Southeast. Tonight, his pride radiated as he examined each painting before reaching her.

"These are extraordinary, Bella," he said, embracing her. The familiar scent of cedar and coffee enveloped her.

"The evolution is clear."

"Thanks, Dad," she replied—the word settled now, yet always sacred. "I worried about the balance: landscapes, abstracts."

"They complement each other," he said. "Precision beside intuition, like reflections from different angles of the same journey."

His gaze shifted to *Reclaimed*—a portrait of himself with the faint silhouette of baby Abbeline layered behind him. It had marked their reunion and now stood as the emotional center-piece of her career.

"You've created something only you could make," he said. "Not your mother. Not me. Just you, and it's extraordinary."

The words brought unexpected tears to her eyes. Though Edward and Beatrice often spoke of her resemblance to Abbie, this wasn't comparison—it was affirmation. He saw her not as a reflection of the past but as an artist in her own right.

As more guests arrived—critics, collectors, Atlanta's social circle—Abbeline found herself explaining technique, inspiration, and process. Some guests leaned close to admire her brushwork; others took in entire canvases from across the room, drawn by the emotional resonance.

"I think I see Randolph," Edward said, his voice low.

She followed his gaze to the entrance. Her grandfather stood just inside, cane in hand. At seventy-seven, his movements were measured, yet still commanding. His tailored gray suit fit perfectly, though his grip on the ebony cane betrayed the effort beneath the elegance. His signet ring glinted as he unconsciously turned it—three slow, clockwise rotations.

"He came," she murmured, a small smile forming as she watched him step inside. Randolph rarely appeared in public now.

"Of course he did," Edward said, his tone free of bitterness. "He wouldn't miss this."

It was simple, but profoundly generous. Despite their complicated history, the two men had forged a truce: a peace crafted not from affection, but from mutual commitment to her.

"I should greet him," she said, passing her glass to Edward.

She crossed the gallery, accepting congratulations with grace. The creak of hardwood beneath her heels grounded her as she approached Randolph, noting the slight tremor in his hand.

"Glad you could make it, Grandfather," she greeted, embracing him warmly. His cologne—leather and sandalwood—triggered childhood memories of library shelves and polished desks.

"Wouldn't miss it," he said, his voice lighter than usual.

He looked at her—truly looked—not at the image he once tried to mold, but at the woman she'd become.

"The work is remarkable," he said. "Your mother's talent, your father's clarity. A powerful combination."

It still surprised her, these easy acknowledgments. Since Thanksgiving, Randolph had begun speaking openly about Abbie, as though memory itself were a kind of atonement.

"Let me show you the new pieces," she offered, taking his arm gently.

They walked slowly. She explained techniques and meaning, and he listened with real attention. At *Forest Whispers*, inspired by the path to Edward's cabin, he paused.

"There's a journey here," he murmured. "That light—it draws the viewer forward."

"That's exactly what I hoped," she replied.

Before they could continue, Beatrice arrived with Abigail and Bau. At thirteen and nine, they'd grown fully into their family—their nervous beginnings replaced by confidence.

"Hi, Grandfather," the kids said in unison.

Beatrice smiled at her father as Randolph returned their greeting with a warm, genuine smile.

"Aunt Bella!" Bau burst out. "The *Washington Post* critic was staring at your forest painting for like ten whole minutes!"

"Inside voice," Roderick reminded, smiling as he walked up to the group.

"Good news about the critic," Abbeline said, ruffling Bau's hair.

Abigail stood beside her mother with quiet poise, sketchbook in hand. "The forest series is beautiful," she said. "Especially the contrast. The shadows have so much... depth."

Abbeline smiled. "Thank you. That means a lot coming from a fellow artist."

Around them, the gallery's noise softened, forming a small bubble of closeness. Edward and Abigail talked technique, Randolph and Bau discussed bridge designs, Beatrice and Roderick hovered nearby. The fragile healing begun at Thanksgiving had deepened into something real.

Still, her gaze drifted to the door. Chance's absence left a quiet space.

Beatrice noticed. Linking arms with her, she said gently, "He called while we were parking. Said to tell you he's devastated to miss it, and that you have his heart, even when he's not here."

Abbeline smiled. "Thank you. I just wish he could see this—all of it."

"He will," Beatrice said. "If not tonight, then soon."

The evening continued, steady and warm. Miranda circled with practiced grace. Red dots marked seven sold pieces, and quiet interest built around several more.

"A tremendous success," Miranda said, appearing beside her. "The Seattle pieces are striking a chord. People are connecting with the emotion beneath the landscapes."

Abbeline nodded. The journey to find Edward had transformed her art as deeply as her life. Presence and absence were no longer abstract concepts—they were lived experiences.

A ripple near the door drew her attention. The crowd parted.

And then he was there.

Chance—rumpled from travel, suit creased, hair tousled. Her heart lifted at the sight of him.

He scanned the room, then found her. That smile—the one that never failed to undo her—broke across his face.

He moved toward her with purpose, apology, and relief in every step. When he reached her, he swept her into an embrace, lifting her gently off her feet.

"I'm so sorry," he murmured into her hair. "Meeting ran over. Flight delay. Traffic. I didn't think I'd make it."

"You're here now," she said, wrapping her arms around his neck.

When he set her down, his hands lingered at her waist. "Show me everything," he said. He smiled and offered a quick wave to the gathered family—Edward, Beatrice, Roderick, the kids—before turning back to her. "I want to see it all through your eyes."

They moved through the gallery hand in hand, pausing at each piece. He asked insightful questions, remembered details from past visits. His thumb traced familiar circles on her palm, a quiet rhythm of reassurance.

Before *Reclaimed*, he paused. "This one still moves me every time."

"It was the turning point," she said. "Everything after this felt honest."

The evening wore on. Fifteen pieces sold. Family gathered near the refreshment table, forming their own orbit within the crowd.

"I think this calls for a toast," Edward said, raising his glass. "To Abbeline—whose courage and talent inspire us all."

"To Abbeline," echoed around the room.

A soft smile spread across Abbeline's face as she lifted her glass—grateful, and just a little overwhelmed.

As the last guests trickled out, Chance helped pack up. Across the gallery, he chatted easily with Edward, two anchors in her life, their quiet understanding growing.

Beatrice approached, Abigail beside her. "From that day in the attic to this," she said.

"I couldn't have imagined any of it," Abbeline replied.

"That's what truth does," Beatrice said. "It opens doors we never knew were there."

Later, with the gallery dark behind them, Chance pulled her close against the cool night air.

City lights shimmered in puddles from an earlier rain.

"I was thinking," he said. "That review clause in my contract—it's up in six months."

She turned toward him. "And?"

"There's an opening in Atlanta. Smaller team, but promising. I've already requested the transfer."

She blinked. "You're serious?"

He nodded. "Distance worked. But I want the ordinary days too—morning coffee, grocery runs. You."

"What about your career?"

"There are opportunities everywhere. But you're here. This is where your work is thriving. Your family. And maybe... our home?"

Her heart caught on the quiet proposal nestled in those words.

"I want that," she said, her arms looping around him. "More than I can say."

His smile lit up his whole face. Their kiss was a quiet promise.

As they walked to his car, Abbeline looked back once more at the darkened gallery.

Each canvas had been a step—from hiding to truth.

And in that truth, she'd found not just herself, but the shape of a future she hadn't dared imagine.

***

Six months after the gallery opening

Chance Bianchi studied his reflection in the hotel mirror as golden morning light filtered through half-drawn curtains. The sunrise painted the Atlanta skyline in amber hues—a view he'd specifically requested. His fingers trembled as he adjusted his tie for the third time.

Stepping back, he rubbed the stubble on his jaw—deliberately left unshaven to temper the formality of his crisp blue shirt and tailored slacks. On the nightstand, his phone lit up again.

Marco: *Don't chicken out, cuz. She's gonna say yes.*

Chance: *Not nervous about her answer. Just want to do this right.*

That was the truth. After two and a half years navigating love across cities and time zones, he had no doubts about

Abbeline. What mattered now was honoring their journey—and the family that shaped it.

The velvet ring box sat on the bed. He picked it up, its weight familiar after weeks of carrying it, waiting for the right moment. Inside, the diamond sat in a setting designed to reflect Abbeline's painting style—gold curves that flowed like brushstrokes.

His phone buzzed again—Marco, this time sending a GIF of a man hyperventilating into a paper bag. Chance chuckled. "Not quite," he murmured, slipping the box into his jacket pocket. He checked his watch: 7:30 AM. Edward would be expecting him soon.

The elevator ride to the lobby provided sixteen floors of second-guessing. Should he have worn the gray jacket? Was the tie too much? Would Edward see through his calm exterior?

Traffic cooperated for once. He passed galleries and studios that had become familiar, reminders of the life Abbeline had built—and that he hoped to join.

Edward's workshop occupied a renovated brick warehouse. Chance pulled in beside the familiar truck and sat for a moment. Through the windows, Edward moved with measured grace around a lathe.

His phone buzzed one last time before he silenced it:

Marco: *Remember what Nonna says—speak from your heart, not your head. Love you, cuz.*

The message steadied him. Drawing a breath, Chance stepped out into the earthy scent of spring and approached the door.

The moment he stepped inside, the scent of cedar and pine enveloped him. Dust motes swirled in shafts of light. The hum of machinery and the occasional clatter of tools created a rhythm that felt almost meditative.

Edward looked up. His eyes scanned the room instinctively before landing on Chance. He smiled, setting aside his tools with the same care he brought to everything he did.

"Chance," he said, wiping his hands. "Right on time."

"Morning, Mr. Stuart," Chance replied. The respectful title remained a habit. He wiped his palms on his trousers, the ring box pressing like a stone against his side.

Edward motioned toward the office. "Coffee's fresh."

They entered the small glass-walled room. It smelled of wood and coffee, its walls lined with photos—many of Abbeline, in both gallery finery and casual moments.

Edward poured two mugs, handing one to Chance before settling into his chair. "I assume this isn't just a social visit."

Chance nodded, grateful for Edward's directness. "No, sir. I'd like to talk to you about something important."

Edward's expression was neutral but attentive. "I'm listening."

Chance took a breath. All the rehearsed speeches fell away. What remained was truth.

"I love Abbeline," he began. "I think I've loved her since the day I saw her sketching at that fundraiser instead of networking. I'm going to ask her to marry me, and I wanted you to know first."

Edward studied him, expression unreadable. The clock ticked. A truck rumbled past.

"That's a significant commitment," Edward said eventually. "Especially with your current living arrangements."

"I've accepted a transfer to Karrington's Atlanta office," Chance replied. "Starting next month. I'll be heading their new sustainable investment division."

"She doesn't know yet?"

"Not yet. I wanted to be sure before telling her."

Edward nodded slowly. Chance watched his hands—strong, calloused, always precise—wrap around his mug.

"I don't want to just visit her life anymore," Chance added. "I want to build one with her."

Sunlight slanted through the windows, catching floating sawdust like stars.

Edward smiled faintly. "You've thought this through."

"Very carefully," Chance said. "Abbeline is... she's home."

Something in Edward's expression shifted—recognition, maybe. He rose and retrieved a framed photo from the shelf: his wedding day with Abbie.

"When I married her," he said quietly, "we had nothing but love. Minimal family support. No promises life would be fair. But we were certain."

He set the photo between them. Abbie's joy-filled face smiled from the frame.

"Are you certain, Chance?" Edward asked. "About loving her through everything—supporting her career, respecting her independence, continuing to grow together even when it gets hard?"

"I am," Chance said. "I've seen her rebuild everything—her name, her career, her family. And every part of it has made me want to be part of what comes next."

Edward considered that, then nodded. "Then you have my blessing. And my respect."

Relief swept over Chance like cool water. He drew out the velvet box and opened it.

"I had it designed to reflect her painting style," he said. "Flowing, distinctive."

Edward examined it without touching. "She'll see the thought behind it. It's perfect."

"Like the woman herself," Chance said, closing the box.

Edward rose and extended a hand—then pulled him into a brief, firm hug instead. The scent of wood and varnish grounded the moment.

"Welcome to the family," Edward said. "Though I think you've been part of it for some time."

Outside, Chance leaned against his car and exhaled. The sun had climbed higher, warming the metal beneath his hands. A delivery truck passed, its driver offering a casual nod.

"One down," Chance murmured. He checked his watch—10:15. Forty-five minutes until meeting Beatrice and Roderick.

A message buzzed from Marco:

Marco: *Mission accomplished or funeral arrangements needed?*

Chance: *Still breathing. Edward's blessing secured. Proceeding to phase two.*

Marco: *Of course the military guy approved. Strategic operations. Good luck with the lawyer—she'll be the real interrogation.*

Beatrice's home greeted him with fresh coffee and the scent of roses drifting through open windows. It was the opposite of Edward's world—softened by family life and blooming with warmth.

"You're exactly three minutes early," Beatrice said with a half-smile, ushering him in. Dressed in jeans and a blue sweater, she still carried the posture of a courtroom closer. "Roderick's just made coffee."

The hallway gleamed with lemon oil polish and quiet order. Roderick met him in the kitchen, French press in hand.

"Twenty seconds left," he said, focused on the timer.

Beatrice arched a brow. "You're wound tight this morning."

"Is it that obvious?" Chance asked, setting his keys down.

Beatrice arched a brow. "Power tie. Polished shoes. You called last night to meet both of us. We've been expecting this."

Roderick poured coffee and handed him a mug. "Especially after that transfer news last month."

"You knew?" Beatrice asked

"I may have helped with some of the contractual work," Roderick admitted.

Chance chuckled. "Hope that's not a conflict of interest."

"On the contrary," Roderick said, motioning toward the living room. "It's all been quite promising."

They settled in. The garden outside was alive with color, the windows framing a peaceful scene. Beatrice and Roderick took the couch. Their attention was full and expectant.

Beatrice set her mug down. "Abbeline makes her own decisions—we all know that. But your perspective is important to us."

"I'm not asking permission," Chance said. "But I do value your opinions. You've both stood by her through everything."

Beatrice nodded. "What about timing? Her career is accelerating—Seattle, possibly New York."

"We've talked about that a lot," Chance replied. "I want to support her, not slow her down."

"Good answer," Beatrice said, her expression softening.

"When?" Roderick asked, removing his glasses and polishing them.

"Tomorrow evening. At the coffee house where we first really talked."

"She'll like that," Beatrice said. She and Roderick exchanged a glance of approval.

Chance glanced toward the fridge, where Abigail's art and Bau's schematics covered the surface. "How are they adjusting to school?"

"Very well," Roderick said, pride easing into his tone. "Abigail's on track for advanced placement in art. Bau's been invited to the robotics team."

"They'll be thrilled," Beatrice added. "Abigail's been asking when you and Abbeline would 'make things official.'"

As they chatted, Beatrice stepped out to take a call. Roderick leaned in.

"One more thing," he said quietly. "Consider visiting Randolph."

Chance hesitated.

"He's not well," Roderick added. "Beatrice hasn't told Abbeline the full picture to spare her worry. But I think Randolph would want to be included."

Chance nodded slowly. "I'll go. Before dinner."

Roderick's approving nod closed the conversation. Beatrice returned, and as Chance prepared to leave, she hugged him.

"You've been good for her," she said. "More than I ever expected. You've been family since the day you helped clean her studio. This just makes it official."

He nodded, still absorbing the quiet weight of her words. Then he turned toward the final visit of the day.

The Hartwell mansion stood in dignified stillness under the afternoon sun, its white columns and manicured lawn casting long shadows. Chance's car crunched up the gravel drive as magnolia blossoms perfumed the air—familiar and oddly comforting.

Martha opened the door with a warm smile. "Mr. Bianchi. A pleasant surprise."

"I was hoping to speak with Mr. Hartwell." He smiled back.

"He's in the solarium. Been reading since breakfast—it's a good day."

She led him through halls lined with new additions: candid family photos, including one of Abbeline and Edward at her gallery opening. The quiet visual shift told its own story— Randolph's rigidity softening over time.

In the solarium, Randolph sat in a leather chair, a book open on his lap, tea cooling beside him. His skin looked thinner, his frame more frail. But his eyes remained sharp.

"Mr. Bianchi," he said, setting the book aside. "Unexpected."

"Apologies for the unannounced visit," Chance said. "I wanted to speak with you, if you have a few minutes."

Randolph gestured to the opposite chair. "About my granddaughter, I presume?"

"Yes, sir. I plan to ask Abbeline to marry me. I wanted you to hear it from me."

Randolph's fingers moved to his signet ring. "And you're here for my blessing?"

"I'm here because you matter to her," Chance said. "Whatever your past, you're part of her life. I thought it was right to tell you."

Randolph nodded, gaze drifting to the garden. "I never gave Edward that opportunity. Judged him by what I feared, not who he was. That mistake cost me dearly."

Chance remained quiet, letting the moment hold.

"I've watched you," Randolph continued. "Seen how you supported her—through the search, the distance, her career. I see in you what I failed to see in Edward."

Then, softer: "You have my blessing. And my respect."

Chance swallowed, surprised by the depth of the response. "Thank you. That means a great deal."

Randolph leaned back, the chair creaking under his slight frame. "When will you propose?"

"Tomorrow evening."

"She'll appreciate something meaningful over something grand." He reached into a drawer and retrieved a small box. "This belonged to my grandmother. Intended for Abbie. It should be Abbeline's now."

Inside was a delicate antique comb—silver filigree, inlaid with pearls and emeralds.

"It's beautiful," Chance said. "She'll treasure it."

"You needn't tell her it came from me," Randolph added.

"With respect," Chance replied, "I think she'd want to know. Truth is the standard in this family now."

Randolph met his gaze and gave a quiet nod. "Well said. Bring her by after the engagement. If I'm strong enough, I'd like to share the piece's story myself."

Outside, the light had softened. Chance left with the heirloom safely stored in his car—and a deeper understanding of the man who had once stood between Edward and Abbie, now offering something that resembled peace.

Back at Beatrice's, the living room smelled of paint, glue, and cookies. Abigail was finishing a watercolor; Bau was mid-cityscape with foam and tape.

"Uncle Chance!" Bau launched into a hug. "Did you bring the special foam core?"

"In the car," Chance said. "But first, I need to tell you both something."

Abigail looked up, already smiling. "The proposal."

"How do you know these things?"

"You're not subtle. And Mom's been humming all morning."

"What proposal?" Bau asked, climbing beside him.

"I'm asking Aunt Bella to marry me."

Bau's eyes widened. "Like, with a ring? Like in movies?"

"Exactly like that."

"So you'll live here? Help with science projects?"

Chance laughed. "Yes—both."

"He's already said yes," Abigail said, turning back to her painting. "You haven't even asked her yet."

"I'm confident she'll say yes too."

"She will," Abigail said simply. "She paints better after your calls."

The remark hit him with unexpected force. He managed a quiet, "Thank you."

"I wanted to tell you first," he added. "You're important to her—so you're important to me."

"So you'll be our uncle for real?" Bau asked.

"That's right."

"She'll say yes," Abigail said again. Then stood. "I'm making something for her."

"Me too!" Bau cried, scattering glitter and tape as he began building.

Beatrice appeared in the doorway, arms crossed, smiling. "Looks like you've engaged the creative team."

Chance nodded. "More than I expected. Especially from Randolph."

Her brow rose. "Really?"

"He's changed. More than I realized."

"Pain and regret are powerful teachers," she said. "Some of us just take longer to learn."

Later, Abigail handed him a sketch—two hands entwined, one with a ring. "For when she says yes."

"It's beautiful," Chance said, genuinely moved.

Bau followed with a silver-covered box, blueprints scrawled on the lid. "For the ring. It's the exact size."

Chance accepted both gifts with care, struck by the thoughtfulness of it all. These children—so fully part of Abbeline's life—had claimed him as family too.

***

Abbeline stood in front of her mirror, fluffing her light brown curls threaded with natural blonde highlights, her fingers restless with nerves. Afternoon light streamed through the window, catching her hair in a halo that still startled her—even three years into embracing her curls. The emerald dress hugged her gently, its color echoing the stone in her mother's silver necklace resting against her collarbone.

"Why am I so nervous?" she murmured. "It's just dinner," she told herself. "With Chance."

But something felt different. Maybe it was how specific he'd been about the time. Or that he'd chosen the Buckhead Coffee House—the place where their real connection had begun.

A text from Beatrice chimed: *Have a wonderful evening. Call me tomorrow.*

Abbeline replied: *Thanks,* the simplicity of her response at odds with the growing suspicion that something important was coming.

Outside, early summer settled over Atlanta in a warm hush. She drove with the windows cracked, the scent of honeysuckle and magnolia drifting in. The coffee house looked the same—weathered brick, copper sign aged with character, like their relationship. But a "Closed for Private Event" sign in the window gave her pause.

The door was unlocked. Inside, candles flickered on every table, casting golden light. The scent of coffee mingled with roses and lilies. And in the center stood Chance, hands clasped in front of him, dressed in a navy suit that brought out the blue in his eyes.

"What's all this?" she asked, stepping inside.

"I wanted to recreate our beginning," he said, voice steady though his flushed neck betrayed his nerves. "Do you remember that night?"

"Of course." She moved closer. "The fundraiser. You found me sketching the bartender instead of working the room."

"You looked so embarrassed," he said with a smile. "Tried to hide your sketchbook."

"I thought you'd report me to Grandfather," she laughed. "Instead, you asked about my technique."

"Best decision I ever made."

She noticed the walls then—lined with photographs in chronological order. She moved to the first one: their first selfie. Her hair still straightened, her smile hesitant beside Chance's easy grin.

"What is all this?" she whispered.

"Our story," he said, joining her.

The images captured it all—coffee meetings, gallery openings, family dinners, their search for Edward. In each, her smile grew more open, her posture more sure. Her natural curls returned. Her confidence, too.

"I didn't know some of these existed," she said, pausing at a photo of her asleep on his shoulder during the flight back from Seattle.

"I enlisted a stranger," Chance chuckled. "Beatrice and Marco supplied the rest."

The final photo showed them at her gallery opening, standing before *Reclaimed*. Beside it, an empty frame.

"This one?" she asked.

"For tonight," he said. "For what comes next."

He took her hand and led her to a small table in the center of the room—where they'd sat three years ago. Champagne and two flutes waited.

"Do you remember what we talked about that night?" he asked, voice low, pulling out her chair.

"Art," she said. "And truth."

"You told me your sketches revealed what people hid. That's what drew me to you. You didn't just look—you saw."

She smiled. "You didn't even flinch when I showed you your sketch."

"Because you saw me. Not the Bianchi heir. Not the finance prodigy. Just a guy, nervous about his speech, wondering if any of it mattered."

He took both her hands. His warmth calmed her.

"That night changed me," he said. "I started finding excuses to see you. Because for the first time, I wasn't performing—I was just being."

Her breath caught. The private setting. The photo wall. Beatrice's text.

"Chance—"

"When you started discovering who you really were, I saw the real you, too. Not just the parts you shared, but everything— the artist, the daughter, the woman becoming herself."

He released one hand and reached into his pocket, kneeling beside her with a velvet box in his palm.

"These past three years—watching you reclaim your name, your family, your art—it only deepened what I felt that first night," he said. "I love you, Bella. Not the polished version from society events, but the woman brave enough to be entirely herself."

He opened the box. The diamond gleamed, embraced by curved gold bands like brushstrokes.

"Will you marry me?"

Her vision blurred with tears. "It looks like my painting style," she whispered.

"It is," he said. "I had it made for you—for the artist who taught me to value truth over perfection."

She slid to the floor beside him, cupping his face. "Yes," she said. "Yes, I'll marry you."

His smile outshone the candles as he slipped the ring on her finger. When their lips met, it was salt and laughter and everything they'd built.

Then—a camera shutter clicked.

They looked up to find Marco, grinning from behind the counter.

"For the empty frame," he said, holding up an instant photo. "Don't worry—I'll vanish in sixty seconds."

"You might as well stay for champagne," Chance laughed.

"Nope. I'm on Nonna-call duty." Marco placed the photo beside the timeline and disappeared.

Chance helped her up. The cork popped. Bubbles foamed into their glasses.

"To us," he said.

"To us," she echoed, their flutes clinking.

She sipped, then paused. "Does this have anything to do with your mysterious errands yesterday? Beatrice wouldn't stop giving me that look."

"I may have spent the day collecting blessings," Chance said.

"Blessings?"

"I talked to your dad first. Then Beatrice and Roderick. And..." he hesitated, "your grandfather."

"You went to Grandfather?"

"I did. He surprised me. He gave me something for you."

He pulled out a small antique box. Inside lay a silver hair comb, inlaid with pearls and emeralds.

"It was your grandmother's. Intended for your mother."

She traced the filigree, overwhelmed. The gift wasn't just historic—it was personal. Restorative.

"He hopes to share its history with you himself," Chance said. "If you're willing."

She nodded, moved beyond words. It wasn't just a gift—it was restoration. A bridge between past and present, given freely. On both sides.

"There's more." Chance handed her two items: a detailed drawing of entwined hands from Abigail and a glittery ring box from Bau, covered in blueprints.

"They've already assigned themselves wedding roles," he grinned. "Abigail's lobbying for flower girl duties."

Abbeline laughed, clutching both gifts. "They knew before I did!"

"Everyone did," he admitted. "Keeping this secret was harder than New York."

He hesitated. "Speaking of which—one last thing."

Her smile faltered slightly. "What is it?"

"I've accepted a transfer to Karrington's Atlanta office. Starting next month."

"You're... moving back? For good?"

"I am. I don't want to visit your life anymore. I want to live it with you."

"But New York—your future—"

"Is flexible," he said. "My real future is here. With you."

She stood and wrapped her arms around him. "We should call our parents."

"They're waiting at Beatrice's," he confessed. "Unless you want tonight just for us."

"No," she said. "Let's go tell them."

As they gathered the photos and gifts, Chance placed the new image in the empty frame.

"The next chapter begins," he said.

"And all the ones after that," she replied, slipping her hand into his.

Outside, Atlanta shimmered under a warm sky. The city that had once held secrets now held promises. The woman who had once hidden now walked forward in truth.

"I love you," she said, pausing beside her car. "Not just for the proposal, but for always seeing me."

"I love you too," he said, kissing her hand. "For teaching me to see myself clearly."

They drove toward Beatrice's, toward family, toward the future. The ring on her finger wasn't just a promise.

It was a foundation—truth-shaped, freely chosen, exactly as they were.

***

Morning sunlight streamed through the studio windows, casting long shadows across canvases in various stages of completion. The familiar scent of linseed oil and turpentine hung in the air, accompanied by the distant sounds of Atlanta stirring awake.

Two weeks had passed since Chance's proposal, yet Abbeline found herself pausing at unexpected moments, captivated by the ring on her finger. Whether sketching, driving, or pouring coffee, the diamond would catch the light—reminding her she was engaged. The journey that began with attic discoveries and family secrets now extended toward a future she hadn't imagined three years ago.

The studio door creaked open, pulling her from her thoughts. Expecting Beatrice or perhaps Chance with coffee, she turned to find Randolph standing hesitantly in the doorway.

"Grandfather," she said, setting aside her charcoal. "I wasn't expecting you."

"I called Beatrice," he explained, lingering at the threshold. "She mentioned you'd be here this morning." His voice held an edge of emotion. "I hope I'm not intruding."

"Not at all," she assured him, gesturing to a chair near her worktable. "I'm just sketching concepts for the Seattle commission."

Randolph stepped into the studio, his gaze taking in the organized chaos with genuine interest. Though still impeccably dressed, his clothes hung more loosely than before his heart attack. The signet ring on his finger—once a symbol of authority—now slid slightly as he adjusted it, a habitual gesture from her childhood.

"Your work continues to gain recognition," he observed, carefully navigating between canvases. "The gallery in Seattle—that's significant."

"It is," she agreed, watching him settle into the chair with deliberate movements that hinted at fatigue. "They're commissioning a series on family legacies. I'm experimenting with combining traditional portraiture and abstract elements."

"Appropriate," he nodded. "Families are rarely as straightforward as conventional portraits suggest."

The observation—self-aware in a way the Randolph of three years ago could never have managed—created a moment of connection between them. Not the false harmony of her pre-discovery childhood, but something more authentic, built on acknowledged truths rather than careful omissions.

"How have you been feeling?" she asked, noting the fatigue around his eyes.

"Managing," he replied—the word carrying more honesty than ever before. "The new medication regimen is effective, if not entirely pleasant."

Abbeline nodded, recognizing the effort it took for him to acknowledge vulnerability. "Aunt Bea mentioned the doctors were pleased with your last visit."

"Doctors are easily impressed by small improvements," he said dryly, a flash of his old sardonic humor emerging. "But yes, things are stable." His gaze drifted to a half-finished canvas near the window. "Is that Beatrice's house?"

"Yes," Abbeline confirmed, surprised by his recognition. "I'm painting it as a wedding gift for her and Roderick. Their one-year anniversary is next month."

"They've been good for each other," Randolph observed, fingers unconsciously turning the signet ring. "Better than I initially understood."

The admission—one of many small acknowledgments that had emerged over the past three years—hung in the air between them. Randolph's earlier disapproval of Roderick had stemmed not from any objection to the man himself, but from the same controlling instinct that had separated Abbeline's parents decades earlier.

"They have," she agreed simply.

A quiet silence settled between them, filled with the hum of the heater, a distant birdcall, and the soft shift of paper beneath her hand. This, too, marked a change from the past—when silences had been charged with unspoken expectations.

"I came to speak about the hair comb," Randolph said at last, his voice gentler than usual. "Chance mentioned he'd given it to you."

"He did," Abbeline nodded. "It's beautiful. Thank you for entrusting me with something so significant."

"It belongs with you," Randolph replied, his gaze turning toward the window, where sunlight illuminated dust motes dancing in the air. "My grandmother wore it at her wedding in 1893. She passed it to my wife on our wedding day, with the understanding it would continue through the generations."

He paused, adjusting the ring again before continuing. "Elisabeth had intended it for your mother. After her passing, I held onto it—perhaps always with the thought that, one day, it might find its way to Abbie's daughter."

The phrasing was gentler than expected—not evasive, but reflective. It wasn't a full confession, but it acknowledged more than he once would have dared.

"Did my mother know about it?" she asked.

"She did," Randolph confirmed, something softening in his expression. "Elisabeth showed it to her on her sixteenth birthday, explaining its history. Abbie immediately began sketching designs for how she might wear it someday."

This glimpse into her mother's life—a simple moment of joy—felt like a precious gift. Though Beatrice had shared many stories and Edward had offered his own memories, Randolph rarely spoke of Abbie directly.

"I have something to show you," she said, moving to a flat-file cabinet. From its depths, she retrieved a leather portfolio Edward had given her. "Dad saved these—sketches Mom made during their time together."

She returned to Randolph, carefully opening the portfolio to reveal delicate drawings. Though many depicted Edward or landscapes, one page showed an elegant hairstyle with a distinctive comb nestled among upswept curls.

"I believe this is it," she said softly, pointing to the drawing. "She must have been planning how she'd wear it for her wedding."

Randolph's hand trembled slightly as he reached toward the sketch without touching it. His composure faltered—grief, regret, and something like wonder passing briefly across his face before he gathered himself again.

"She had extraordinary talent," he said finally, his voice rough with suppressed emotion. "Like you."

The simple comparison—acknowledging both her mother's gift and her inheritance of it—felt like another step in their evolving relationship.

"I've brought something else," Randolph continued, reaching into his jacket pocket. He withdrew a small velvet pouch, its fabric faded with age. "This belonged to my mother. She wore it on her wedding day as well."

From the pouch, he extracted a delicate bracelet of interwoven gold and pearl. Though clearly antique, it had been well-maintained—the gold still gleaming in the studio light.

"It's tradition," he explained, "for Hartwell brides to wear both the comb and the bracelet—something from the paternal line, something from the maternal." He held it out to her.

"Should you wish to continue that tradition, of course. There's no obligation."

Abbeline accepted the bracelet, its weight more substantial than expected despite its delicate appearance. The metal warmed quickly against her palm.

"Thank you," she said sincerely. "I would be honored to wear them both."

Randolph nodded, satisfaction briefly smoothing the lines of his face. "Good. That's... good." He adjusted his position in the chair, discomfort flickering across his features as he shifted his weight.

"Would you like some tea?" Abbeline offered, noticing his fatigue. "I have a kettle in the corner."

"Please," he accepted—another small sign of his evolution.

As Abbeline prepared the tea, she reflected on the journey that had brought them to this moment—not just her discovery of family secrets, but the gradual, halting reconciliation that had followed.

She handed him a steaming mug of Earl Grey, his preferred blend that she now kept stocked in her studio. He accepted it with a nod of appreciation, his fingers curling around the ceramic for warmth.

"Have you and Chance set a date?" he asked after taking a careful sip.

"Not yet," she replied. "We're thinking next spring—after he's fully settled in Atlanta."

Randolph nodded, sipping his tea thoughtfully. "His move is significant—leaving New York, an established position..."

"It's not a sacrifice," Abbeline said gently. "It's a choice. He loves his work, and it can flourish here as well. Our family is here."

He placed his cup down, gazing at her engagement ring. "The Hartwell house was built for family," he said lightly. "Provide room for studios or offices, and it's a convenient commute to Karrington's Atlanta office."

Abbeline met his gaze, understanding the invitation rather than a demand. "That's something Chance and I will consider. It's complicated—historically and logistically."

"Of course," his tone softened, surprise at his own empathy showing. "I merely thought it worth mentioning."

Their conversation drifted—Abigail's art, Bau's robotics, Edward's projects—flowing comfortably under the morning light. They spoke easily, occasionally pausing as he adjusted his ring or shifted in his seat, small gestures of growing intimacy.

An hour later, Randolph rose to leave. Slowly, he donned his coat, a twitch of fatigue in his movements.

"The children are performing next Friday," he mentioned. "Beatrice invited me."

Abbeline offered to help. He allowed it—another small but meaningful cooperation.

"The bracelet should be professionally cleaned before the wedding," he added. "I know someone." There was no dictation—only suggestion.

"I'd appreciate your help," she replied, grateful for the practical care beneath it.

He paused in the studio doorway, studying the canvases and sketches, the heirlooms laid out beside the charcoal drafts.

"Your mother would be proud—of the woman you've become, the artist you are, the family you're building," he said, voice thick with emotion.

Before she could answer, he turned and left, moving steadily down the stairs toward the waiting car.

Abbeline lingered at the studio entrance until the car pulled away, then returned to her workspace.

She moved to the window again, gazing across the rooftop trees toward the skyline. The city had witnessed her transformation—Hartwell heiress to Stuart artist, daughter discovering her truth, beloved fiancée forging the future with the man she loved.

Abbeline returned to her easel. Charcoal moved in slow, confident strokes—figures beginning to take shape, not fully formed but reaching, connected. On the table behind her, the comb and bracelet caught the morning light, casting soft reflections across her sketchpad.

She didn't need to look at them to feel their presence. The ring on her finger, the heirlooms beside her, the conversation still echoing—all of it lived in her hands now, in the lines she drew, in the story she chose to tell.

Outside, the wind shifted, rustling the trees just beyond the studio window. She looked up once, took a breath, and kept drawing.

Chapter 11

A House Made New

AUTUMN SUNLIGHT SLANTED through the windows of the Hartwell mansion's dining room, casting golden patterns across the table, now buried under fabric swatches, flower arrangements, and seating charts. A year after Chance's proposal, wedding preparations had transformed even this once-formal space into a living blueprint of joy.

Abbeline stood by the window, curls loose around her shoulders, honey-blonde highlights catching the light as she watched workers construct the garden pavilion where she would soon say her vows.

"I still can't believe we're having the wedding here," she murmured, her fingers drifting to the silver necklace that had belonged to her mother, a gesture she always made when the past pressed gently against the present.

"It makes the most sense," Beatrice replied from the head of the table, where she was carefully organizing the final guest list by color. "The gallery's too small for this many people. And after you two decided to move in…" She gestured toward the room, the house, and the history.

Chance glanced up from the music selections he was reviewing with Marco. "Living here has changed how I see it. It's not just Randolph's fortress anymore."

"A home," Abbeline finished for him, moving to his side and gently squeezing his shoulder. "Ours, eventually."

Their most surprising decision had been accepting Randolph's offer to live in the mansion after the wedding. What had once symbolized control and silence was being reshaped by new choices. Randolph had retained his suite in the east wing, but the rest of the house was gradually becoming theirs.

"And the symbolism is perfect," Marco added, his enthusiasm undimmed by detail fatigue. "Getting married in the place that once kept your parents apart—it's like rewriting the story."

Beatrice shot him a look, but Abbeline smiled. "It's okay. He's right. That's part of what makes it so special."

The door swung open with the quick scuff of sneakers on polished floors. Bau burst in, eyes bright. "Uncle Edward's here with the wooden arch pieces! He says he needs strong helpers to carry them."

Marco sprang up, flexing with theatrical flair. "Did someone call for muscle? Let's go, architect."

As they left, Abigail entered, balancing a sleek portfolio case. At fourteen, she moved with the quiet poise of someone older. Her artistic eye and stillness mirrored Abbeline's.

"I finished the place cards," she said, placing the case on the table. Inside were seventy-eight hand-lettered cards, each in soft watercolor tones that complemented the wedding palette.

Chance leaned in to admire them. "These are professional quality, Abigail. Really impressive."

She flushed with pride. "The Gs took forever to get right."

"They're perfect," Abbeline said sincerely. "Thank you for putting so much care into them."

"I wanted to help," Abigail said softly. "You're the reason we found our family."

The room stilled for a beat. The simple acknowledgment—of how Abbeline's search for truth had widened their family circle—settled in the air like a shared breath. Beatrice reached out to squeeze her daughter's hand, her expression unreadably full.

From the hallway came the low murmur of Edward's voice, met by Randolph's sharper tones. Once adversaries, the two men had found an uneasy civility, held together not by liking but by love for the same people. The wedding had only accelerated their truce. Edward had crafted the arch; Randolph had opened his home.

"They're debating wood stain," Abigail reported, eyes dancing. "Grandfather wants dark to match the pavilion. Uncle Edward says natural's better with the flowers."

"Five bucks says the dad-to-be wins," Chance murmured, referring to Edward by the nickname he'd adopted since proposing to Abbeline.

"No bet," Abbeline whispered back. "Dad's patience beats everything."

The door opened again. Randolph entered with a leather portfolio tucked under one arm, his movements careful, deliberate. Though he still carried himself with an old boardroom grace, Abbeline noticed the subtle changes: slower steps, the way his hand rested briefly on the back of a chair before sitting. His face, however, was animated—a warmth rarely seen in his eyes.

"I found something you might want to see," he said, setting the portfolio on the table. "While cataloging heirlooms for the insurance adjusters."

Abbeline moved closer, curious. Randolph had been meticulously organizing the mansion's contents ever since she and Chance had agreed to move in—a gesture equal parts control and concession.

"What is it?"

"Your grandmother's wedding portfolio," he replied. "Elisabeth kept detailed records of every major family event—our wedding, and the plans she began for our daughters."

Inside, pages of photographs, fabric swatches, handwritten notes, and delicate sketches unfolded like petals—Elisabeth's vision laid out with astonishing precision. Her elegant script annotated every detail, from floral themes to seating configurations.

"She was organized," Chance murmured, flipping through the pages with reverent hands.

"It gave her peace," Randolph said, touching the edge of a page. "Her family lost everything in the Depression. Order was how she found safety."

Abbeline turned each page with growing awe, feeling as if she were opening a door to the women who had come before her. As she neared the end, the mood subtly shifted. They reached a section labeled *Abigail's Wedding*. The notes grew sparse, the sketches uncertain—possibility interrupted.

"She started this when Abbie was young," Randolph said quietly. "She added ideas over the years—right up until she passed. Things she hoped her girls might want someday."

Abbeline's hand hovered over the page, her throat tightening. Among the clippings was the same hairstyle from her mother's sketch with the antique comb. Proof that Abbie had seen this, dreamed with it, been inspired by it.

"What a gift," Abbeline whispered. "To see their dreams still waiting here."

Randolph nodded, adjusting his signet ring. "Elisabeth would be pleased to know the comb and bracelet are being used as she hoped."

The silence that followed was full, not empty. Connected. Then, footsteps echoed in the hallway again.

Roderick appeared, a garment bag draped over his arm.

Roderick entered with the quiet gravity of someone carrying more than fabric. He laid the garment bag at the cleared end of the table, giving Randolph a wordless nod before turning to Abbeline.

"It's ready," he said. "Final alterations are done."

He unzipped the bag with deliberate care, revealing a wedding gown of ivory silk. Its delicate lace overlays caught the sunlight, the silhouette classic and elegant, a dream once imagined, now brought to life.

Abbeline's breath caught. "Is that the final fitting?"

"Yes," Beatrice said, stepping beside her. "The alterations are done on your mother's dream wedding dress—the one she would've worn, had she and your dad not eloped."

Abbeline approached slowly, her fingers brushing the fabric. "Wow, they did a fantastic job finishing it."

"I agree," Beatrice said gently. "The tailors really captured Abbie's design and your input, sugar."

Randolph, who had stood quietly nearby, spoke with unexpected softness. "She insisted on having one that was entirely hers. Said she could see it perfectly in her mind."

The words pulled Abbeline's and Beatrice's attention from their quiet admiration. Their smiles faded as they turned to him, taking in the expression on his face.

He wasn't looking at them—his eyes stayed fixed on the gown. And for once, there was no edge in his tone, only a distant tenderness.

The control he used to wear like armor had slipped for some time now, and Abbeline could see how deeply the sight of the dress shook him.

Knowing how this must have crushed him, she didn't speak, just rubbed his back. He looked at her, eyes rimmed with unshed tears. She leaned into him with a side hug, fully feeling the quiet weight of his pain and regret.

Beatrice leaned into them as well, wiping tears from her eyes, the emotion of the moment settling over all of them.

They stayed like that for a while before Abbeline gently pulled away and returned to the dress.

"It's beautiful," she murmured, tracing the embroidered lace. "Wearing Mom's dress, with Grandmother's comb and bracelet... it brings everything full circle."

In the doorway, Edward appeared, his boots quiet against the floor. He paused when he saw the dress, his expression shifting—surprise, recognition... then something deeper, something aching.

"Abbie's dress," he said softly, stepping in. "I remember the sketches. The fabric samples."

He approached the table slowly, stopping across from Randolph. The gown lay between them—once a quiet point of division, now perhaps a step toward reconciliation.

"She would've been beautiful in it," Edward said.

"Yes," Randolph replied quietly. One word, weighted with years they'd never spoken of.

The weight of that unspoken history hung in the air. Not forgiveness. Not forgetting. But a shared truth neither could deny.

"Dad," Abbeline said, gently shifting the mood, "what do you think of the finished dress? Would Mom have liked the additions?"

Edward's smile lit his face. He leaned in, hands precise, examining the seams with the ease of long habit.

"Beautiful additions, Bella," he murmured, tracing a line of stitches. "Your mom would have loved it." He looked up at her. "You are your mother's daughter—and you're going to look amazing in this dress."

Abbeline's heart pulled at that—another quiet inheritance, stitched into her story.

Abigail, who had watched in reverent silence, stepped closer. "May I look?"

Abbeline nodded, and the girl leaned in with the serious focus that always accompanied her art.

"The embroidery on the bodice..." she pointed. "Lilies of the valley. The same flowers in the chapel wedding photo."

Edward blinked, then smiled. "You're right. Those were her favorite."

"We should use them in your bouquet," Beatrice said, already making a note. "And maybe in the pavilion."

That detail sparked a new wave of energy. Beatrice and Abigail dove into floral sketches, referencing Elisabeth's portfolio for continuity. Roderick jotted notes for the ceremony, while Chance returned with Marco, laughing about song choices.

Abbeline stood still amid the movement, watching these people—her people—make something together. Not just a wedding, but a new narrative. The mansion, once a place of closed doors and silenced voices, now echoed with creative noise.

Bau barreled back in, cheeks flushed. "Uncle Edward! The arch is up, but Marco says we need your eye on the anchor points."

Edward nodded, returning the dress gently to Roderick's care. "Let's make sure it can hold Abigail's design."

As he followed Bau, Randolph cleared his throat. "I should oversee that as well. Pavilion installation requires proper oversight."

The room paused. That Randolph would willingly join Edward, unsupervised, would have been unthinkable a year ago.

"I'll come too," Chance said, exchanging a quick glance with Abbeline. "Another set of eyes can't hurt."

The three men departed, leaving Abbeline, Beatrice, Roderick, and Abigail in a rare moment of quiet.

Sunlight stretched across the table, touching each artifact: Elisabeth's portfolio, Abigail's place cards, Abbie's wedding gown. Three generations threaded together—not by seamless harmony, but by love earned and wounds healed.

"It's really happening," Abbeline said softly, more to herself than anyone else. "We're getting married. Here. With everyone present."

"Together," Beatrice replied, sliding an arm around her. "Exactly as it should be."

Abigail glanced up, eyes thoughtful. "Is it strange?" she asked. "Having your wedding where your mom couldn't have hers?"

Abbeline hesitated. Beatrice started to speak, but Abbeline gently raised a hand.

"Not strange," she said. "Healing. We're taking something that once hurt and turning it into something beautiful." She looked at Abigail. "It's like your paintings—layers and color over pain. A new image, but one that remembers."

Abigail nodded slowly. "That's what I thought."

Outside, the murmur of tools and voices floated in from the garden. Abbeline returned to the window. Edward knelt by the arch, checking anchor points. Randolph stood nearby, offering suggestions. Bau darted between them, full of purpose. Chance and Marco adjusted beams, working in sync.

This—this was the real ceremony. Not the vows or the aisle, but the unspoken choice to build something new from what was broken.

"Three more days," Beatrice said beside her. "Are you ready?"

Abbeline smiled, the answer blooming clear and strong in her heart. "More than ready. I've been walking toward this my whole life—even when I didn't know it."

Outside, Edward glanced up. Their eyes met through the window. He smiled—a reflection of hers. A father's pride, a daughter's peace.

And in three days, she would walk down the aisle on his arm. Not just to marry the man she loved, but to step fully into a story rewritten with truth, forgiveness, and love.

***

Moonlight silvered the pavilion in the Hartwell garden, casting long shadows over the arch Edward had completed just hours earlier. The house, after a day of joyful chaos, had finally quieted. Abbeline sat alone on the terrace, a steaming mug of chamomile tea in hand, breathing in the autumn night—the scent of late roses mingling with fresh wood and cool air.

From her vantage point, the mansion stretched before her, no longer Randolph's fortress but a home slowly becoming her own. The thought still surprised her—that she had returned to the place she once fled. But she wasn't the same woman, and this wasn't the same house.

The French doors opened behind her, spilling warm light. Edward stepped out, two gift-wrapped packages under his arm.

"Can't sleep either?" he asked, settling beside her.

"Too many thoughts," she replied, smiling at him. "Tomorrow, the past, how we got here."

He nodded, the silver at his temples catching the moonlight. Time had changed them both since their reunion three years ago—marked by healing, discovery, and the building of their bond.

"I brought something," he said, placing the larger package on the table between them. "A tradition in my family, though one I never expected to pass on."

Abbeline unwrapped it carefully, revealing a handcrafted wooden box, its intricate carvings flowing over the lid and sides—forest, meadow, and tiny scenes that emerged gradually in the low light. She opened it. A soft melody drifted out—one of her mother's favorites.

"It's beautiful," she murmured, tracing the carvings.

"My father made one for my mother before their wedding. His father before him." Edward's voice softened. "I'd planned to make one for Abbie, but... things happened too fast. This time, I had the chance."

She leaned closer, the details revealing themselves: a carved studio with an easel, a market stall, the pavilion framed by trees.

"Your journey," he explained gently. "There's your studio. The booth in Seattle. And tomorrow's pavilion."

Tears welled in her eyes. In the carvings, she saw the attic where she'd found the truth. The coffee house where Chance had proposed. The gallery of her first solo show. It wasn't just a box—it was a chronicle, a tribute to her becoming.

"There's more," Edward said. "Bottom compartment."

She pressed the catch. Inside lay a delicate paintbrush with a carved wooden handle.

"It was your mother's," he said. "She called it her 'dream brush.' Used it only for her most important work."

Abbeline held it with trembling fingers. "She would've used this for our portrait," she whispered, recalling the unfinished painting.

Edward nodded. "She started it the week before..." He didn't need to finish. Before everything changed.

"Thank you," she said, returning the brush to its place. "For saving this. For being here now."

His smile held joy and grief in equal measure—undeniable, and earned.

"There's nowhere else I'd be."

He reached for the second package. "This is from Desiree and me."

Abbeline opened it to find a leather-bound journal with handmade paper and a fountain pen. A note in Desiree's looping script read, *For your next chapter. Some stories are too precious not to record.*

"She suggested it," Edward explained. "Said the day would blur, and writing it down might help preserve the details. She's been incredible throughout all this."

"I'm glad she'll be here tomorrow," Abbeline said. "She makes you happy."

"She does," he admitted, quietly amazed. "Something I didn't expect again."

They sat in silence, the music box still playing, the night humming around them. Crickets sang. A breeze stirred the roses.

"Nervous?" Edward asked eventually.

"Not about marrying Chance," she said without hesitation. "That's the easy part." She twisted her engagement ring—a new reflex. "But doing this here, in this house... sometimes it still feels surreal."

He nodded. "Places carry power. But power can be re-directed. You're doing that tomorrow—turning a symbol of separation into connection."

His insight mirrored what she'd told Abigail. Even after so many lost years, they often arrived at the same truths from opposite directions.

"That's exactly it," she said. "Full circle."

"Your mother would approve," Edward said quietly. "She never saw places as fixed. She once told me she could imagine this house filled with light and laughter."

The image brought unexpected comfort. Even in a space Abbie had once needed to escape, she'd seen its potential.

"Did you see Grandfather with the florists today?" Abbeline asked, shifting gently. "He actually smiled when they used Grandmother's silver vases."

"I noticed," Edward said, wonder flickering in his tone. "Three years ago, I couldn't have imagined working beside him without tension—let alone like this."

"He's trying," Abbeline said.

"In his way," Edward agreed.

It wasn't absolution. Randolph still stumbled, still bristled at vulnerability. But the effort was real.

The French doors opened again. Beatrice emerged, wrapped in a cashmere shawl.

"I thought I'd find you two here," she said, joining them. "Reflection? Nerves?"

"Reflection," Abbeline answered. "Everything's ready."

"Almost," Beatrice said, drawing a cream envelope from her shawl. "This arrived an hour ago. From your grandfather."

Abbeline took the envelope, recognizing the familiar weight of Randolph's stationery and the unmistakable Hartwell crest. Her name, written in his formal script, felt less like possession now and more like continuity.

"He asked that you read it privately. Tonight."

Edward rose slightly. "Do you want some space?"

"No," Abbeline said. "Stay. Please."

She broke the seal and opened the letter. Randolph's precise handwriting filled the page.

> *My dear Abbeline,*
>
> *On the eve of your wedding, I find myself reflecting on journeys—yours, mine, and those of our family. Journeys completed, interrupted, and just beginning.*

As she read, tears threatened. The tone was stripped of pretense—just a man speaking plainly. He admitted regret: over Abbie and Edward, over the control he had once mistaken for protection, over years wasted in silence.

> *Your choice to marry here reveals a generosity of spirit I don't deserve but deeply value. You've brought light to this house. Truth where there was once silence. Forgiveness in place of pride.*

His words spoke not just of change, but of legacy. He described the creation of a foundation in Abbie's name, and updates to his will—practical actions that honored the values she and Chance had voiced for years.

This house is your inheritance in more than legal terms. It is your canvas—to fill with the life and love that should have always existed here.

Abbeline lowered the letter slowly, the emotion settling into her chest.

"He wrote this himself," she said quietly.

"Is it okay?" Beatrice asked.

"It's more than okay," Abbeline said. "It's a blessing. In his way."

Edward reached for her hand. She held on.

"I should try to sleep," she said, gathering the gifts and the letter. "Tomorrow's a big day."

They rose. The garden lights flicked on, bathing the arch in gentle radiance.

At the doorway, Abbeline paused and turned. The house behind her, the garden ahead—both changed, not by forgetting, but by choosing what to remember.

"Thank you," she said, looking from Edward to Beatrice. "For everything. For being exactly who I needed."

Beatrice hugged her first, her familiar perfume grounding the moment. Then Edward wrapped his arms around them both.

"Get some rest," Beatrice said, wiping away tears. "Dress fitting at nine."

"I'll see you at four," Edward added. "To walk you down the aisle."

Abbeline nodded, too full for words.

Golden afternoon light bathed the Hartwell gardens, transforming the space into something ethereal. The pavilion stood adorned with cascading autumn florals—deep burgundies, rich golds, and soft creams, accented by lilies of the valley in memory of Abbie. Edward's handcrafted arch framed the space, its carved curves embedded with tiny mirrors that scattered light like stars across the seated guests.

Inside the mansion, Abbeline stood before a full-length mirror in what had once been her grandmother's dressing room. Her mother's wedding dress fit perfectly now—the ivory silk catching the light, the lace overlay casting delicate patterns across the fabric. Her honey-blonde curls were swept into an elegant updo that showcased her natural texture and the antique comb nestled among the spirals.

"You look beautiful," Beatrice said softly, fastening the bracelet—Randolph's maternal heirloom—at Abbeline's wrist. "Like you've stepped out of another time, while remaining entirely yourself."

Abbeline smiled at her aunt in the mirror. Beatrice, in a soft plum dress that echoed the silver in her hair, stood steady and elegant—her eyes reflecting years of guardianship, sacrifice, and love.

"Thank you," Abbeline said, turning to face her. "For all of it. Standing up to Grandfather, helping me find Dad, supporting me even when I made choices you didn't expect."

Beatrice's composure flickered, emotion catching at the edges. "You never needed my protection as much as you needed my love," she said, squeezing her hands. "Everything else was just logistics."

A knock interrupted them. Abigail stepped in, radiant in her burgundy junior bridesmaid dress. Her usual poise was tempered by a flush of excitement.

"Everyone's seated," she reported, her voice practiced and formal. "Bau is ready with the rings. Dad says it's almost time."

Roderick followed her in, dapper in a tailored suit. "Edward's waiting at the stairs. And Chance is at the altar—somewhere between terrified and ecstatic."

Abbeline laughed, light and clear. "That sounds about right."

Abigail approached with care, holding a bouquet of cream roses and lilies of the valley, tied with silk ribbon. "These are for you," she said, presenting them with quiet gravity.

"They're perfect," Abbeline told her. "Thank you for everything."

Pride spread across Abigail's face, softening her composed expression into something open and joyful. "I wanted it to be special."

"It is," Abbeline assured her. "Because of you."

Beatrice glanced discreetly at her watch. "It's time."

With a final look in the mirror—not to check her appearance, but to acknowledge everything that led to this day—Abbeline followed them out. The hallway was lined with framed photographs—now including her parents' wedding and recent family gatherings. The house felt different today: lighter, fuller.

At the base of the grand staircase stood Edward, poised in his suit, silver hair neatly combed. When he looked up and saw her descending, something raw moved through his expression—a tangle of pride, wonder, and memory.

"Bella," he said softly. "You look just like your mother."

The words, once painful, now filled with grace, brought tears to her eyes. "Do I really?"

"Yes," he said, offering his arm. "The same light shines through you both."

Behind them, Beatrice wiped at her eyes before guiding Abigail to the doors. "We'll take our places. Roderick will cue the music."

Alone in the entrance hall, Edward and Abbeline shared a stillness that held all they had lost—and all they'd reclaimed.

"I never thought I'd get this chance," Edward said. "To walk you down the aisle. To witness your beginning when I missed so much."

"But you're here," she said, squeezing his arm. "That's what matters."

He nodded, posture softening. "Your mother would be so proud. Of your art. Your strength. Your heart."

"I think she'd be proud of us both," Abbeline said. "Of how we found our way."

From the garden, the string quartet began to play. Roderick appeared at the doors and nodded.

"Ready?" Edward asked.

"More than ready," she answered.

The doors opened to reveal the garden transformed. Rows of white chairs lined a petal-strewn aisle. Chance stood beneath the arch, Marco beside him, grinning. Beatrice and Randolph sat in the front row, Bau holding the rings with ceremonial care. The Bianchis and guests from every chapter of their lives filled the seats.

Desiree sat beside Edward's empty chair, offering a warm, steady smile. Across the aisle, a single bouquet of lilies rested on a vacant seat—a silent tribute to Abbie.

The music swelled. Edward guided Abbeline forward, each step deliberate. She took in the scene—the culmination of three years of searching, growing, and choosing truth over performance.

Chance's gaze never left her. As they reached the arch, Edward placed her hand in his—a gesture ancient, but weighted with personal meaning.

"Who gives this woman in marriage?" the officiant asked.

"Her father," Edward said, voice steady. Then, with a smile that acknowledged their family's full truth, he added, "And her aunt, who has been her guardian and guide."

Beatrice gave a quiet nod of affirmation. Randolph sat composed, his expression surprisingly open. Edward joined Desiree, their hands brushing briefly.

The ceremony unfolded with quiet rhythm—traditional structure threaded with intimate touches. When the time for vows arrived, Chance spoke first.

He took a breath, then looked at her like she was the only person in the world. His fingers flexed in hers, grounding himself before he spoke.

"I knew I was in trouble the moment I saw you."

The guests chuckled, a ripple of warmth moving through the garden.

"Not the polite kind of trouble. The kind that rearranges you. You were sitting alone at that fundraiser, sketching on the back of a program, surrounded by noise but completely in your own world. And all I could think was—I have to know her. I need to know her."

He laughed softly, the sound laced with wonder. "And the more I did, the more certain I became. You weren't just brilliant—you were brave. You let yourself break and rebuild. You opened yourself up to truth, even when it hurt. You faced down silence, secrets, grief, and you didn't run. You created from it."

Abbeline's lips trembled, her eyes fixed on his. He pressed her hand gently, continuing.

"There's this moment I think about all the time. That kiss. On that Seattle street, right after we found your father. I wasn't expecting it. Not even close. But when it happened..." He shook his head with a crooked smile. "It felt like the world slipped sideways. Like someone hit pause on reality and said, 'This right here—this is it.'"

The audience laughed softly, touched.

"And I'll admit it," he added, grinning. "That night I couldn't sleep. Not a wink. I lay there like a middle schooler at summer camp, kicking my feet under the covers and staring at the ceiling."

A louder burst of laughter echoed around them. Abbeline's eyes glistened with tears, her hand covering her mouth in a smile.

"That was the night I stopped wondering if this could be something," Chance said, voice softening again, "and started hoping it would be everything."

He paused, emotion tightening his voice.

"I love you, Bella. Not just because of who you are, but how you see. You notice the broken edges most people skip over—and you turn them into art. Into connection. Into meaning."

His voice steadied, full of promise.

"I vow to love you with the same courage you've shown me. To protect the space where you can grow, and to never fear your strength. I promise to laugh with you, to fight beside you, to make our home a place where honesty and wonder live side by side."

He exhaled, then added with quiet certainty:

"And I promise that wherever life takes us—whether it's art shows or house renovations or a backyard full of kids with paint in their hair—I'll always be the guy who can't believe he gets to walk beside you."

He squeezed her hand, eyes locked with hers.

"Forever."

Her fingers tightened around Chance's hand as Abbeline drew in a steady breath. The words she'd written and rewritten so many times settled on her tongue with surprising calm. When she began, her voice was clear—but tender, edged with emotion that trembled just beneath the surface.

"Chance, you saw me before I could fully see myself—not just the artist or the woman I was becoming, but the fractured pieces I was still trying to hold together."

She paused, and a soft murmur moved through the seated guests. His gaze stayed locked on hers, unwavering—shining with unshed tears, lips parting slightly as if to steady himself with a breath.

"You never tried to fix or shape me," Abbeline continued, her voice dipping softer. "You simply stayed—steadfast, gentle, patient—through every turn of the journey."

A few quiet sniffles rose from the front row. Beatrice dabbed discreetly at her eyes. Edward leaned forward, hands clasped tightly in his lap.

"When I was buried in grief," she said, her throat tightening slightly, "you carried hope for both of us."

She smiled through it, a breathy laugh escaping as Chance's thumb stroked her knuckles—grounding, wordless, his way of telling her: I'm here.

"When I doubted the road ahead, you cleared space for me to dream again. You scrubbed my studio floors, held the weight of silence when I couldn't speak, and gave me the courage to search for answers I wasn't sure I wanted to find."

A ripple of emotion passed across his face—humble pride, disbelief, wonder. He blinked hard, jaw tightening as though trying not to cry.

"You believed in the best of me—even when I struggled to see it," she said, her voice trembling now, "and you reminded me that love doesn't have to be loud to be powerful."

A breeze moved through the garden, lifting the edge of her veil. Someone in the back exhaled a quiet "Wow." Abbeline steadied herself, lifting her chin with the quiet strength that had defined her journey.

"Today," she said, "I promise to hold you with the same devotion you've shown me."

Chance exhaled softly, his lips parting again—this time in a stunned, slightly crooked smile that made her heart lurch.

"To support your vision, as you've supported mine. To create a life rooted in honesty, laughter, and unwavering trust."

Her voice had grown stronger now, anchored by conviction.

"I vow to walk beside you, not just in joy, but in every quiet, complicated, beautiful moment that follows—because you are my home, my calm, my truest companion."

A hush settled over the garden—reverent, suspended.

And then, as if on cue, the wind rustled the lilies beside the arch. Abbeline blinked back tears that finally escaped, one sliding down her cheek. Chance reached up and brushed it away with exquisite tenderness.

The moment held—real, sacred, and entirely theirs.

Bau stepped forward with the ring pillow cradled in both hands, his face set with exaggerated solemnity. He paused at the arch as if awaiting some sacred cue, then adjusted the pillow with theatrical care before holding it aloft. A soft chuckle rippled through the guests—gentle, affectionate.

Chance knelt slightly to accept the rings, his voice low but clearly heard. "Thanks, buddy." Bau puffed with pride and retreated to his place, his job complete.

As Chance gently took her hand and slid the ring onto her finger, Abbeline's gaze flicked to the faces around them. Edward's eyes shimmered with quiet pride. Beatrice dabbed at the corner of her eye, trying to remain composed. Randolph sat taller than usual, his hands clasped tightly in his lap. Abigail's cheeks glowed as she wiped away a tear with careful precision. Marco looked as though he might burst from joy, his grin irrepressible.

The officiant's voice wrapped around them like ribbon. "By the power vested in me, I now pronounce you husband and wife."

Their kiss was soft, sure—an exhale of years of waiting, of wounds mended, of love chosen again and again. The garden burst into applause, not just for a marriage, but for everything it represented. Restoration. Reclamation. Homecoming.

The receiving line became a steady tide of warmth and connection. Beatrice hugged Chance with fierce affection, pulling back just long enough to murmur something only he heard before embracing him again. Edward greeted the Bianchis with genuine ease—shaking hands with Chance's father, exchanging words with his mother that left her blinking back tears.

Abigail and Bau flitted about like miniature diplomats, directing guests with the kind of pride only children trusted with serious jobs could possess.

Aunt Margo arrived next—Marco's mother, her signature smile radiant, eyes brimming with emotion. She cupped Abbeline's face with both hands, whispering, "You've made our boy's heart whole. Welcome to the family, sweetie," before kissing both her cheeks in turn.

Miranda arrived last. Sleek bob immaculate, her tailored dress a perfect blend of edge and grace, she leaned in with a quiet smile. "You were always worth the risk," she said simply. "Thank you for proving me right."

Abbeline watched it all unfold, her heart a mix of wonder and stillness. When the line of guests ended, she saw Chance slip away. As she finished hugging the last guest, he returned to her side with two glasses of champagne, offering one with a gentle tap to her arm.

"Taking a mental snapshot?" he asked.

"Or framing my next painting," she replied, lips curving into a smile.

"These are the moments," he murmured, wrapping an arm around her waist. "From attic dust to this."

"And it's just the beginning," she said.

"We still have the renovations, the foundation..."

"And whatever comes after," she finished, grinning.

The band began the first notes of their song. As they crossed to the dance floor beneath the garden's twinkling canopy, Abbeline caught a glimpse of Randolph from the corner of her eye. He was watching them—not sternly, not formally, but with a softened gaze that hinted at hope. His hands rested loosely in his lap, the corners of his mouth tugging almost, not quite, into a smile.

In Chance's arms, beneath the arch Edward had built and the stars emerging in the dusk above them, Abbeline felt everything settle into place. Her mother's dress moved with her, the antique comb and bracelet catching the light with each turn. Symbols of love that had once been deferred, now lived and real.

The Hartwell mansion stood behind them—no longer a place of shadows, but a home transformed.

As Chance pulled her a little closer and whispered something only for her, she closed her eyes and breathed. A future reclaimed—not from silence, but from the truths their secrets had waited to tell.

Epilogue 1

The Heart of the Mansion

Three years after the wedding

Randolph Hartwell sat in his favorite armchair by the east wing window. Autumn sunlight warmed his shoulders as he gazed at the garden below. The once-formal landscape had been gently reimagined, traditional hedges softened by whimsical touches, symmetry giving way to paths that invited exploration, especially by the children soon to arrive.

In his early eighties, Randolph found himself in a late season marked by unexpected transformation. The man who had once shaped the Hartwell legacy with iron resolve now looked forward to a role he had never envisioned: great-grandfather to the twins Abbeline carried. Her seventh month of pregnancy had brought not just anticipation, but a sense of continuation—something deeper than the visible or expected.

"Are you comfortable there, Grandfather?" Abbeline's voice, soft and steady, came from the doorway.

He looked up to see her framed in the light, the confidence she'd grown into over three years of marriage glowing quietly around her. Her painting career had flourished. Exhibitions in major cities marked her rise, yet she remained grounded in the authenticity that had defined her earliest work.

"Perfectly situated," he replied, his voice softened in unguarded moments. "The light is exceptional."

Abbeline crossed the room and eased into the window seat opposite him, her movements deliberate with her pregnancy's weight. Sunlight caught her curls—so like her mother's— momentarily stealing his breath, grief remembered, gratitude newly felt.

"Chance will be home soon," she said, glancing at her watch. "The quarterly board meeting should be finishing up."

After two years at the Atlanta branch of Karrington Financial, Chance had moved into a new role as Finance Director at his father's company, part of a plan long in motion. The position challenged his intellect and honored tradition, not as a gift but as an earned step forward, a reflection of the values he and his father shared.

"Abigail called from school," she added. "She's staying late with her art club. Asked if she could bring three friends for dinner."

Randolph nodded without hesitation. The idea of spontaneous guests, once unthinkable in the mansion's former life, was now commonplace.

At seventeen, Abigail had become a poised, perceptive young woman. Her artistic eye and analytical mind blended into quiet leadership, her paintings showing a maturity that sometimes caught even Abbeline off guard.

"And Bau?" Randolph asked, though he already knew.

"Robotics club until five," Abbeline replied with a smile.

At thirteen, Bau thrived between his school's robotics program and time with Edward in the workshop. He spoke the languages of engineering and craftsmanship with equal ease. One wall of Edward's space now displayed Bau's detailed architectural plans, each one carefully preserved and dated to mark his growth.

"Chance and I have been talking," Abbeline said, her voice gently turning thoughtful, "about making some changes to the west wing."

Randolph nodded, sensing significance beneath her calm delivery. Over the past three years, the west wing had transformed from formal entertaining spaces into warm family rooms filled with comfort, children's drawings, and the quiet mess of real life.

"We're thinking of converting the old library into a nursery," she continued. "The light's perfect, south-facing, with those beautiful bay windows."

The mention of the twins—identical girls, according to the ultrasound—brought another wave of gentle awe at the thought of two new lives soon to join them. They would never know the rigid patriarch he once was, only the version of him softened by time into something more enduring.

"That sounds ideal," he said, adjusting his signet ring, a familiar gesture in moments of emotional weight. "Excellent ventilation, too. Important for a nursery."

Abbeline smiled, recognizing the way he cloaked affection in practicality.

"It's close enough to our suite that we'll hear them at night, but still gives the rest of the house some peace."

Their practical planning revealed just how fully she and Chance had made the mansion their home. What began as a tentative arrangement—Randolph in the east wing, the newlyweds in the main house—had evolved into a true coexistence, generational lines respected, and lovingly blurred.

"Have you told your father?"

"We're having dinner with him and Desiree tomorrow," she replied. "They're driving up from the cabin."

Edward and Desiree had quietly married the previous year, splitting their time between Atlanta and her landscape projects on the West Coast. Their relationship, built on mutual respect and shared artistic rhythms, had grown strong despite the distance.

"They'll approve," Randolph said. "Your father always appreciated how you've balanced preservation with function."

The comment held no defensiveness, only quiet respect, a sign of how far he and Edward had come. Not easy camaraderie, but a kind of mutual understanding rooted in their shared love for Abbeline.

The sound of the front door opening signaled Chance's return, and Abbeline's face brightened. Even now, their daily reunions carried an ease and joy that hadn't dimmed.

"Just in time," she said, rising slowly from the window seat. Randolph instinctively offered his hand—support given freely, no longer weakness.

Chance appeared in the doorway, professional but radiant with warmth.

"There are my favorite people," he said, kissing Abbeline, then nodding to Randolph. "How are the three of you today?"

"Active," Abbeline replied, guiding his hand to where her dress shifted with movement. "One of your girls is practicing gymnastics."

"While the other seems to be conducting an orchestra," Randolph added with an amused glance. "Quite the little maestro."

That light-hearted observation—remarking on his great-grandchildren's personalities—was a quiet marvel in itself. Decades ago, he'd met Abbie's pregnancy with disdain. Now, he embraced this new chapter with wonder he'd learned to receive, not control.

"I've got news from the board meeting," Chance said, loosening his tie as he sat near them. "The foundation's educational outreach expansion was approved. We'll be funding ten more schools next year."

The foundation—established in Abbie's name after the wedding—had grown into a vital force in Atlanta's arts education. It merged Chance's acumen, Abbeline's vision, and Randolph's legacy into something profoundly new.

"That's wonderful," Abbeline said, her face lighting up. "The waiting list's been growing since the cultural center showcased the kids' work."

"Your board presentation was strong," Randolph told Chance. "Especially the data on academic improvements. Very persuasive."

Though retired from active leadership, Randolph still advised the foundation, lending his experience while allowing the younger generation to steer its future. This balance, offering guidance without command, had become a new rhythm for them all.

As Chance described the board's response, Randolph found himself simply watching—his granddaughter and her husband, so aligned in thought and gesture. Their shared vision, mutual respect, and quiet joy echoed everything he and Elisabeth had once hoped for. The road to get here had been difficult, but the result was something even more enduring.

"Abigail and Bau will be here soon," Abbeline said, glancing at the clock. "I should check on dinner."

"Right behind you, babe," Chance offered, instantly attuned to her increasing fatigue. "Martha said she's adjusting the menu for Abigail's guests."

As they left together, still talking easily, Randolph remained in his chair. Afternoon light now fell across the hallway they'd passed through, his corner in shadow, a quiet, fitting metaphor for his season of life.

Three years ago, when he suggested Abbeline and Chance move in, he'd framed it as practical—just shared space, nothing more. He hadn't imagined how thoroughly they would remake the emotional architecture of the mansion.

The house that once guarded secrets and projected power now echoed with laughter and love. Formal rooms had become play spaces. Corridors once silent were filled with music, conversation, and children's footsteps.

Soon, the twins would arrive. The library would hold handcrafted cradles from Edward and murals from Abbeline. Abigail and Bau would become proud older cousins, eager to share their passions. The foundation would grow, bearing Abbie's legacy forward.

And Randolph would continue, not as a relic of a bygone era, but as great-grandfather to a family who knew him not for who he had been, but for the man he had chosen to become.

Lost in quiet contemplation, he hadn't noticed how much time had passed.

He rose carefully, mindful of his slower pace, and followed the sound of teenage chatter drifting in from the kitchen. Afternoon light streamed through windows once shuttered against intrusion, casting warmth over walls now adorned with Abbeline's artwork and children's drawings—past and present hanging side by side.

As he neared the kitchen, he paused. Abigail's laughter blended with Bau's excited description of his latest robot design. Martha passed snacks, Chance and Abbeline listened with interest. It was an ordinary moment, all the more extraordinary for its simplicity.

"Join us, Grandfather," Abbeline called, motioning to the chair prepared for him. "Bau's explaining how his robot won first place."

Bau waved to him. "Hi, Granddad," he said before diving back into his explanation. Abigail walked over, kissed him on the cheek, and slipped her arm through his as they made their way to the island.

As he took his seat, accepted naturally into their orbit, Randolph felt the truth settle over him—quiet, clear, undeniable.

This—this connection, this living, evolving love—was the true inheritance worth preserving.

Not legacy as once defined by wealth and power, but the kind born of honesty, forgiveness, and grace.

Epilogue 2

Full Circle of Love's Foundation

Ten years after the twins' birth

Morning sunlight streamed through the Hartwell mansion's renovated kitchen, casting warmth over the familiar rhythm of breakfast. Abbeline moved between the island and the stove with practiced ease, flipping pancakes while navigating a debate between ten-year-old twins Layla and Lara.

"But historical fashion *is* literature," Lara insisted. Her sketchbook lay open beside her plate, Victorian silhouettes detailed in pencil. "I need context to represent the clothing accurately."

"That's not the same as appreciating the writing," Layla countered, sliding a bookmark into her well-worn copy of *Jane Eyre*. "You just look at the pictures."

"Girls," Abbeline interjected gently, seasoned by a decade of twin debates, "reading takes many forms. Both are valuable."

Chance entered the kitchen with three-year-old Chance Jr. perched on his shoulders.

"Papa here?" the little boy asked, looking around. "Him make cheese sandwich!"

"Not yet, buddy," Chance replied, lowering him to the floor with ease. "But he and Desiree are on their way."

"Papa makes the best cheese sandwich in the wold," Chance Jr. announced, beaming with certainty, as if the household could forget.

"We know, honey," Abbeline laughed, kissing the top of his head and sliding the last batch of pancakes onto a plate. "You tell us every day."

The bond between Chance Jr. and his grandfather had been evident from the start. Edward had embraced his role as "Papa" completely, often working with his grandson perched beside him in the workshop, "helping" with handcrafted projects made just for him.

"Abigail called," Chance said, pouring coffee while watching their son build a napkin fortress. "Her flight lands at two. She asked if Bau could pick her up—he'll be done with morning classes by then."

At twenty-seven, Abigail had flourished. Her talent earned her a Royal Academy fellowship in London, a natural extension of the quiet independence and creativity nurtured since childhood with Beatrice and Roderick's care.

"I'll text Bau," Abbeline said, already reaching for her phone. "He wanted to show her his latest project anyway."

Now twenty-two and a senior at Georgia Tech, Bau had channeled his childhood energy into architectural engineering. His dorm walls were covered with designs for sustainable structures, many informed by conversations with Edward about merging traditional craftsmanship with modern design.

The front door opened, its familiar sound prompting Chance Jr. to leap up and dash toward the entry.

"Papa! Papa! Cheese sandwich?"

Edward's laugh mingled with Desiree's voice as they greeted him. Minutes later, Edward entered the kitchen with Chance Jr. riding high on his shoulders.

"Not quite lunchtime, little man," he said, reaching into his pocket. "But I brought something for your fortress."

He revealed small wooden knights, carved and painted in fine detail. Though seventy now, Edward's hands remained steady, his skill undiminished.

"These are amazing," Layla breathed, eyes wide. Lara, inspired, sketched new costume ideas beside her plate.

"Just something I made on the drive over," Edward said, clearly pleased. He hugged Abbeline, clasped Chance's hand, and surveyed the room with affection. "Smells incredible."

Abbeline hugged Desiree next, the warmth between them long familiar. "Morning, Mama Ree," the twins chimed in unison, grinning as Desiree bent down to kiss them both. "How are my two halves?" she asked. The girls just giggled at their nickname.

"Pancakes now, world-famous grilled cheese later," Abbeline said to Chance Jr. "Perfect Saturday lineup."

They gathered around the table, conversation flowing easily—Abigail's return, Bau's competition, the twins' school projects, Desiree's restoration work in Savannah, Edward's latest furniture for a children's hospital.

Chance Jr., absorbed in his fortress, narrated epic adventures for the wooden knights. No one minded the interruptions. This was their family rhythm: layered, lively, and unmistakably interconnected.

"I heard from Beatrice this morning," Abbeline said, passing fruit to Desiree. "They're cutting their cruise short to be here by Thursday."

"Because of Randolph?" Edward asked, his voice quieting.

Abbeline nodded. "The doctors called yesterday. They don't think he has much time left."

A hush settled. The twins exchanged looks, old enough to grasp the weight of those words.

"Is Great-Grandfather going to die?" Layla asked, her tone direct but steady.

"Yes, sweetheart," Abbeline answered gently. "His heart's very tired."

"That's why we're all coming together," Chance added. "So we can say goodbye."

"Will he go to heaven with Great-Grandmother Elisabeth?" Lara asked, eyes on her sketchpad but ears attuned.

"I believe so," Edward said. His quiet answer, from the man who had once lost everything because of Randolph, carried weight. "He's not the same man he was. People can change."

Edward's quiet grace rippled through the room—simple, profound, and wholly unexpected.

"Abigail's coming home early because of that," Abbeline explained. "And Bau's been visiting him every day."

"And we're making his favorite lemon cake?" Lara asked, connecting it all.

"Exactly, sweetheart," Chance said. "It's important to show love while we still can."

The conversation turned to memories. The twins recalled chess lessons and Boston stories.

"Gweat-Papa wead stowies," Chance Jr. said, not looking up as he marched his knight across the table.

Abbeline smiled at her son, surprised by how closely his young mind was following the conversation.

Each recollection painted a portrait not of who Randolph had been, but of who he had become.

After breakfast, the family dispersed—Edward and Chance Jr. to the workshop, Desiree and the twins to the living room to catch up on the latest teenage gossip, and Chance to the study.

Alone in the kitchen, Abbeline loaded the dishwasher, emotions stirring beneath routine. On the counter beside her sat a faded recipe card—Elisabeth's lemon cake, its corners worn soft with time.

Seventeen years had passed since the attic photographs. Seventeen years of healing and rebuilding, of reclaiming something lost and making it whole again.

A car in the drive drew her to the window. Bau's blue hybrid pulled up. He emerged quickly, his usually buoyant energy tempered now by concern.

"Is it true?" he asked as he entered, concern softening his voice.

"Yes," Abbeline said. "The doctors say maybe days."

Bau nodded, absorbing the news. "I'll bring Abigail straight here. She'll want to see him first."

"She'll be glad," Abbeline said. "Your mom and dad will be here by Thursday."

"A final gathering," Bau murmured. "Full circle."

The words landed with a quiet, precise truth.

By Thursday afternoon, the mansion thrummed with quiet preparation. Family arrived from every direction—Abigail from London, Beatrice and Roderick fresh from their cruise, Edward and Desiree settled into the east wing. Bau moved between campus and home.

Randolph now lay in a hospital bed in his study, the former seat of power transformed into a sanctuary overlooking the garden. His mind was sharp, his voice thinner but still laced with that old rhythm.

The family visited in shifts, sharing stories, exchanging silence, allowing space for both presence and parting. The mood was reverent, not bleak. There was no clinging, only gratitude and grace.

That evening, with the children in bed and the house quieting, Abbeline sat beside Randolph.

"Thank you," he said, his voice no more than a breath.

"For what?" she asked, adjusting his blanket.

"For this," he said, gesturing faintly to the home around them. "For giving me a place in your children's lives. For a second chance I didn't earn."

His clarity—so different from his guarded past—was itself a form of legacy.

"You're their great-grandfather," Abbeline replied. "They needed to know you. And you needed to know them."

"They've taught me more than I ever expected," he said with a flicker of humor. "Especially young Chance. No one questions authority like that child."

Abbeline chuckled. "He gets it from me."

Randolph's eyes warmed. "Asking the hard questions. Just like your mother."

The moment stretched between them, simple, honest, rooted in the journey from estrangement to understanding.

"I've made arrangements," he said, lifting his hand to adjust his ring with effort. "The house will transfer to you and Chance. And the foundation funding is locked through a perpetual trust. Beatrice and Roderick will remain executors until they choose to pass it on."

His practical care—a final offering of stability—touched her more than any sentiment could have.

"One more thing," he added. "In the wall safe, behind Elisabeth's portrait. A letter. For Edward. I wasn't brave enough to give it to him myself. Will you?"

"I will," she promised.

He nodded, eyes slipping shut.

She stayed, watching the man who had once broken so much find peace not through erasure, but through truth.

Stars appeared outside the window, steady above the mansion that had witnessed their family's long arc from secrecy to connection.

***

Three days later, with family gathered in the study, Randolph took his last breath. Chance Jr. sat by his side, reading about knights and dragons, his small hand curled in Randolph's until it slowly relaxed.

In the days that followed, the house filled with friends and stories. The public memorial honored achievements, but the private gathering in the garden held the soul of his legacy.

"He wasn't perfect," Beatrice said, raising her glass as twilight settled. "But he changed in ways I never thought possible."

"To growth," said Roderick.

"To family," Abigail added, her voice soft.

"To healing," Edward said, voice even. Desiree took his hand.

Abbeline watched her children, faces lit by fading sunlight, expressions open. They were not the descendants of who Randolph had been, but of who he had chosen to become.

That night, with the house quiet again, Abbeline retrieved the letter.

She found Edward in the garden. Without a word, she offered the envelope.

"Stay," he said, patting the bench.

She sat as he opened it. His face shifted as he read—surprise, sorrow, and something softer.

"He apologized," Edward said. "No excuses. Just acknowledgment. And thanks."

He opened a box that had come with the letter. Inside lay Randolph's signet ring.

"He wanted me to have this. To pass to my grandson, if I choose."

"What will you do with it?"

"I'll keep it. Not to wear. But to honor what it represents—change, and the family we built anyway."

Abbeline leaned against him. "Mom would be proud. Of you. Of all of us."

"She believed in growth," Edward said, his eyes on the stars. "Even when it seemed impossible."

They sat quietly, listening to the house breathe behind them—the soft hum of life continuing.

Upstairs, Chance's voice calmed a nightmare. Somewhere, the twins read. Abigail sketched. Bau drafted designs.

Different threads in the same tapestry—not perfect, not painless, but true.

"We should go in," Edward said, rising slowly.

Abbeline took his arm. They walked together toward the lighted terrace where Chance waited.

"The kids want a story," he said. "The one about the attic. And the photographs."

Abbeline smiled. "We can manage that. Especially the part about what came after."

They stepped into the home they'd made, where legacy wasn't about bloodlines, but about the love and truth that bound them together—like the photograph tucked in the attic drawer, now framed on the hall wall.

Thank You for Choosing Change

I hope this story touched your heart and lingers in your mind long after the final page. If you enjoyed spending time with these characters, I'd be truly grateful if you took a moment to leave a short review on Amazon.

Reviews help future readers decide if a book is right for them—and they make a huge difference for indie authors like me. Your feedback helps this story reach more people and keeps independent publishing alive.

Review on Amazon U.S
http://bit.ly/3J03W3g

Review on Amazon (Global)
http://bit.ly/42vKRwB

Thank you so much for your support. Your words matter more than you know.

About the Author

A.T. Rhode is a storyteller drawn to the quiet "what ifs" of everyday life. With a background in IT and a mind that's always troubleshooting, she brings the same curious spirit to her writing—exploring how ordinary moments can shift in unexpected, meaningful ways.

She lives in Georgia with her husband and two sons, balancing her creative pursuits with a career in quality assurance. Whether she's writing fiction, roller skating, learning something new, or crafting homemade lotions, A.T. is happiest when building something real from scratch.

Her passion lies in creating grounded, emotionally resonant stories—narratives that feel lived-in, with characters you can almost reach out and touch. Her books are published under **Vailed Pen Publications**, a small press devoted to stories that leave a lasting impression.

Connect with her at: facebook.com/VailedPenPublications

More Titles from Vailed Pen Publications

Nonfiction

Stop Negative Thinking Now – Science-backed strategies to rewire your thoughts and reclaim your peace. http://bit.ly/4gTV5g0

Discover what's next from Vailed Pen Publications, where one pen brings many voices to life:

https://www.facebook.com/VailedPenPublications